EMILY ADRIAN

the foreseeable future

 Dial Books

DIAL BOOKS
An imprint of Penguin Random House LLC
375 Hudson Street, New York, NY 10014

Names: Adrian, Emily, author.
Title: The foreseeable future / Emily Adrian.
Description: New York, NY : Dial Books, [2018] | Summary: "High school
senior Audrey Nelson is ready to move far away from her small coastal California
town after graduation, but that all changes when she falls for Seth O'Malley, saves
his ex-girlfriend's life, and becomes a viral sensation in the process"— Provided
by publisher. Identifiers: LCCN 2017039685 | ISBN 9780399538995 (hardback)
Subjects: | CYAC: Celebrities—Fiction. | Dating (Social customs)—Fiction. | Family
problems—Fiction. | Nursing homes—Fiction. | Family life—California—Fiction.
California—Fiction. Classification: LCC PZ7.1.A27 For 2018 | DDC [Fic]—dc23
LC record available at https://lccn.loc.gov/2017039685

Printed in the United States of America
1 3 5 7 9 10 8 6 4 2

Text set in Horley

For my mom,
Ellen Adrian,
who taught me independence

ONE

"It's an adorable town, right on the water. There's a surf shop, a gas station, a restaurant called the Fish Shack, and that's basically it."

My host, a freshman named Vanessa, paused her spiel to check the time on her phone. She had already warned me about the risks associated with being late to dinner; apparently, the dining hall ran out of veggie burgers fast on Friday nights. "The problem with Crescent Bay is that it's about a twenty-minute drive from campus, so you have to befriend someone with a car. But I totally recommend going into town as soon as you get a chance. It's really quaint. I think the population is less than a thousand."

Signing up for an overnight preview of life at Whedon College had been my parents' idea. So far, my preview had entailed following this girl around while she took a lot of pride in scanning her ID card to open doors marked STAFF AND STUDENTS ONLY. Vanessa had a tangle of dirty-blond hair and wore, attached to her belt with a carabiner, a noisy collection of keys and small tools. She was the kind of person whom my best friend, Sara, would describe as *mountain grunge*. Letting her show me around felt sort of disingenuous—like I was pretending to be some city kid who had picked Whedon for its proximity to the Pacific, or because I'd heard people in northern California were uncommonly chill.

Really, the campus was as familiar to me as my own backyard.

"The population is over four thousand," I said. "Four thousand, three-hundred and fifty-five." I knew the number from a salt-eroded highway sign bearing my hometown's slogan: RELAX, YOU'RE IN CRESCENT BAY!

"Whoa." Vanessa had a dramatic habit of lowering her sunglasses every time she wanted to look me in the eye. "You really did your research before deciding on a school."

"Actually, I'm from here."

"For real?" Her surprise was sincere. "I don't think I've ever met anyone who's *from* here."

I believed her. Most local kids didn't have the grades or the money to attend the only college within our zip code. Arguably, I didn't have the grades, either. What I did have were two tenured professors for parents.

"It must be nice to love where you're from so much, you don't ever want to leave," Vanessa said.

I was on the verge of correcting her. My decision to stay in Crescent Bay after graduation—still two months away— couldn't be reduced to anything as easy as love. Forming an official opinion of this place would have been like trying to articulate my feelings for my thirteen-year-old sister. Obviously, I loved Rosie. We shared a room, a history. We had identical splashes of freckles across the bridges of our slightly oily noses. Almost every day of our lives contained a moment when one or both of our parents said something so off-putting that only a shared look of sisterly commiseration could comfort me. And yet, the last thing I'd said to Ro was, "If you don't stop leaving your dirty balled-up socks on my bed I will literally carry your entire wardrobe into the yard and set it on fire."

Toward Crescent Bay, I felt a similar combination of loyalty and irritation—the kind that makes you grind your teeth, exhale through your nose. My tour guide was from a suburb outside of Chicago. I didn't think she'd really understand, so I just said, "Someday, I'll leave."

"Oh, totally. But why rush it? This is the most beautiful place I've ever been."

I nearly thanked her, as if the compliment had been for me and not the landscape. The truth was that I agreed;

everyone who stepped foot in our town agreed with Vanessa. The refrain you heard all the time, as families arranged their collapsible chairs in the sand—or as your dad, piloting the minivan, rounded a particularly scenic bend of Highway 101 for the third time that week—was, *Does it get any better than this?*

TWO

That night, Vanessa and her mountain-grunge boyfriend were excited to bring me to a party. At the boyfriend's insistence, Vanessa and I leaned against the brick exterior of an ivy-draped dorm and posed for a picture, which the boyfriend uploaded to Instagram. Before we went inside, he showed me the caption—*Baby's first college party!*—and the list of people who didn't know me but had promptly liked the photo anyway.

It was true that I'd never attended a party at Whedon; the only parties anyone in Crescent Bay really cared about centered around the weekly bonfires we built on top of Cape Defiance. There, Friday after Friday night, we perched on Igloo coolers and drank beers filched from our own garages. The boys stuck fallen branches into the fire and ran around threatening one another with their makeshift torches, while the girls discussed how long it would take us to wash the smoke smell out of our hair.

This party was different. And not in a way I found especially refreshing. Everyone was sitting on the carpeted floor or else squeezed onto one of two narrow beds. Music played faintly through someone's laptop, and a kid with a knit cap slipping from his head welcomed me to *Cali*, not even bothering to ask where I came from. I was bored and, for the first time in my life, feeling a little claustrophobic. The whole experience was like being trapped in an elevator with a lot of wasted strangers.

On our way back to Vanessa's dorm, she and her boyfriend laughed until their knees stopped functioning. Because I had avoided the shot glasses lined up on the edge of someone's desk, filled with ominous blue liquid, all my joints were in working order.

"I just need to rest awhile," Vanessa announced, collapsing in the grass beneath a statuesque tree. We were right outside the political science building where my mother—Professor Iris Cox Nelson, chair of the department—had her office.

"Right on," agreed the boyfriend.

I joined them on the ground, at first sitting cross-legged and then letting myself fall backward. Above us, leaves shivered in the breeze. I could still locate the exact limb from which my brother had fallen, age ten. After landing in a heap, Jake had at first regarded his left arm—fractured in two places, like a staircase—with detached horror. A beat later, he began to scream.

As Vanessa and her boyfriend discussed how it was possible that the moon looked "sometimes huge and sometimes tiny," I texted my brother. Locating his name in my phone made my heart surge with a level of affection I felt for Jake only when he was nowhere near me.

Hey. Why did it take you a second to start screaming after you broke your arm?

It was three a.m. in New York City, but my brother wrote back right away.

It didn't really hurt until I looked at it up close.

In the morning, under the assumption that I'd woken up with a hangover to rival hers, Vanessa tried to persuade me to stay and consume one of the infamous infant-size burritos from the dining hall, but I was done previewing college life. Leaving campus felt essential. Driving back toward town, my stomach growling, I tried to reassure myself. The past twenty-four hours had not actually revealed what my life would be like next year. For one thing, I was going to live with my parents, not sleep on the floor between Vanessa's bed and the one containing her congested roommate.

Furthermore, no one would force me to attend parties in tiny, crowded rooms. Wasn't the whole point of college that you could spend your time however you wanted?

Or, in my case, exactly as I'd spent time all my life: wandering the beach, driving north and south down the highway, listening to my parents' rapid-fire dinner conversations in which they referred to *Academia* as if it were a distant and sophisticated nation.

It was Sunday, and still early. I had what was left of my weekend to search for a summer job. At the moment, securing seasonal work felt more crucial than coming to grips with my college plans. Sara would be leading tourists on horseback trail rides beginning and ending at her family's barn, as she did every summer, and our friend Elliot had already been offered three months of evening shifts at the Qwick Mart. I wanted something semi-interesting—a job where I wouldn't have to sit still or answer any phones, ever. Something that would make people raise their eyebrows and ask questions, years from now, when I described the first job I ever had. Crescent Bay was not exactly rife with employment opportunities, but there was one place in town where I had yet to try my luck.

The Crescent Bay Retirement Home was glassy and modern, sprawled out across the top of a bluff, presumably so no one inside had to deal with any stairs. As I pulled into the parking lot, I observed that Seth O'Malley and Chelsea Hamilton were messing around outside the main entrance. She had on pale blue nursing scrubs. Seth was just in regular jeans, his lips elastic with laughter. Every few seconds he would lunge at her, arm outstretched, and she would spin in a frantic circle.

It appeared he was trying to steal the rubber band from the end of her braid.

I got out of the car and walked toward them, preparing my face for the moment they noticed me and I would have to pretend to be noticing them for the first time. But because they were engrossed in their game, and also blocking the doors, I was forced to say, "Hey, guys."

Seth snapped to attention, like a daydreaming kid called out by his teacher. "Hey, Audrey." He clasped his hands behind his back. "How can we help you?"

Still giggling, Chelsea, who had graduated two years ago, stepped closer to Seth. "Yeah, how *can* we help you?"

"Please, let us help you." Seth was grinning. He looked older than he had whenever I'd last given him a second thought; laugh lines edged his eyes and something resembling a beard shadowed his cheeks.

Seth and I were the same age and had gone to school together since kindergarten. He had a ponytail and had been known to wear cowboy boots to places other than the rodeo.

In school, he was always giving people hugs. These long, meaningful hugs that blocked the hallway and inspired both parties to close their eyes. It wasn't uncommon to overhear one Crescent Bay girl ask another, "Have you seen Seth? I could really use a hug," as if pressing your face against the guy's Levi's shirt was some holistic cure for heartache and insecurity and period cramps.

"I was just going to see if they're hiring servers." I nodded toward the entrance. I knew of kids who, over previous summers, had waited tables in the dining room. Allegedly, the uniform included a necktie patterned with tiny bottles of red wine, and the residents tended to be picky about the number of prunes adorning their morning oatmeal. But the retirement home was supposed to be fancy. A billboard erected beside the exit for Crescent Bay featured three silver-haired women walking on the beach, their arms linked. The ad promised, *Friendship never grows old.*

I figured the job might pay.

"Oh, damn," Chelsea said. "There aren't any openings right now."

"But they're always looking for CNAs, aren't they?" Seth asked her.

Chelsea made eye contact with him as she said, "But Audrey's not a CNA."

"What's a CNA?" I asked.

"Certified Nurse Assistant. Key word being *certified*, I'm afraid." Her smile was convincingly apologetic.

"How do you get certified?"

"You have to take a course. Night school. It's pretty grueling."

I pictured myself wearing blue scrubs, like Chelsea's. I pictured myself rushing down a long sterile hallway, responding to an urgent call for nurse assistance in Room 12. The job, in my imagination, would be superior to manning the front desk at the hair salon, or getting personal with the deep fryer at the Fish Shack.

Seth's eyes were fixed on my profile. I wondered if my cheek still bore the imprint of a standard-issue dorm room carpet.

"Well. . . ." Chelsea sighed, as if we were nearing the end of a phone call.

"Maybe you could join the janitorial staff," said Seth, inadvertently providing an explanation for the bleach stains on his black jeans. "I'll show you how to mop a mean floor."

"I'll think about it," I lied. To Chelsea I said, "I'm sorry I interrupted your, uh, conversation."

She relaxed her arms. "No problem."

Clearly, she expected me to turn back toward my car.

It's not inaccurate to assume, as everyone does, that people in small towns are friendly. We never cross paths in the supermarket without smiling broadly and saying hello. We know the names and birth orders of one another's siblings and pets. But we can also be territorial, determined to separate what's ours from what's communal. Pissing off Chelsea wasn't my goal; she could have Seth O'Malley all to herself, for all I cared. But she couldn't prevent me from going inside the retirement home and asking about a job.

"Good luck," Seth called as I moved past Chelsea and pushed through the glass doors.

Turning to thank him, I was caught off guard by the expression on his face. Both his grin and his slightly raised eyebrows suggested we had history—some enduring past we were hiding from Chelsea, and also from the world.

I swear, I barely knew the guy.

It was April. I would graduate from high school in two months—the exact amount of time my mother had already been gone.

When she first told us that she'd won a grant and would be spending the duration of her sabbatical in Italy, I wasn't entirely upset. I loved my mother, but when the five of us Nelsons were together, I sometimes felt like I was trapped on a television show that had been renewed for too many seasons. All of the plotlines were stale, all of the once-charming characters reduced to caricatures of themselves.

We would recycle the same arguments and one-liners and family legends until the writers finally had one of us murdered in an effort to boost ratings.

But when Jake was away at college, the four remaining Nelsons relaxed. We went off-script, gave one another more space. Rosie stopped scrawling FOR RO'S LIPS ONLY across bags of Goldfish crackers. Dad stopped making us bet on who would be the first to get married, have kids, commit accidental tax fraud. And I was less prone to flinging insults, as if drawing attention to everyone's weaknesses—Jake's pride, my sister's paranoia that she was the butt of every joke, Mom's desperation to be perfect, and Dad's sensitivity, which he masked with a perpetual scholarly gloom—would force them all to conclude that I, Audrey, must be flawless.

That my brother's summer at home would coincide with Mom's trip seemed, potentially, ideal. Like maybe what our family needed to achieve domestic equilibrium was to exile one member at a time. But Mom had been gone since the first week of March, and already it was clear that she had, all along, been the most crucial member of our clan. Evidently, she had kept the mess of our lives below a certain threshold. In her absence, the mess had crossed that threshold. Laundry had swallowed the bathroom. Sand had seeped between every cushion, every crack in the floorboards. Some kind of black mold was spreading across the shower wall—granted,

Google had declared the growth "common and harmless" and we weren't too concerned.

Maybe the main reason we missed our mother was that she was kind. Her kindness wasn't constant; when we pissed her off, she was quick to lay down the law, shouting rules and restrictions that hadn't previously existed—like the time Jake let a half-consumed container of strawberry yogurt slide between his bed and the wall, where it dripped and hardened and soured over a period of three days. Now we weren't allowed to eat anything, not even ice, in our rooms. Other times, Mom forgot we were not her political theory students. Rosie would say something like, "I got so lucky today; a fire drill interrupted gym class!" and Mom would crease her forehead and ask, "But what *is* luck? How would you define it, Ro-Ro?"

Otherwise, Mom was the kind of person who would casually announce "I love you" when you hadn't been doing anything lovable, just eating carrot sticks and idly wiping ranch dressing from the corner of your mouth. She was a dispenser of back rubs and small gifts. As a parent, Dad was perfectly adequate. He hung out with us all the time. When he was in the mood, he paid close attention to our stories and analyzed our actions as if we were characters in the books he wrote. But he wasn't *kind*. A fun experiment, conducted often by Jake and Rosie and me, was to tell Dad you loved him and watch as he struggled to repeat the phrase.

He did love us, presumably, but the words sounded foreign in his mouth.

These days, the Nelsons were scattered across the globe, with Mom already in Italy and Jake still in New York until June. Every Sunday night we gathered around our laptops for a group video chat. When it was eight p.m. in California, it was only five a.m. in Naples—bizarrely, the hour at which my mother preferred to begin her day. Tonight, Dad and Rosie and I squeezed onto the couch, bowls of Cherry Garcia ice cream balanced on our knees and the computer centered on the coffee table.

Jake was the first to appear on the screen, his hair wet from the shower and dripping onto the shoulders of the Taylor Swift shirt he wore often and only semi-ironically. He waved to us, and in another second our mother's call came through. The box containing my brother shrank to accommodate a box of Mom.

"My family!" she cried.

Dad and Rosie and I monotoned a low "Hi," spoons clanking against our bowls. It was always awkward at first. There was something depressing about accepting these blurry, jerky images as stand-ins for our actual relatives.

Jake was always the first to break the tension. "Mom, I stayed up so late reading the new draft of your paper. It's astounding."

Astounding was a word my brother and mother used a lot—usually to flatter each other—and it always made my insides cringe.

"Oh, thank you," Mom said. "It's still rough, but the ideas are really coming together. I've been so immersed in it. Even in my dreams I'm reading Machiavelli. I'm not kidding; entire pages of *The Prince* appear word for word!"

"In English or Italian?" Dad wanted to know.

Mom thought for a second and answered, "Italian!"

"I'd like to read this article," Dad said, wrapping his lips around his spoon.

"No," Mom said. "It's not ready. You're too critical."

With his mouth still full of cutlery, Dad looked crest-fallen.

"Audrey, you spent last night at Whedon, didn't you?" Iris would have known how I'd spent the previous night, no matter how I'd spent it. Even from six thousand miles away, she probably knew when I'd last brushed my teeth.

"Yup," I said.

"And how was it?"

"It was . . . okay."

Jake said, "Don't let the big kids intimidate you. You're going to love college."

"I promise you, I was not intimidated."

"And are you still looking for a summer job?" Mom asked.

"Yeah," I said. "I talked to someone at the retirement home today."

Beside me on the couch, Dad looked surprised. "The old folks' home on the hill?"

I wondered if *old folks' home* was an offensive turn of phrase. Despite the word *old*, it seemed sort of infantilizing. "They need nurse assistants, starting in June. I would have to go to night school over the next few weeks to get certified, but it pays twice as much as anything else in town."

"Honey, that sounds kind of intense." Mom's eyes drifted, presumably locating Dad's grainy image on her own screen, though she appeared to be frowning into the corner of our living room.

"And grubby," added my father. "That line of work is mostly bedpans and sponge baths, is it not?"

I shrugged. Mom took my lack of conviction as a good sign, and relaxed. "You know, you don't *have* to work this summer. You could spend time with your friends . . . get ready for your first semester. . . ."

"I'd get bored," I told my mother. "Besides, everyone works the summer after high school."

"I didn't," Jake said.

I opened my mouth to remind Jake that he and I were entirely different people—but Rosie interrupted me.

"Mama, you look tan."

My sister was right. Through the harsh shadow cast by a desk lamp, Mom's face glowed, luminous.

Dad said, "I was thinking the same thing."

Mom laughed. "Well, I admit I've made it to the beach a *few* times. Not that it was easy to tear myself away. You know me."

"I do," Dad said cautiously, "and yet, I've never known you with a tan."

"You look great," Rosie said. "You should grow your hair out."

Mom ran a hand through her gray pixie cut, not so different from Dad's regular guy cut. The image froze briefly with the blur of her fingers obscuring her forehead. "You think so?" she asked.

"Rosie," my brother said, "Mom's in Naples to *write*, not to get some European makeover."

Rosie shrugged. "Do both. That way, when you get home, everyone will be jealous."

My father snorted, a little too loud.

THREE

Before first period on Monday, I waited for my friends in front of the oceanic mural—ecstatic sharks, mournful orcas—that some kid had won the right to paint on the wall, decades ago. It was our usual meeting spot, close but not too close to a broken drinking fountain whose spray always pummeled the face of the person bending over it. Sara and Elliot and I took pleasure in watching the occasional ninth grader get soaked. We could be cruel that way.

"Is it just me," I asked my friends as they emerged from the crowd, "or is everyone acting especially unhinged?"

A football kept sailing over the hallway's shifting sea of heads and backpacks. Each time the ball descended into the mob, kids tripped and protested and a different boy shouted, "Got it!" The early morning swell of voices was always loud, but today it was high-pitched and deafening, as if all five hundred students were competing to tell the stories of their weekends before the bell rang.

"It's the weather." Elliot gestured to the end of the corridor, where unfiltered sunlight—the kind Crescent Bay normally didn't see until July—poured through the open doors. The heat had not dissuaded him from wearing the puffy green vest I was pretty sure he'd been born in.

"It's not the weather," Sara argued. "It's the promise of freedom. Only thirty-one more days!"

Elliot wrinkled his nose and performed some mental math. "You left out the weekends." He was always tempering Sara's exaggerations.

"Weekends don't count," she said.

"Won't you miss your friends?" I asked her, moving closer to the mural and stroking the painted sharks.

Sara considered the sharks. Their manic, toothy grins. "No."

Elliot humored me, saying, "We'll miss *you*, though."

"Oh, totally," Sara said. "But not at seven a.m. After graduation, I'm never going to think about you guys before noon."

In the fall, Sara was headed to UC Davis to study veterinary science. Elliot was even farther southbound for UCLA. My friends never made me feel inferior for agreeing to stay and live at home, but sometimes I felt it anyway.

"Duck," Elliot said, shielding his head with his arms.

Sara yelped and nearly knocked me over in her attempt to avoid a broken nose. Somehow, before I even realized what was happening, I had caught the ball.

"Nice," said a gravelly voice to my left. "Also, so sorry."

I turned. Pieces of hair had escaped his ponytail and were hanging in his face. Seth O'Malley looked pleased and sheepish at the same time, as if remembering what his mother had told him about roughhousing in crowded places. He raised his hands, indicating I should toss him the ball, but whatever reflexes had prompted me to snatch the thing out of midair failed me now. I stepped toward him, placing the football directly in his arms.

"Uh." Seth bit down a smile. "Thanks."

"No worries," I said, then cleared my throat. *No worries* was one of those California-casual expressions I'd never used before in my life. Now I was overly conscious of my friends, their incredulous stares. Seth O'Malley was not our kind.

"It was cool running into you yesterday," he said.

"Oh, yeah." As if I'd forgotten all about it. "That was."

His upper lip twitched as he selected his next words. "About Chelsea . . ." Seth hesitated. Had either of us ever had a conversation before? "I hope she didn't, like, discourage you or anything."

"Oh, no. She didn't." Part of me wanted to laugh. Seth sounded as awkward as I felt, but his eyes told a different story. I kept expecting him to wink.

"I've worked at the retirement home since I was fifteen. They're always looking for CNAs, especially on the night shift."

I already knew this. It was exactly what the receptionist behind the front desk had told me. As I'd driven home, I'd constructed a night-shift fantasy sure to distract me from whatever I was supposed to learn in school today. As a nurse I would exchange caffeine-fueled banter with my coworkers. I would memorize my patients' names and ailments and hustle from room to room—my presence, for some reason, invaluable.

"And working nights can be fun, in a way," Seth went on, as if deliberately vying for a cameo in my vague fantasy. He was cradling the football against his chest, as you would a newborn. "Anyway, I just thought you should know they're hiring. Do with that what you will." Seth waved good-bye before crossing the hall and disappearing inside the room where I, too, had first period. That we shared a math class had only ever dimly occurred to me.

"Weird," Elliot observed.

"Extremely weird," Sara said. "Why is Seth O'Malley so invested in your summer job prospects?"

"I have no idea," I answered honestly.

"I can't stand that guy," said Elliot.

"Why not?" I asked.

"He's always looking for an excuse to get nude. You'll be at his house, and he'll be like, 'Just give me a sec to change my shorts!' And before you know it, you're staring at O'Malley's bare ass."

"That's awful," Sara said.

I studied Elliot. "When were you last at Seth's house?"

He thought. "Second grade?"

"Is it possible Seth has changed since second grade?"

"He was the kind of kid who always wanted to play doctor. Do those kids ever change?"

"Nope," Sara answered.

When she and I had been about seven, we had gone through a phase of pretending that some malicious, unseen force wouldn't let us use the bathroom or indulge in an afternoon snack until we kissed each other. Eventually this unforgiving god raised the criteria and made us kiss with tongue. I could still remember the precise twist of shame and excitement I'd felt as we'd mashed our mouths together.

"Everyone changes," I said. Sara and I no longer made out for sport. Elliot no longer hung around with the kids who had grown into jocks and cowboys.

Sara rested a hand on my shoulder. The bell began to ring, earsplitting and rude. "Maybe," she allowed. "But it's not like Seth's developed a reputation for keeping his pants on."

At the beginning of the year Mr. Longo had assigned seats, but by second semester his attempt at order had been overthrown. Now we set up camp wherever we wanted and, unless notoriously disruptive pairs of best friends sat side by side, Mr. Longo pretended not to notice. The desk beside Seth's wasn't my only option that morning; I could have chosen a spot in the front row, or over in the corner, which always smelled faintly of the sponge festering in the sink.

I sat next to Seth.

It didn't make any sense, because he'd been around forever, but I couldn't shake the feeling that Seth O'Malley was the first interesting thing to happen to me in a long time. I dropped my bag in the aisle between us and he stared straight ahead, his fist blocking his mouth so I couldn't tell if he was smiling.

"Hi," I said.

Seth nodded toward Mr. Longo, who had assumed his position at the front of the room.

"Good morning, boys and girls," our teacher intoned. "Let's talk last night's homework. Anyone have any trouble?"

Several hands shot into the air. Seth refused to break his

gaze, as if he couldn't bear to miss a word. The snub was slight, but I felt my cheeks redden anyway.

With one glance Seth noted my complexion and he grinned, triumphant.

I'd been played.

He scribbled something onto a blank page of his notebook. As discreetly as possible, he tore it out and passed it to me. I was charmed; at some point after junior high, Sara and Elliot and I had switched from paper notes to covert text messages.

Do you remember the night my girlfriend puked on you?

I blinked, at first wondering whether Seth still had a girlfriend—he normally did, but I'd never felt any need to keep track of them—and then wondering what he was talking about. When Mr. Longo turned his back, Seth swiped the note and added:

The night I drove you and Rusty home from that party on Cape Defiance and then, since you're girls, you made me take you to the Taco Bell drive-through.

The night came back to me in flashes. I'd been going through a phase of wanting to seem whimsical and childlike and so had worn a black romper that made it impossible to pee. Crescent Bay was a strange place. For example, it was possible to be convinced you'd had next to zero contact with a person, and then remember the night he gave you a ride home from a party in his maroon Jeep Cherokee.

What's girly about the drive-through? I wrote back.

Not the drive-through, Seth scribbled. *Taco Bell. All girls love Taco Bell.*

I frowned. *Actually, girls are varied and complex and we all love different things.*

For sure! There's just this one exception, which is that, when drunk, y'all demand to be taken to Taco Bell.

I was having a hard time recalling what had possessed tenth grade–me to leave the party with Seth's ex-girlfriend, Rusty Tillman. Rusty's real name was Danielle and nobody could ever remember why she was called Rusty. The girl had a gap between her front teeth and perpetually skinned knees that were somehow sexy. What I remembered clearly now—both its smell and its awful, ground beefy consistency—was the torrent of vomit Rusty had, without warning, deposited into my lap as Seth drove us home. The two of us had been riding in the back together, eager to split our feast of crunchy tacos.

I remember. I wrote to Seth. *That was unfortunate.*

His leg bounced as he composed his reply. He had the longest legs I'd ever seen. *That's exactly what you said at the time! I thought you were either going to get mad or get sick, but instead you were just like, "Well, this is unfortunate."*

It was!

You were so chill. I was impressed.

It took me a second too long to realize that Mr. Longo was hovering above my desk—that the entire class had craned their necks to stare at Seth and me. With his hand outstretched, our teacher demanded the note.

I could sense Seth struggling not to smile.

"You know," Mr. Longo began, drifting back toward the front of the classroom, his chin raised proudly, "I understand that the majority of seniors believe what happens inside this building has *ceased* to matter, that all you need now are your diplomas before you go galloping off into the sunset—"

We couldn't gallop anywhere near the sunset. We lived on the coast; we'd drown.

"—But I've been teaching calculus for twenty-five years, and I'm here to tell you that the people who go on to do great things with their lives are always those few students who remain respectful and *focused*"—Mr. Longo locked eyes with me, not Seth—"until the moment that final bell rings."

With a slight shake of his head, he moved on.

Seth leaned sideways into the aisle and whispered, "Sorry."

I shrugged it off. In general, teachers were disappointed in me. Most likely they remembered and still pined for my older brother. When Jake had lived at home, when Columbia University was a goal but not yet a sure thing, he would frequently declare his intention to pull an all-nighter. Never out of necessity—procrastination was not his vice—but out of ambition for ambition's sake. Our dad was always quick to say, "That sounds nice. I'll join you," as if Jake had proposed a relaxing few hours of Boggle. Then, after finishing the dishes, the laundry, ensuring that Rosie and I had everything we could desire in terms of late night snacks, counsel, and toiletries, Mom would pull up a chair at the kitchen table. The three of them would remain hunched over their books until dawn.

Even my sister, too young for term papers and AP exams, lived for our family's yearly trips to Office Depot. Her fetish for paper clips shaped like animals and sparkly gel pens didn't exactly scream *budding genius*, but her collection of novels—organized by color on a shelf above her desk, their pages slightly warped from all the hours she spent in the bath—proved she was our father's daughter.

I had tried.

I wanted to love reading. I wanted to participate in heated family arguments over which twenty-first-century authors would contribute to the canon and who among the ancient Greeks had best understood democracy—but I didn't actually care. Whenever I opened a book my fingers always itched to text Sara. My legs craved a hike and my ears missed music. In ninth grade, after I'd nearly failed my midterms in both English and European history—"You didn't let me edit your essay!" cried Dad; "I would have quizzed you on the Peloponnesian War!" mourned my mother—I had turned my attention to math and science, supposing I might be the first ever left-brained Nelson. And while I was a tiny bit better at solving for X and memorizing the periodic table of elements, I still had to enlist Sara and Elliot to help me with my homework. By junior year, Sara had exhausted her patience explaining simple chemistry equations to me.

"I am not your science teacher," she said finally, shoving my textbook across our wobbly cafeteria table. "You have one. She's called Mrs. Delaney. Have you ever tried paying attention in class?"

Paying attention in class was, for me, an impossibility—like trying to count how many times you blink in a day. I would sit down, stare at the teacher, endeavor to hang on her every word. Then the drone of her voice would become a soothing sound track to whatever was actually on my mind—something funny Rosie had said at dinner. Whether Elliot would be willing to steal beer from his mom for a party. Where my family would travel this summer and if my siblings and I would get our own hotel room, like last year in Orlando, when we'd snuck out, hopped the fence surrounding the pool, and admitted how many people we'd kissed so far.

Rosie: one girl, on a dare.

Me: three boys.

Jake: also three boys, but hoping to increase his numbers during his second year at Columbia.

In the fall, my parents had ever-so-gently suggested I apply early decision to Whedon. "It's a good school, honey," my mother said. I sat on the couch, picking at a hole in my jeans. "To be honest, it's superior to any school that's going to accept you with your current GPA."

She was referring to my collection of low Bs. They stung worse than Cs, the grade you got when you didn't particularly care. Teachers gave out Bs to acknowledge when you'd tried.

"What makes you think Whedon will let me in?" I asked, wishing my voice hadn't cracked.

"They will," Mom said firmly.

She had already talked to someone.

"There's also the not-insignificant matter of Whedon covering tuition for the children of faculty members," Dad added, summarizing: "No loans."

Last September, I had filled out a completely symbolic application to Whedon College because I was tired of trying. My unsurprising acceptance letter had thrilled Mom and Dad, and now my mind could wander guiltlessly. I could half-ass my papers, and guess on my tests, and pass notes with scruffy football players if I wanted to—all the while maintaining lazy faith in my parents' claim that at college, this fall, I would learn to love learning.

I would get a second chance.

At the end of first period, Seth slung his bag over one shoulder and lingered. Glancing up at him, all I could think to say was, "Hi."

How many times was I going to greet him today?

"Sorry again," he said.

"For what?"

"For getting you in trouble."

"You didn't get me in trouble. I mean, I'm sort of always in trouble."

"Oh, I see. Didn't realize I was dealing with such a badass."

"I didn't realize you were *dealing* with me."

The look he gave me was one of amusement and acknowledgment. We had started something. A math class friendship or a promising flirtation or just an inside joke to which we'd refer, casually, if we ever ran into each other in the grocery store. *Remember the time my girlfriend puked on you?* Whatever we'd started, our next encounter would have to be different. We'd have to say something more than *Hi*.

Seth grinned. "You know what's weird?"

"What?"

"How you've never sat next to me before."

Sliding my textbook into my bag, I released a note of laughter. "Why is that weird?"

"I don't know. I just think it's strange."

"You're not actually in class that often," I pointed out.

"True." He sighed, wistful, as if his attendance record was beyond his control. "Anyway, Audrey, I'll see you around?"

"See you," I confirmed.

His boots thumped against the floor as he walked away. In Crescent Bay you could always tell whether someone lived close to the beach or up in the woods by what clung to their shoes—sand or dirt. Seth's boots were streaked with hardened mud. He moved differently than most boys of his height. Rather than propelling himself forward with his shoulders, he stood up straight and sort of glided.

Before today, I had never once considered sitting next to Seth O'Malley, but he was right—that the idea had never occurred to me now seemed unlikely, and strange.

FOUR

"This house is full of tourists," Sara complained into the phone.

"That's because you live in a hotel."

On a rural road about ten miles outside of town, the Quintero family's B&B was one of my favorite places in Crescent Bay. It was the only home in which I'd spent a significant amount of time that didn't smell vaguely like a wet dog, and where the floors weren't always coated with a thin layer of sand. Sara's mother hung modern art instead of dead starfish on the walls. The bathroom sinks were edged with tiny bottles of perfume and eucalyptus-infused shampoo. Tourists—usually up from San Francisco or Silicon Valley—happily forked over two hundred dollars per night to stay in the carefully curated guest rooms.

"There's this couple here"— Sara's voice was low, but I could hear floorboards squeaking and horses snorting, suggesting she had already escaped the main house for the solace of her barn. Sara spent a lot of evenings hiding in her hayloft, armed with homework and TV shows downloaded to her laptop—"and they want me to take them on a trail ride tomorrow night. At *sunset*. They have a very specific need to canter across the sand *at sunset*. Which, fine. But they showed me all this gear they brought with them—boots and pants and helmets. And this stuff is so brand spanking new, you can tell they bought it all for this one vacation."

"Are you jealous?" I teased her.

"Maybe of the boots," she admitted. "They look like Brogini's."

In spite of the way she slandered them behind their backs, Sara was always nicer to her customers than I would have expected. And I didn't think it was just because some of them tipped. Secretly, I suspected my best friend of wanting to be the kind of person who could pass through Crescent Bay and absorb its charms without feeling its limits.

Still, I understood that the boots and jodhpurs were overkill. When Sara and Elliot and I went riding on the beach, we wore cheap sneakers and jeans, no helmets. We were always fine.

"I have a question for you," I said, slipping out the front door and onto the porch. My dad was grinding coffee beans for the morning and bellowing along with a Loudon Wainwright song, but I didn't want to risk him falling silent, overhearing.

"Go for it," Sara said.

"Would you be alarmed if I became a Certified Nurse Assistant?"

"No. Wait, maybe. What's that?"

I laughed, then explained. The job entailed bathing and dressing patients, monitoring their vital signs, helping them get around and go to the bathroom, reporting major concerns to the RNs or doctors on staff. For days now, I had been poring over forums on which nurse assistants, nationwide, compared their salaries, supervisors, horror stories, and favorite patients. *The best part of this job,* one girl had written, *is that you're never, ever bored!*

Sara was slow to respond, and I felt my excitement deflate. I'd hoped she would see the appeal immediately, or at least agree that the job sounded like something I'd be good at. Finally, she asked, "Wouldn't that be a lot of work for a summer gig?"

"I could switch to part-time after school starts. First I need to take this class at Steeds County Community College. It starts next week."

"And what about, uh, high school?"

"The class meets at night. A lot of people do it while they're still in high school."

Sara cleared her throat. "This is the thing Seth O'Malley was telling you about?"

"Yeah."

"What does Seth know about it?"

"He mops floors at the retirement home."

Again, Sara was quiet. "You'd be so busy. Especially after August."

"That's kind of the point. . . ."

"But you'd be working nonstop. You'd never have time to hang out."

"Um," I said, waiting for Sara to be struck by the obvious. "Hang out with *who?*" Come September, she and Elliot would be long gone.

"I'll be home some weekends. And you'll make friends at Whedon."

I remembered Vanessa. She had so relished describing the dining hall's weekly rotation of offerings—from Meatball Mondays to Falafel Fridays—I'd wondered about her childhood in some Chicago suburb, if maybe her mother had served nothing but roast chicken.

Of the two of us, Sara was more likely to arrive at school and assemble a fast group of friends. None of the kids in her veterinary science program would leave campus after class; they would crowd into one another's dorm rooms to study heartworm prevention, methods of tranquilization.

And I doubted she would ever drive home for the weekend. UC Davis was seven hours away.

Sara sighed. None of this needed to be said aloud; she was leaving town and I wasn't. "I guess my question is just . . . *why?* Why even bother training for this intense-sounding job? It's not like you desperately need the money. You're going to live at home."

The sun had set since the start of our call, and now the air was cold, perfumed by the rosebushes in my backyard. "Exactly," I said, shivering.

"Come again?"

"I'm going to wake up in this house every day for the next four years. Just like the last four years, and the four years before that. I'm going to live with my parents. They're going to be my professors at some point—you can't even graduate from Whedon without taking my mom's political responsibility seminar. Basically, if I don't do *something* different this summer, nothing will ever change."

"College won't be anything like high school."

"Are you sure about that?"

I regretted the question instantly. I knew Sara was excited for college; my best friend loved school, in theory, but had long been forced to make the best of Crescent Bay High's meager offerings. She'd never fully forgiven the administration for accidentally putting her in ninth-grade Spanish after she'd registered for French. Madame Casey's class already full, Sara was stuck listening to us white kids laconically butcher the language she'd been speaking at home all her life.

Overlooking my skepticism, Sara continued. "So many people would kill to go to Whedon! Did you know this magazine just ranked it the second best liberal arts college in North America? The article raved about one *Professor Iris Cox Nelson*."

"I'm still going," I reminded her. "But does my whole life have to revolve around college? I don't even *like* school. I never really have."

"Shouldn't you have thought about this, like, six months ago?"

"I was hoping I had enough time to sort of . . ."

". . . become a different person?" Sara supplied.

"Correct."

"So far, the new you seems really similar to the old you."

"Do you think I could do it? Work as a CNA?"

"You're asking if I think you're capable of helping other people's grandparents go to the bathroom?"

"Don't judge. You've logged a lot of hours dealing with literal horse shit."

"Horses eat oats, Audrey. For breakfast, lunch, and dinner."

"There's more to the job than the gross stuff."

"Okay, but do you even like the elderly?"

"Definitely."

"Really?" she pressed. "Like, you have a specific interest in them?"

"They're just people, but with wrinkles. And I like people. I think I could do it."

"Of course you could do it." Sara always withheld her confidence in me until I desperately needed it, then acted like her faith in my abilities was a given, something she shouldn't have to assert at all. "You'll be great. You'll be the first-ever college freshman moonlighting at an old folks' home."

"Lots of people have jobs in college," I argued.

"Maybe," she said. "But not people at Whedon."

Crickets were chirping in the long grass of our yard. Farther down the gravel road, the neighbors' cat sounded indistinguishable from a baby crying. Living in the country was supposed to be quiet, but it was actually deafening most of the time.

"They're all going to think I'm a townie, aren't they?" I asked Sara.

"You're not a townie," she assured me, avoiding the actual question. "Seth O'Malley, on the other hand . . . there's your townie."

"He's not *my* townie." Alone on the porch, I could feel myself blushing.

"He's somebody's townie," she said.

FIVE

The back of my father's T-shirt said PROFESSOR "NELSON" NELSON, the letters cracked and faded from too many cycles in the washing machine. Dad's given name was Hunter, but it didn't suit him; everyone had called him Nelson since he was a teenager. After drawing his name in the English department's game of Secret Santa, five Christmases ago, Dad's secretary had gifted him with the custom tee. Mom despised it—which explained why he'd hardly taken it off since she'd left.

Neither Dad nor Rosie seemed aware of me as I entered the kitchen the next morning. My sister was leaning way back in her chair—bare ankles crossed atop the table, a lot of bagel crumbs spilled down the front of her camisole—while Dad drummed his fingers against the cover of a novel Rosie had been reading all week.

"What did you think of that climax?" he asked her.

"Didn't you feel like your heart was going to escape your chest?"

"Oh my God," Rosie confirmed. "I died."

I decided to make my announcement all at once, no build-up. Like ripping off a Band-Aid.

"Hey, Dad? Remember the job I was telling you guys about? At the old folks' home?"

He shifted toward me, a smile lingering on his face. "I think so."

I took a breath. "I've decided I want to go to night school to get certified."

My sister's mouth hung slightly ajar.

Before our mother had left for Europe, she'd instructed us to go to Dad with our requests and complaints, with all the blank permission slips we normally reserved for her signature—but lately, when it came to executive decision-making, Nelson had been painfully slow to engage.

"That's probably fine," he concluded.

I locked eyes with Rosie. With her feet still on the table, she shrugged.

"Really?" I couldn't help pressing him. "You don't want to discuss it with Mom? You don't want to have a lengthy chat about *presenting a united front*?"

"Audrey has a point," Rosie said. Frequently, my little

sister's only contribution to a conversation was to comment on who had a point. "You guys normally opt for the lengthy chat."

Dad took a second to examine the linoleum, which was spangled with drops of tomato sauce. "Do you imagine Iris will mind?" he asked.

It was a complicated question. Iris would mind anything that distracted me from the final exams and papers of my senior year. She would mind if she knew that the nursing home was likely to assign me to the night shift, compromising my REM sleep and limiting my exposure to vitamin D. She would definitely lose her cool if September arrived and I told her I didn't want to quit, didn't have it in me to devote myself entirely to my studies, after all.

"Nope," I told Dad.

Strictly speaking, I didn't think my mother would forbid me from signing up for night school and becoming a CNA.

I would assure her it was just a summer job.

Night school, it turned out, was exhausting.

The classroom at Steeds County Community College was small and hot and windowless. It was always too dark to see the decades-old dust hovering in the air, but by the end of each three-hour session I could feel it coating my tongue, invading my nostrils. Everything in the room was either broken or breaking; it took our instructor forever to successfully project her PowerPoint onto the battered pull-down screen. Inevitably, the screen would snap back toward the ceiling with a loud *thwap* and no warning. In those moments, when all of us prospective CNAs were just sitting around, waiting to be taught, I would forget I wasn't still at Crescent Bay High. I would check the clock on the wall, thinking it must be past three thirty and time to go home, only to remember that it was nine at night and I was here by choice.

More than once over the six-week course, I almost fell asleep at my desk. To avoid collapsing I developed an addiction to the muddy coffee spat out by the vending machine in the hall. The caffeine, entering my bloodstream so late in the evening, mostly just made my temples ache and my eyes water—but there was something about constant fatigue that worked for me. When the instructor—a retired RN named Joan—finally got her PowerPoint working, her lecture rolling, I found it easy to absorb every word. Maybe it was just because the information was so obviously essential to the job I wanted. If I was going to be a CNA, I was determined to be a good one, and that meant knowing the precise way to assist a patient with a bedpan, minimizing mess and embarrassment. It meant studying the ideal body temperatures and heart rates for people of different ages, genders, and sizes. It meant defining *Aphasia* and *Embolism* and *Bradycardia*.

Arrhythmia and *tachycardia* and *rigor mortis*.

None of which was entirely riveting by itself, but when Joan asked us questions about bedside manner and patient safety—about actually taking care of people—I wasn't just interested; most of the time I could guess the answers. On a night toward the end of May, our instructor put her fists on her hips and said, "Okay. Say you have a patient who's recovering from a stroke. Over the last few months he's regained some mobility in his arms and legs, but he's still shaky, still struggling with his exercises. And he won't let you feed him. He wants to feed himself. What do you do?"

A girl named Felicia stuck her hand in the air. She was close to my age, maybe nineteen, and always wore a faded sweatshirt advertising an aquarium in Newport, Oregon. "I would tell him he has to let me do it," Felicia said. "Respectfully, of course. But otherwise he'll make a mess, right? And then I'll have to clean him, change his sheets. I don't have the time. I have other patients to take care of."

Joan's expression was hard to read. "Anyone else?"

I raised my hand. Joan called on me, her lips twitching into a preemptive smile. Never once had a teacher looked at me like that.

"I would let him feed himself," I said.

"Why?" Joan asked.

"Because he wants to."

She nodded. "Good answer."

During our ten-minute break, Felicia followed me to the bathroom. As we washed our hands in front of a warped mirror, she asked if I knew where I wanted to do my clinicals. Assuming we didn't fail our written exams, we would all have to work two weeks of unpaid shifts at the hospitals or clinics that would eventually hire us.

"Retirement home in Crescent Bay," I told her.

Officially, we were supposed to submit our top three choices to our instructor, and Joan would do her best to match each of us with our preferred employer. But, on one of the rare mornings he'd shown up to math class, Seth O'Malley had all but promised I would get my first pick.

"I know a guy," was all he would say, when pressed.

"You know a guy?" I'd repeated. Seth's hair was always damp in the mornings. He smelled like the kind of cheap shampoo that's advertised exclusively to men—more spicy than sweet. I imagined him setting his alarm for the last possible minute, rolling out of bed, his mind still mired in dreams.

"Well, *technically* I know a lady," Seth had said.

Pulling paper towels from the dispenser, I asked Felicia, "What about you? Where do you want to train?"

"Anywhere. But as soon as I pass my clinicals, I'm looking for a job in LA."

"Really?"

"There's a ton of work in LA," she said, "and it's my favorite city. Have you ever been?"

"Sure." My parents were always combining academic conferences with family vacations; I had been all over.

"It's awesome, right?"

I shrugged. LA, in my experience, was all traffic and billboards and drive-through car washes. The palm trees lining every massive boulevard weren't enough to make the air smell like something you should breathe. "I like Seattle better."

"Is that where you'll look for work?"

For a few seconds, before I remembered I had already accepted a spot at Whedon, my heart lurched at the idea. Sometimes, I wished I had the nerve to tell my parents I wasn't particularly interested in college, that I would rather move to any big city, get a job, and see what happened. But more often than not, such a plan seemed so vague as to be completely terrifying.

Whedon College was my best option. There was nothing vague or unknown about it.

"Maybe," was all I told Felicia.

"You should get out of here," she said firmly. "We should *all* get out of here."

Felicia made it sound like Crescent Bay would soon be swallowed by a tidal wave.

To be fair, it was a real possibility.

Sara wouldn't stop declaring everything we did a milestone: last ever cafeteria breadstick. Last time filling in Scantron bubbles. Last assembly at which we had to watch the football team—including Seth, who wore a bandanna tied around his neck—perform a mortifying dance routine in the name of school spirit. On a Thursday in June, I exited the bathroom in the south hallway, saying, "That tampon dispenser ate my quarters again," and Sara cried, "That tampon dispenser has robbed you for the last time! Less than one menstrual cycle until graduation!"

Dutifully, Elliot said, "T-M-I," as if we'd never before subjected him to a conversation concerning our bodily fluids. As Sara spun in dreamy circles, it dawned on me that she was correct. And also that, soon, we probably wouldn't see each other often enough to discuss things as banal as tampons. That maybe, after people grew up and got lives and mortgages, they stopped discussing tampons altogether.

It seemed like a loss.

And then, despite incessant reminders from Sara, and also from the posters plastering the walls at school, I accidentally scheduled my CNA exam for Saturday evening, also known as prom night. We had chosen our time slots at the end of an especially long class—the projection screen had rebelled; our instructor had refused to stop quizzing us on heart attack symptoms—and in that moment, prom and Sara's recent obsession with it had been far from my mind. Taking the exam required driving forty miles south to a testing center in another town. I wouldn't be back in Crescent Bay until eight, at the earliest.

"I'm sorry," I groaned into the phone. "I guess I could throw a dress in my car and change in the parking lot."

"But who am I going to get ready with?" Sara asked. "*Elliot?*"

It was Friday night. I was lying with the phone pressed between my ear and the pillow. On the top bunk, Rosie was tossing from side to side, letting her bedsprings voice her annoyance. "Sure," I yawned. "Get him to French braid your hair."

Elliot had two little sisters. His braiding was top-notch.

"I wanted to get ready with *you*." Sara pouted.

I didn't know what to say. Maybe once, in seventh grade, Sara and I had idly wondered who our prom dates would be. In general, it wasn't a fantasy on which we'd dwelled.

"Since when do you care about prom so much?"

"I don't care about prom so much. I care about you so much. I miss you."

"You're the one who's leaving," I snapped, as if Sara Quintero spending her college years in Crescent Bay had ever been an option. She had a perfect grade point average, had known she wanted to be a veterinarian since she was six.

"And you're the one who's making sure we have no time to spend together before I leave!"

"It's not like I'm avoiding you. I'm just trying to . . ."

Trying to do something different. Trying to make my life in Crescent Bay feel as fresh and as daunting as Sara's would feel, the moment she arrived in Davis. But I couldn't make myself say any of this out loud. I worried Sara would think my efforts were pathetic, that in reality I was turning into the kind of girl who would get a job in town, marry a boy from school, and have three kids by the time she was twenty-four.

"Meet me at the dance," Sara said, excusing me from finishing my sentence.

"I'll throw a dress in my car," I agreed.

"By *a dress*, do you mean the only dress you own, which you already wore to your cousin's wedding in Baltimore two years ago?"

I took mental inventory of my closet. "I do."

"I'll loan you a dress. Text me when you get there and I'll do your makeup in the bathroom."

"Deal."

The exam took longer than I had expected, but I was pretty sure I had passed. Only two questions gave me pause—one about the precise definition of a stage-three bedsore, and one about the common signs of deep-vein thrombosis. On the drive back to Crescent Bay, I kept hoping for some kind of post-test adrenaline rush to kick in—some feeling I could exchange for prom-worthy levels of excitement. But I only felt beat. By the time I pulled into the school parking lot, I was trying to gauge the consequences of letting Sara down.

Every few minutes, the metal doors to the gym would fly open and eject a group of giggly, glittery seniors. The bass line of a pop song thumped, deafening, until the doors fell shut.

Seth O'Malley appeared in my passenger-side window.

My heart raced as I scrambled to lower the glass. As soon as there was space, Seth reached inside and unlocked the door. I watched, amused, as the guy struggled to fit his long legs between the seat and the glove compartment. My dad's car was a MINI Cooper, suited to people of average height, or else large numbers of clowns.

"Uh, what's up?" I asked him.

"Just taking a break." Seth flashed me the broad, unself-conscious smile of a little kid saying *cheese* for the camera. His tux had been tailored for someone much shorter and wider than he was.

"In my car?"

"I just came out to get something from my Jeep real quick. Then I saw you sitting alone in the dark . . . and I thought, *there's Audrey Nelson again.*"

"Again?"

"You're everywhere, lately."

"I'm exactly where I've always been."

"Well, now I see you."

"I see you, too."

"So it's mutual. We're both visible."

"Neither of us is a ghost."

He poked me in the arm, then nodded, satisfied. "So did you pass your exam?"

I had told Seth the date of my CNA exam whenever he'd last been in class, but I was surprised he remembered. "I think so."

"Good. As long as you passed, you'll be joining the exemplary staff at the Crescent Bay Retirement Home."

"According to the lady you know?"

"The director of the nursing home. We had a chat, and I vouched for you. Of course, I had to fudge some of the details—didn't mention your drug habit, or your snaggle-tooth."

Reflexively, my tongue sought each of my canines, but three years of orthodontia had forced my teeth into alignment long ago.

"Just kidding," Seth went on. "The only thing I had to say was that you're up for a long-term commitment."

I blinked.

"To the job," he clarified. "You're not planning to quit the moment you pass your clinicals, right?"

"Right." My dread of going inside the gym, of dancing, began to dissolve. The pieces of my summer were falling into place. "Thanks, Seth." Experimentally, I angled my right knee closer to his left.

Our legs remained separated by the gearshift.

"No problem," he said. "Working nights gets lonely. I like to try and sync my breaks with whoever's around, so I don't forget how to interact with other humans."

Socializing seemed like the last thing Seth O'Malley would ever forget how to do.

"I thought you worked days," I said.

"Only during the school year. Every summer I go nocturnal."

My phone vibrated against the cup holder. Sara's message lit up the screen: **Where are you??**

"You know—" I reached for my phone. Suddenly, I couldn't wait to see Sara. "Your tux doesn't really fit you. Like, at all."

"That's what my date said!"

"Who's your date?"

"Manda Hastings." All I knew about Manda Hastings was that her parents owned the surf shop in town, and also that her hair was the exact color of uncooked pasta. "Anyway," Seth said, gesturing to my body, making my skin feel tight, "you're the one wearing jeans."

"I'm about to change. Shouldn't you get back inside before they crown you prom king?"

Seth winced.

"Were you actually nominated?" I asked, starting to laugh.

"I'm very popular."

I cracked up, hard.

"Don't laugh," Seth said, but his shoulders were shaking. "We can't all be mysterious loners."

"I'm not a loner!"

"Oh, pardon me. I forgot about your two friends."

"Two is plenty!"

"If you say so, Audrey." He pronounced my name carefully, taking his time with both syllables. "Will I see you inside?"

"I thought we established that you see me everywhere."

Seth grinned. "That's right. How could I forget?"

"You'll see me inside. You'll see me in class. You'll even see me at graduation."

"And I'll see you at work, all summer long."

"All summer long," I echoed.

Seth climbed out of my car. I watched him glide across the parking lot, tucking loose strands of hair behind his ears. Crescent Bay's prom king had worn cowboy boots to the dance.

I texted Sara: **I'm here, I'm here.**

Her reply was a row of exclamation points.

SIX

At graduation, Seth and I sat in the same row of folding chairs, waiting for our turn to line up at the base of the stage. Separating us were Annie Nichols and Brian Oakley. On the school bus in fourth grade Brian had, for a reason I no longer remembered, pulled my hair until I screamed. Now he was jiggling his leg beneath his aquamarine robe, casting nervous glances at the sky, muttering, "Totally gonna rain." Somewhere far behind us sat Sara Quintero and Elliot Slate, banished to the back by virtue of their last names. If I had been allowed to sit with my friends, maybe graduating from high school would have felt more momentous. Instead I just felt detached, and annoyed.

Seth caught me glaring at Brian. Leaning forward, he said, "Brian, bro? Could you chill with the leg-shaking?"

Obediently, Brian froze. "Sorry, man."

A minute later we were shuffling toward the stage erected temporarily in the middle of the football field. I smiled only because my brother was in the audience; if my face looked weird, Jake would taunt me with pictures of the next three minutes for the rest of my life.

My name sounded awkward in the school principal's mouth. I'd never met the guy. Beside him, a receiving line of teachers beamed and mouthed, "Congratulations," dabbing at their eyes as I reached to shake the principal's surprisingly clammy hand.

"Tassel," he said under his breath.

Facing the audience for the few seconds it took to move the tassel from one side of my cap to the other, I grinned maniacally. I heard Sara's squeal, Elliot's baritone, and my brother hollering, "Nelson!" like I was his favorite baseball player stepping up to the plate.

After hurrying down the steps, I looked over my shoulder, expecting to see Seth close behind.

He was still onstage. He was holding up the entire show, keeping so many seniors from their long-sought diplomas, as he leaned toward one tearful teacher after another and wrapped each of them in a patented Seth O'Malley bear hug.

The whole process took forever.

A fan of graduations, Mom hadn't committed to going to Italy until I'd sworn up and down that I would not be devastated if she missed my ceremony. Now, in the parking lot, Dad insisted we needed to send her a family photo. In lieu of asking me who would be an appropriate choice, he flagged down the nearest graduate, Cameron Suzuki, to serve as our photographer.

Of all the girls in Crescent Bay, Cameron was the most widely beloved. While most of us had been born in one of three windowless delivery rooms at Steeds Memorial, Cameron had lived in Tokyo until she was a kindergartner. Every other July she traveled back to Japan with her parents, effectively ruining our teachers for the rest of our "How I Spent My Summer Vacation" reports. By high school, Cameron was so secure in her popularity she broke every rule associated with being adored by several hundred teenagers. For example, in eleventh grade she'd been voted homecoming queen but hadn't shown up to claim her crown. Later she explained she'd taken an impromptu backpacking trip with her father in Yosemite.

Now, she accepted my own father's battered phone and began sweetly bossing us around: "Jake, put your arm around your sister," and "Audrey, try to look happy! High school's over!"

She snapped what must have been fifty pictures before concluding, "You guys are adorable," returning Dad's phone, and jogging after a crowd of her friends.

"What a nice young lady," Dad said in a perfectly neutral tone that launched Rosie into a fit of giggles.

"Yep," I agreed, pulling my robe over my head and tossing it into the trunk of the car. Underneath, I was just wearing jean shorts and a thermal. A lot of kids had donned dresses and heels, curled their hair so it wouldn't look so oppressed beneath their caps. I hadn't seen the point.

"Was that the first time someone's described you as *adorable*?" Jake wanted to know. My brother had been home for less than twenty-four hours. His final exams had wrapped up halfway through May, but he'd spent the last couple of weeks with his new boyfriend's family in some suburb of New York.

"I doubt it. I was a baby once, you know."

"Yes," Dad confirmed, "but you were bald and prone to rashes."

"Gross," said Rosie.

For dinner we got takeout from the Fish Shack and carried our order down to the beach. In my life, I'd consumed more fried clams from the Fish Shack than was probably safe. Even before Dad passed me my food, I could taste the bland, rubbery shellfish, the lemon-soaked breading. It was the taste of Crescent Bay, the taste of boredom. And at the same time, the food was delicious—especially with some extra salt and the wind whipping my hair into my tartar sauce.

As my family ate, we leaned against a log and watched the sun sink into the ocean, flares of orange visible through the clouds. Dad said, "I can't believe two-thirds of my children now boast high school diplomas!"

"We would never boast about our diplomas," said my brother, tearing open a packet of ketchup.

"Yeah," I agreed, "that would be hella uncouth."

Rosie giggled some more.

Ignoring us, Dad said, "What do you think you'll study, Aud?" as if the question was brand-new, a topic over which no one had ever fretted.

Jake answered through a fake cough: "Poli-sci."

"Maybe I'll study business," I said lazily, knowing Whedon offered no such degree.

"Perfect," Dad said. "You can support me in my infirmity."

"That's the eldest child's burden, I think."

Jake scoffed. "Please. I won't even be done with my PhD by the time Dad's demented."

Our father dipped his chin to conceal a combination of amusement and dismay. "We've talked about this, Jakey," he said, recovering. "Five years. Nelsons write their dissertations in five years flat."

"Nobody cares what I want to study," Rosie whined.

"That's because you're the youngest," Jake explained.

"By the time you're eighteen, Mom and Dad will be so worn out from raising me and Audrey, they'll let you join the circus."

"I don't want to join the circus," Rosie said. "But maybe I want to major in Marine Biology."

The rest of us stared at her. She wiggled her butt deeper into the sand. "Or else English," she amended.

Dad retrieved his phone from his pocket. "Let's wake up Iris."

"Don't do that," Jake protested. "Let her sleep."

But Dad was already scrolling through his contacts. His eyes brightened when Mom answered on the first ring. "Say hello to Whedon's most promising incoming freshman!" he shouted before passing the phone to me.

I reached across my siblings. "Hi, Mom."

"Hi, honey." Her voice was thick with sleep. "Congratulations. I'm so sorry I couldn't be there."

"That's okay." I raked my fingers through the cold sand. Even when I hadn't been actively missing my mother, the sound of her voice always drilled a hole in my heart. I wondered if it was a permanent weakness or something I'd grow out of.

"You start at the old folks' home tomorrow, right?"

"Yeah," I said, unsurprised that she remembered. My mother could probably recall the date and duration of my last head cold, along with the precise circumstances under which I'd lost my final baby tooth.

"That's great. That'll be such an interesting experience to have before college." I knew my mother was bluffing. She thought that if she objected to my choice of a summer job, the work would only appeal to me more. Not because I was so rebellious, constantly scheming to piss off my parents, but because my mother was a woman of theories.

Sometimes, I wasn't sure she could see me through all those theories.

"Yeah, I think so," was all I said. Because even if her support was contrived, it still felt good. The way ice cream still tastes like ice cream, even when you're five years old and someone's bribing you to behave.

"When does your shift end?"

"Five a.m."

"Well, if you want to talk afterward, you know who to call."

Beside me, my brother was staring intently at the ocean. Allusions to my new job always made him uncomfortable. That I wanted to be a CNA was confusing to him, and Jake had that big-brother inability to cope with confusion. It was like he needed to know me better than I knew myself.

"Thanks," I said to Mom.

I could hear her yawning. "I better let you get back to your celebration."

"Want to talk to Dad again?" I tried to catch his eye, but he had joined Jake's staring contest with the Pacific.

"No thanks," she said. "I'll catch up with him later."

The speed with which she hung up unsettled me. It wasn't normal for my parents to decline a chance to exchange last-minute good-byes, reminders, instructions. Even when they weren't separated by half the world, just a mile or two, their communication tended toward constant.

"Okay, Ro," I said, in need of distraction. "Tell us about your future as a marine biologist."

The tips of my sister's ears turned pink. "I heard that you get to swim with dolphins. I was mostly kidding."

Dad jostled her shoulder. "Pick English. One of my kids should write a best-selling memoir about what it was like to be reared by the aloof-yet-charming novelist Hunter Nelson. The opportunity is my gift to you."

Rosie took a noisy slurp of her soda, sucking up the dregs from beneath the ice. "Work on the *charming* part, and it's a deal."

Dad grinned at the three of us, like he had never been so proud of his sandy, salty brood.

When I turned fifteen, Sara and Elliot came to my backyard birthday party. They were the only guests to whom I wasn't directly related by blood. Afterward, the three of us were alone in my room when Elliot said, appalled, "Your family is so *mean*."

"What are you talking about?" I asked, looking from Sara to Elliot, wondering who had hurt them and how I'd missed it.

"Not to us," Sara clarified. "You're mean to each other."

At fifteen, I vaguely understood that my family members had the potential to strike outsiders as rowdy and rude. I knew, also, that our behavior was extra abrasive on special occasions, such as birthdays, and that my mother—who didn't even participate in the aggression—provided the security we needed to proceed with it. Because even if someone started crying, Iris would be there to bandage his or her wounds. What I hadn't realized was how purely heartless we seemed, until my friends began listing examples.

First, ten-year-old Rosie had emerged from the bathroom having blow-dried her hair for the first time ever, and Dad had said, "Whoa, who invited Tom Petty?"

Jake challenged our father to name a single Tom Petty song and, when he couldn't, tried to call Dad a dilettante but accidentally said *debutante*. Dad guffawed and feigned concern over my brother's soon-to-be-released SAT scores. And I, bored of the vocabulary mishap, asked the group, "Who do you guys think would win if Mom and Dad arm wrestled?"

Mom won, and the rest of us made sure Nelson never lived it down.

But I didn't really believe we were mean. On nights like tonight, when we shared dinner in the sand, lightly ridiculing one another in a way that proved we *knew* one another—then coming home and drifting wordlessly, comfortably into our respective corners—I wasn't sure I'd ever completely belong to anyone aside from the Nelsons. Our meanness was a by-product of our closeness. We strove to offend one another just to prove it wasn't really possible; we were indivisible.

Before bed, I checked my phone one last time, curious to see if I'd been tagged in the background of any graduation selfies captioned, *We did it!* or *What a wild ride!*

My only notification was for an unread e-mail. It was from a blogging platform I had signed up for years ago and never used. I would have dismissed the message as junk if not for its subject line: *Someone you know* (Iris Cox Nelson) *has started a blog!*

Automatically, I followed the link. In general my mother was blind to the nuances of the World Wide Web; she couldn't have defined *meme* or *troll* or *clickbait*. But even Iris made the occasional attempt to get with the times. For instance, she had a Twitter account featuring a single tweet—*Enjoying a night off w/my girls!!*—referring to the time she and Rosie and I drove forty miles to see *The Hunger Games*, and also a Facebook profile with a picture she hadn't changed in seven years.

I was expecting to find unorganized bits of her research, or else a dumping ground for photos of the Mediterranean. The blog's title, **SPRUNG FREE IN ITALY!**, didn't bother me until I read the subhead:

An anonymous account of my trial separation from my husband of twenty-five years.

It was a joke. A prank.

I reminded myself that the Internet was not real life— that anyone could impersonate anyone. Meanwhile, my chest tightened uncomfortably and my eyes skimmed the post. It was a list. A list of reasons.

- **He still hasn't forgiven me for being the first to get tenure.**

- **Claims to be a feminist but doesn't pull his weight with the kids or housework.**

I felt dizzy, even though I was leaning against a dune of pillows. Apparently I'd made some kind of noise; Rosie had been reading a book on the top bunk, but now she was leaning over the edge of her mattress, her hair waterfalling, demanding, "Audrey, what happened?"

- **Last summer, when I wanted to go out to dinner to celebrate a forthcoming publication, he advised me to "choose my celebrations as I would my battles."**

- **Insists upon working at the kitchen table but groans theatrically anytime someone tries to use the room for food prep.**

- **At conference last year, introduced me as "Wife" rather than "Professor N."**

I struggled to think of a response for my little sister. She didn't need to know about the separation because it wasn't real. She didn't need to know about our mother's blog because it would be gone by morning—like when a celebrity accidentally tweets something offensive.

"Nothing," I said. "Mom's just bugging me."

"Oh, yeah." Rosie relaxed. "Did she forward you that article about how kids who do a shitload of extracurricular activities end up making more money?"

- **Needs me more than ever. Loves me less.**

- **Chews ice.**

"Yup," I managed.

"So annoying!" Rosie commiserated. "Like, can we live?"

I powered off my phone, breathing a sigh of relief as the screen went black.

"I wish," I told her.

SEVEN

My supervisor was an RN in her early twenties named Maureen, who wore scrubs patterned with flamingos and seemed to hate me. For the first few hours of my shift, she'd lulled me into a false sense of security, playing with my hair and regaling me with anecdotes starring her twin toddlers, Evan and Eve. Then, as our midnight break approached—mysteriously, it was still called *lunch*—Maureen's veneer of friendliness began to crack. I was helping Mrs. Goldstein brush her teeth when Maureen chirped, "We don't have all night, here!" with an aggressive trill of laughter.

I could have worked faster. The issue was that brushing another person's teeth was just as awkwardly intimate as you would expect—particularly the molars—and it didn't seem right to speed through the task as if scrubbing grime from a toilet bowl. Toward the end of our rounds, Maureen lost it when I failed to pull Mr. Leary's blanket all the way up to his chin. "Try not to give anyone pneumonia on your first night," she snapped, right over Mr. Leary's sleeping body.

I took a breath. I could feel my composure unraveling. Part of me wanted to tell Maureen that it was difficult to focus on every single rule I'd learned in night school when, more recently, I'd learned that my parents were secretly separated. That my mother hadn't been drawn to Italy by the promise of work so much as she'd been driven from home by the presence of Dad. These were facts that broke every rule, every assumption I'd ever made in my life.

But whining to my supervisor about my newly shattered innocence—as if she were my friend, or my guidance counselor—would have felt hopelessly juvenile. I didn't know a lot about being an adult, but I knew it meant not crying on the job.

I apologized. We moved on to the next resident's room.

By lunchtime, I was conflicted. I needed a break from Maureen's hawk eyes, a chance to assess whether I could actually do this job or if my incompetence was a permanent thing. But a break would mean a chance to confirm that my mother's blog had not, in fact, vanished into thin air. Since this morning, she had already updated with a fresh post entitled *Reasons, Part II*.

In the end, I didn't get a choice; Maureen followed me into the break room. The moment I sat down, she sent a clipboard skidding across the table.

"What is this," she demanded.

I swigged from my Diet Coke and answered, "That would be Mrs. Lu's chart."

Maureen massaged her eyelids. Her frustration clashed with her flamingo scrubs. "Please see what you wrote under *oral intake*."

"One hundred and fifty milliliters of apple juice," I recited obediently.

"Is that how much you think she drank before bed?"

"Yes. That's why I wrote it down."

"Audrey? Sweetie? I'm going to need you to start paying attention. Because I was in Mrs. Lu's room with you, and it was obvious to me that she consumed one hundred and *eighty* milliliters of juice. Do you think maybe you were distracted by the TV?"

"Uh." The television in Mrs. Lu's room was tuned to the Home Shopping Network, but Maureen had been the one captivated by gemstones and exercise machines—not me.

"You have to stay focused, all right?" She paused. "Are you hearing my feedback?"

I forced myself to meet her eyes for a single second. When I looked away, I was horrified by the presence of Seth O'Malley, hovering in the doorway. He was wearing his bleach-stained jeans, his hair in a sanitary knot at the nape of his neck. My heart raced as my cheeks burned. I wondered how long he'd been standing there, and how much he'd heard.

Oblivious to our audience, Maureen sang, "I need to know you're hearing my feedback. . . ."

"Yeah," I mumbled, staring down at the linoleum, willing Seth to leave. "I heard you."

Maureen nodded, satisfied, and went to the freezer to retrieve a Lean Cuisine Hot Pocket.

When I finally looked up, Seth was gone.

I found him after work, leaning against the trunk of his Jeep. Sunlight was just starting to seep through the clouds. In one hand, Seth clutched two small bottles of apple juice—in the other, a brown paper bag.

I hadn't planned on acknowledging what had happened in the break room, now or ever, but as Seth passed me a juice, brushing his knuckles against mine, I found I was too exhausted to be embarrassed. Nothing mattered except that I hadn't gotten fired, and that I'd soon be in bed.

"I don't have to tell you how many milliliters are in this, do I?"

Seth scoffed. "Are you kidding? I won't stand for that metric nonsense. I'm an American, and that there is eight fluid ounces of naturally flavored juice beverage."

Next he presented me with the paper bag, still warm.

Inside were two muffins with fresh blueberries and cream cheese centers. I knew about the cream cheese centers only because these muffins were a hot topic among the residents; even on my first night, I'd heard them referenced more than once.

"Courtesy of Chef Tony," said Seth.

I reached into the bag. "Tony's a good man."

"Tony's an asshole," Seth corrected me. "But he makes good muffins."

It was subtle, Seth's way of letting me know that he, too, had a boss who used his minuscule amount of power for evil. I appreciated the solidarity almost as much as the free breakfast.

When I had swallowed the last bite, Seth slumped against the car, pressing his shoulder into mine. I didn't want him to ever move. "Let's walk on the beach," he said.

"It's raining."

"It's not raining. It's just wet."

The distinction only made sense on the coast, but I knew what he meant. Drops never really fell. Instead, humidity and ocean mist mingled to form a constant wall of moisture. You felt nothing and got soaked anyway.

"Okay," I agreed. The muffins had given me a fresh surge of energy, and now I felt like staying close to Seth. I was starting to realize I was happier when he was near me.

We both had cars parked at the nursing home, but I willingly climbed into Seth's Jeep. It meant that later he would have to drive me back up the bluff, but I didn't point this out. The Jeep, I noticed, no longer smelled like Rusty Tillman's puke. It smelled primarily like fresh-cut firewood, and just a bit like dirty laundry.

Dangling from the rearview mirror was a picture of a little kid, his chubby arm thrown around a black lab. When I asked, Seth said, "My nephew."

We parked in the dunes. Predictably, the beach was empty, cold, and decked with fog. My hospital scrubs were a poor shield against the wind and the water. I only had to shiver once before Seth unzipped his hoodie and gave it to me.

"So, how was your first night?" he asked. "Aside from the juice fiasco?"

Before we'd started talking in Mr. Longo's class, I would never have expected Seth to use words like *fiasco*.

I took a deep breath of cold air. "Honestly? It was so, so hard."

"More than you signed up for?"

"I had no idea what I was signing up for. That's why I did it."

"Really?" Seth said. "You were like, 'what's the wildest thing I could do this summer?' and decided it'd be working at the nursing home?"

"Exactly."

"Have you tried sex, drugs? Rock 'n' roll?"

Seth O'Malley saying *sex* did a number on my heart. "Um, sort of," I said, flustered and annoyed by his proclivity for making me blush.

He tilted his head. "You've *sort of* tried sex, drugs, and rock 'n' roll?"

It was an awkward but not inaccurate answer, and I stuck with it. Seth grinned, like my honesty gave him a thrill.

"I thought I was going to be really good at this job," I confessed. "And I think tonight would have been a lot easier, except I just found out that my mom's sabbatical in Italy has been doubling as a separation from my dad."

Sleep deprivation was like a drug, I realized. The inhibition-lowering kind.

"What's a sabbatical?" Seth asked.

I sometimes forgot that not everyone was fluent in the lingo of academia. "It's when you're a professor and you get these insanely long vacations so you can work on, like, improving your intellect."

"Or your marriage?"

"Apparently."

"Had your parents been fighting a lot? Before my mom left my dad, she screamed at him over every little thing. Like him tracking mud across the carpet or forgetting to take the empties to the curb."

"They literally never fight. Sometimes when my mom has an issue she'll write my dad a strongly worded letter, and then he'll write back until they work it out."

"A letter? Like, sent via the postal service?"

"No. She usually leaves it next to the salt and pepper shakers on the kitchen table."

Seth blinked. "That's so strange."

"Professors are a strange people."

"Are you excited about Whedon? Isn't that supposed to be a really good school?"

My stomach flipped. I didn't want to go to Whedon. My lack of desire to go to Whedon had never been more evident than in this moment, on the beach with Seth.

"Yeah," I managed to respond, because I didn't know Seth's plans and didn't want to seem ungrateful. Whedon College was, in fact, a really good school—one that never should have let me in, no matter whose daughter I was.

"I always thought—" For the first time all morning, Seth stumbled over his words. "I mean, not that I *thought* about it that much, but if I had, I would have expected you to get the hell out of here."

"Out of Crescent Bay?" I was flattered.

"Don't you want to?"

"Definitely, someday. What about you?"

Seth shrugged. "Maybe. Someday. But I love it here."

He declared his love so easily.

"Are you going to community college?" I asked.

"Undecided. For now, I need to save some money."

"No one offered you a football scholarship?"

Seth looked at me askance, unsure if I was kidding. "I don't know how many games you caught this year—"

"As many as I possibly could," I joked.

"—but I'm not actually very good at football. I'm too tall and skinny. To tackle me, all you have to do is go for my knees."

"I'll remember that."

Seth lifted his chin and let the wind pummel his face. His lips veered into a smile—either at the thought of me tackling him or just because he found the ocean breeze refreshing. Exhaustion messed with my judgment so that it was hard to tell. Everything was starting to sound strangely remote, as if Seth and I were conversing underwater.

When I remembered Seth O'Malley, the guy from school, I pictured him leaning over a girl—any random girl—his fingers tangled in her hair or hooked through the belt loop on her jeans. Never for a moment had I fantasized about taking that girl's place, and even now, I didn't want anything to do with the kind of boy I had always understood Seth to be.

But I did want to kiss this boy walking next to me. The one who was confident without being cocky, candid without being self-centered. He had made me feel better about my embarrassing first-day-on-the-job performance.

He had stolen muffins on my behalf.

One question was whether I was even tall enough to reach his face. *To be determined,* I told myself—and then, before I could change my mind, I grabbed hold of Seth's arm.

Just as abruptly, he stopped walking. "You ready to turn back?"

The unsuspecting look in his eyes convinced me he would be nothing but alarmed if I kissed him. Seth had no interest in making out with me; all he wanted was to align our lunch breaks. All he wanted was to avoid loneliness on the night shift.

I must have been staring at him with open despair, because Seth's expression went slack, sympathetic. "You look like you need to sleep for a year," he said.

It wasn't a bad idea.

EIGHT

Seth had asked me for a ride to our town's Fourth of July festival, but it wasn't a date. Apparently, one of Seth's buddies needed to borrow the Jeep to tow a boat someplace, and Seth could not, under any circumstances, miss the festival. His fondest childhood memory was of the year he and his brothers had won the sand sculpture contest for their rendering of SpongeBob SquarePants. Each summer, the O'Malley boys had donned their Stars and Stripes and marched in the parade, whereas my family had never even gone to watch. After two decades of living in Crescent Bay, Mom and Dad were still hell-bent against considering themselves locals.

During my first two weeks on the job, Seth had gifted me with countless blueberry muffins, assorted juices, and cups of reheated coffee. For every complaint I shared about my supervisor, he described Chef Tony berating him in front of the rest of the kitchen staff, or forcing him to wear a hairnet just to mop a floor. After our shifts, more often than not, we walked across the sand and watched the sun come up, sharing high school stories as if high school was something that had transpired a long time ago. The night he and his friends busted a tire trying to drive to the In-N-Out Burger in Grant's Pass. The night Sara, Elliot, and I had a sleepover in the hayloft and were woken up at three a.m. by the murderous threats of Sara's barn cats confronting a raccoon family.

We still hadn't kissed. I was beginning to think that I would never gather the nerve, and that Seth had taken some summer-long vow of celibacy—on a whim, or a dare.

On July Fourth, I slept through the afternoon and woke up around six, leaving hardly any time to get ready. The bathroom door was locked; my little sister yelled at me to *suck it up*. Most likely Rosie had taken a box of Popsicles and a stack of novels into the tub. It was her default summer activity.

I picked the lock with a hairpin. Rosie roared like a lion and pulled the shower curtain shut.

"You have to at least let me pee," I said, pushing down my shorts.

"You're disgusting," she observed from behind the curtain.

"And you're a tiny tyrant."

When I had washed my hands and was beginning to

apply eyeliner, Rosie protested again. "Use the full-length," she said. "Jake has it."

The *full-length* was how we referred to the cheap, oblong mirror Rosie and I had bought to lean against the wall of our room, but which Jake thieved constantly.

"I can't go in there," I told Rosie. "It's full of Crescent Bay High graduates." Our brother's default summer activity was to invite all of his pals and their unenthused girlfriends to play video games in his bedroom.

"Yeah, so?"

"So I'd rather deal with you than them."

I could sense Rosie rolling her eyes. On my way out of the bathroom, I yanked open the curtain just to make her scream.

In the kitchen, I found my father hunched over the table, surrounded by loose pages covered in his own chicken scratch. I told him I was going out. Letting him know where I was going had turned into a sort of courtesy. Since his seminars had ended in May, Dad had sunk too deep into his new book to keep track of my erratic schedule. Sometimes I wondered whether Mom had even informed him that they were separated. Maybe the trial breakup was all in her head, a thought experiment she was conducting for her own private reasons. Iris was prone to thought experiments.

She was not, as far as I knew, prone to keeping secrets from my dad.

Ignoring me, he scribbled another sentence, ended it with a forceful period, and declared, *"Done."*

"With what?"

He looked up, finally registering my presence. Some pasta sauce clung to his beard and his Whedon College T-shirt was almost, but not exactly, the same color as his shorts.

"With a full draft!"

Dad's novels were, technically, about a lot of things, but reviews always praised him for capturing *the essence of the Pennsylvanian middle class*. He had grown up in Pittsburgh and hadn't been back since my grandmother's death, five years ago.

"First draft?" I asked my father. Occasionally I tried to read one of his novels, but I always fell asleep before reaching chapter two.

"Second!"

He was beaming in my direction.

"That's great," I said, trying hard to mean it. "Congrats."

"Do you want to go out to dinner? See a film of some kind? We ought to celebrate."

"I'm going to the beach. It's the Fourth of July."

"Right." Dad nodded. "Independence. I almost forgot."

"I think you're the only person in Crescent Bay who could forget."

Dad smiled like I had paid him a compliment, and asked who I was meeting. Something stopped me from saying Seth's name. I doubted Dad knew anything about the O'Malleys, but in a town so small, it was always possible. "Just Sara and Elliot," I told him.

"Have fun," he said.

Leaving the room was harder than I wanted it to be. Celebrating the distinct phases of Dad's manuscripts had always been our ritual. His triumph would inevitably morph into a kind of hyper-focused attention, all for me. We would go to the ice-cream place in town and sit across from each other at a sloped picnic table covered in seagull shit. He liked to ask me specific questions about my friends and my school assignments, until I felt endlessly fascinating, like a celebrity granting an interview to the press.

"Hey," I said, "remember when Mom got that article published last year? Like, around Christmas?"

Dad squinted into the distance. "I think so. Yes."

"I was wondering, why didn't we go out to dinner or anything?"

Dad searched my eyes. "Probably because it was her fourth publication of the year," he said. "You know Iris. Ever modest."

It was my turn to search his eyes for signs of jealousy, for signs of resentment to rival that which Mom had aired to so many strangers on the Internet. But Nelson's gaze was impassive. The question wasn't whether I knew my mother. The question was whether I knew either of them.

At Seth's house, a basketball hoop lay overturned in the grass, beside an aboveground pool that had been drained of water. A tangle of blackberry bushes half-covered the only window visible from the driveway. He had asked me to honk instead of sending a text; cell service got spotty as you went higher into the hills.

It had been a while since I'd seen Seth in anything but the ratty clothes he wore to work. Now, emerging from the house, he had on a clean white T-shirt and stain-less blue jeans. He looked like the prototype of a boy. It had never oc-curred to me that what I most desired in a boy was maximum boyness, but, as Seth crossed the driveway and squeezed himself into the MINI Cooper, my pulse confirmed that this was the case.

Seth had buckled his seat belt by the time I noticed the football in his hands.

"What is that?"

"It's a football," he said, his knees colliding with the glove compartment. "Crucial to a game called . . . football."

"But why do you have it?"

"You said your friends wouldn't be into sand sculpting."

"So you thought we'd all tackle one another instead?"

Seth pacified me with a look. "I thought we could throw it around."

"My friends aren't going to play football with you," I told him.

"Not even Elliot?"

"Especially not Elliot."

"Okay, okay," Seth said, grinning. "Calm down."

Calm was the opposite of how I felt as Seth leaned over the center console and pushed a lock of hair out of my face. The gesture was unprecedented. Occasionally, Seth pressed his shoulder against mine or grazed my hand as he passed me a paper cup. He had never touched me so deliberately.

"Um," I said, staring at him.

He returned his hands to his lap. "Shall we?"

I fumbled with the key in the ignition. Until I started hanging out with Seth, I'd never fully understood the meaning of the phrase *sexual tension*. And I still wasn't sure if it was supposed to apply to two people who had never so much as held hands, but it was the only way to describe the way I felt around him—torn between melting into a puddle of embarrassment and climbing into his lap.

Normally, I wasn't so afraid of kissing the people I wanted

to kiss. With my last boyfriend—Cole Hendrix, junior year—I had initiated everything from our first conversation to our awkward breakup hug. With Seth, I was convinced the stakes were higher. If we did start something, I wasn't sure how fast he would expect us to proceed. The last time the word *virgin* had applied to Seth O'Malley was probably the year Sara finally persuaded me to start shaving my legs. And I wasn't dying to explain to Seth that my own virginity was about half gone, that Cole Hendrix and I had experienced technical difficulties the night of our junior prom.

It wasn't a conversation I could imagine us having. Not yet.

For once, it was eighty degrees in Crescent Bay. The beach had been divided into sections, with a place for sand sculpting and a place to plant chairs and blankets for tonight's fireworks show. The required firefighters were gathered beneath a tent, where everyone's dad but mine stood around grilling hot dogs, passing out drinks. Beneath a neighboring tent, Crescent Bay High cheerleaders painted little kids' faces with flags and cartoon eagles.

Through the haze of barbecue smoke and patriotism, I saw my friends and waved.

From a distance, Cameron Suzuki's proximity to Elliot appeared incidental—the beach was crowded—but as they approached, I could see how hard she was clutching his elbow. Cameron, with her plaited black hair and easy smile, was beautiful, animated, and not someone I had ever expected to find attached to my perpetually poker-faced friend. My confusion must have been evident; the second Seth and I were within earshot, Cameron launched into an explanation.

"So I went into the Qwick Mart the other night, and I saw Elliot working the cash register, and I thought, *that boy is cute!* And I thought, *how have I never noticed before?* Must have been because he was so quiet in school. But then Elliot asked if he could help me find anything, and I was suddenly so nervous, I forgot I'd come in for gum and I bought a box of Duraflame logs."

Cameron tossed her braid over her shoulder and giggled.

"So the next night, I went back and bought a second box, thinking it would be self-deprecating and adorable, like, how embarrassing, I'm so into you I keep buying Duraflame logs. But *this one*"— she nudged Elliot—"didn't get it. He just asked me if I wanted a receipt."

Elliot shrugged. "It's store policy."

"This morning I came clean. I texted Elliot and asked if he wanted to meet me at the festival. He said yes! I mean, obviously."

Cameron began looking all around, like maybe one of her real friends would appear and recuse her.

"Great story," Sara said. "Even better the second time."

Shuffling his feet in the sand, Seth said, "I enjoyed it."

Elliot turned to him. "You brought a football."

"Yeah, man." Seth tossed the ball at my friend, who caught it against his chest, cringing—like when you slap a mosquito and have to deal with the bloody aftermath.

Cameron relieved Elliot of the football. "Go long!" she hollered at Seth.

Obediently, Seth bounded through the crowd and toward the waves. Cameron followed, leaving Elliot solo.

"Well, that was fast," he said, watching them retreat.

"Popular kids," Sara said. "They always find each other."

I knew she hadn't meant to be insulting—but it stung, thinking that Seth automatically shared something with Cameron that he didn't share with me.

Sara draped a skinny arm around each of our necks. The three of us walked like that, out of the fray and over to a log where we could sit and observe Elliot's date playing with mine. The sun had started its descent toward the horizon. Soon the sky would catch fire and we would all take out our phones, like we'd never seen a sunset before.

Seth and Cameron were throwing the football as high

as possible and competing to see who could catch it. Twice they crashed into each other and tumbled into the shallow waves, meaning, I guess, that nobody won. I would have been increasingly jealous if there had been anything romantic about this routine—but they were playing pretty rough, like dogs or brothers.

As usual, Sara knew what I was thinking. "If they were animals they'd both be Labradors," she said. "Too much energy, and too eager to please."

"What would Elliot be?"

"Elliot would be a horse. Aloof, regal."

"Wow," said Elliot, but it was clear he was flattered.

"What about me?" I asked.

Sara turned and squinted, her face extremely close to mine. She had the densest eyelashes of anyone I'd ever known. They were so long they almost touched her eyebrows. "You're like a cat," she concluded. "You know who your friends are."

I was about to ask her to animalize herself—a challenge she wasn't likely to accept—when, down by the water, Cameron stopped running. I watched as she hunched her shoulders and folded at the waist. She attempted to sit in a chair that did not exist, and then she fell to the sand.

"What the hell?" I heard Elliot ask, his voice slow and heavy.

And then I was running. Because a part of me knew exactly what I had seen. In night school, we had watched videos of the moment when a person's heart stops beating. Cameron's collapse was unambiguous. It was textbook.

Another part of me was in denial. Cameron was a kid, and a girl—not an eighty-year-old man. She wasn't sick, as far as I knew. She hadn't been mixing Red Bull and Adderall. She had been playing catch with a boy.

The dry sand squeaked against my heels. The wet sand cut into my toes. The ocean had never felt so far away.

At the edge of the water, Seth was kneeling beside Cameron's body, gently smacking her face. "Wake up, Cam. Wake up."

"Move," I said, pushing on Seth's broad shoulders.

"I think she fainted," he said.

"No. She didn't."

I opened Cameron's mouth to check if she was breathing. She wasn't breathing. "Call 9-1-1," I told Seth, who might as well have been a stranger, he seemed so remote.

"I don't have my phone." He spoke with the vacancy of someone who really was about to faint. But my friends had caught up to us, and they had phones. Sara dialed the number and Elliot took off sprinting in the direction of the tents.

Cameron's lips were faintly blue. "Fuck," I said, and made sure her head was flat against the sand.

"What are you doing?" Seth asked. "You're going to hurt her."

"I'm sorry," I said, apologizing for everything that was about to happen, feeling both like I'd already failed and like I had no choice. "She's not breathing."

I stacked my hands against Cameron's breastbone. I locked my fingers and stood on my knees, so I could press down with the weight of my upper body. Compressions were supposed to match the rhythm of some pop song from the seventies, but I couldn't remember what it was. At first, I could only remember the number three. As in: *Three percent of people are successfully revived by CPR.*

And then I remembered our instructor, Joan, saying, "If you feel the person's ribs break, you're doing it right."

I pressed harder.

Sara was still talking into the phone. Some random people were hovering over Cameron's body, blocking the sun. I wanted to stop. I was in so much searing pain; it felt like someone had lit my arms on fire.

"I have to stop," I said out loud. But no one offered to take my place.

I was supposed to do thirty compressions on Cameron's chest before attempting to breathe air into her lungs, but either I forgot or I was terrified, and I never counted to thirty. And then Elliot was back. He had brought the firefighters with him. One of them grabbed me around the waist and pulled me off of Cameron. The other took over compressions.

I let myself fall backward. The sun was a bruised orange against the black screen of my eyelids. I heard the sirens, the ambulance plowing through the sand, the paramedics unloading a gurney.

One of them asked, "Does the victim have a known heart condition?"

I had forgotten all about Seth, but now I listened to him say, through sobs, "No. She's always been healthy."

And I was gone, way too far gone to wonder how Seth knew anything about Cameron Suzuki's heart.

NINE

I didn't realize I had left my sandals on the beach until I was sitting in the waiting room, staring down at my bare toes encrusted with wet sand. That panicked, vulnerable feeling washed over me—the one you get just before you figure out you're dreaming.

I nudged Sara. "Hey. I'm not wearing any shoes."

She looked at me, her summer tan diluted by the fluorescent lights, and then down at my feet. "Audrey," Sara said, "where the hell are your shoes?"

On my other side, Elliot stood abruptly and went to the vending machine, which was making a sound like a lawn mower. The sound competed with the screams of some kid across the room. Squeezing a carton of two-percent milk, the toddler sobbed, "I want it to be choc-o-*late*," over and over, always exhaling on the last syllable.

Seth had gone with Cameron in the ambulance, after the paramedics shocked Cameron's heart into responding with a weak pulse that convinced no one she would survive. I hadn't questioned Seth's decision to go with them until my friends and I were halfway across the beach, heading for my car. The ambulance had left long, erratic tracks in the sand, swooping around logs and umbrellas.

"Why did he go with her?" I'd asked Elliot. "Why didn't you go?"

The way he stared at me, it was like I'd spoken a foreign language.

Sara's eyes grew wide. She tilted her head, studying me. "Audrey. Cameron is Seth's ex."

I blinked.

"They were together for most of senior year. You didn't know that?"

I wanted to cry, but only because I'd wanted to cry since the back doors of the ambulance had slammed shut and I understood that we were, most likely, never going to see Cameron again. So she was Seth's ex. Seth wasn't my anything. A girl from school had collapsed at the Fourth of July festival and now we needed to go to the hospital. There was nothing else to discuss.

Noticing how hard my hands were shaking, Elliot requested the car key. Sara, sitting up front, accused him of not knowing which corkscrew of a road climbed the hill to Steeds Memorial. He had repeated *Fuck you*, just under his breath and with a lot of space between the two words. As if the words carried less weight when separated. As if he knew he'd eventually want to take them back.

Now Elliot was crossing the windowless waiting room, handing me a bottle of water. I chugged half of it. Looming over my chair, he gave me a nod of approval.

"I did it wrong," I confessed, capping the bottle.

I knew Cameron was dead. And I also knew that if someone else had reached her sooner—one of the firefighters, or a real nurse, or just some guy with strong biceps and a good memory for *Baywatch* reruns—she might have made it.

Holding out hope required more energy than I had left.

"You don't know that," Sara said, a beat too late. She began scratching at the skin above my knee, gently and rhythmically. Sara sometimes forgot that people were not animals—that I, especially, was not one of her barn cats, soothed or excited according to her whims.

But I did know. In night school, our instructor had promised that the trick to effective CPR administration was to stay calm, and I had not stayed calm. I had drenched my T-shirt with sweat and come close to quitting before the firefighters even showed up. Joan had also told us to perform thirty compressions before beginning mouth-to-mouth. I had forgotten to breathe for Cameron. And wasn't that the step literally *anyone* else would have remembered—

from their poolside fantasies, or, at least, from the movies?

I still had no memory of Cameron and Seth together. I didn't know if they had been prone to making out in the hallway, or posing for yearbook photos. Whether they had been the couple most likely to get married, or run the country, or have twenty kids and their own reality TV show.

A set of glass doors slid open on the far side of the waiting room, and Seth appeared. His ponytail had come loose, and he'd upgraded his usual smile to a grin so broad it crinkled the skin around his eyes.

Why did he look so happy?

Seth stood in front of me, gesturing for me to stand. I did and he wrapped his arms around my middle. "You're going to break my ribs," I said, enjoying the pressure of his arms. Not wanting him to let go.

"I don't even care." He shifted to give each of my friends, whom he barely knew, an equally bone-crushing hug. They hugged him back, like Seth had always been one of us. He said that Cameron was going to be fine. Totally, completely fine. She had regained consciousness in the ambulance. She needed a pacemaker. Her life would resume.

More arms wrapped around my waist, making it difficult to breathe.

A fan of the facts, Elliot asked Seth, "Do they know what caused it?"

With minor difficulty, as if trying to pronounce some-thing he'd memorized for a quiz, Seth said, "It was a cardiac rhythm disturbance."

Sara kept shouting my name, which she did when she was mad at me—but also, apparently, when she was ecstatic. "You didn't do it wrong! Audrey Nelson, you saved a person's life!"

And I kept shaking my head. Someone else was responsible—the firefighter with his confident hands, the paramedics with their defibrillators.

Everyone in that waiting room was waiting for me to say something. To jump up and down, or weep with joy, or just bow my head in humble acknowledgment of what I had done.

I could hear that kid sniffling over her milk, which still was not chocolate.

The praise was too much. The roomful of strangers staring at me was too much. My longing to feel Seth's skin against mine—a longing he had triggered just by hugging me—was too much, and also entirely inappropriate.

"I need to go home," I announced. "I'm really sorry. I just feel like I should go home, put some shoes on."

Confused, Seth looked down at my bare feet. In the next moment he recovered and fixed me with an intense stare. "Do you want me to drive you?"

My bottom lip actually shook as I tried to tell him, *No, stay.*

"What about Cameron?" Elliot asked.

Seth threw a glance over his shoulder, toward the glass doors. "She's pretty out of it, but . . ." A sigh made his chest rise and fall. "Yeah. Her parents are here. I should probably stay with them."

It took me a second to realize that Seth *knew* Cameron's parents. He knew them well enough to be a source of comfort.

"I'm okay," I managed, holding out my hand, asking Elliot to relinquish my car key. "I promise."

The indecision in Seth's eyes would mean something to me, someday. Right now, all I wanted was to get the hell out of that waiting room.

So I did.

I grabbed my car keys and abandoned my friends, and Seth, and the girl whose heart had stopped beating. *Rattled* was not a sensation with which I was totally familiar. *All shook up* was not a state in which I often found myself. I needed to catch my breath. Alone.

But then, once I had my hands on the steering wheel and the radio tuned to a familiar Emmylou Harris song, I realized I was okay. Everything was fine. I had been terrified, but it had never been my own life or my own body on the line. And Cameron had lived. Someday she would die for real, but now there was a good chance I wouldn't have anything to do with it.

The hill leading down to the highway was steep, surrounded by colossal trees that, if rotten or storm-cracked, could easily fall and block the road. In Crescent Bay, everything crucial—public schools, emergency rooms—had been built on higher ground. Ordinary storms were not our main concern. People in town loved to talk casually about the tsunami—they called it *the big one*—that would someday take us all down.

It was a source of local pride, this idea that we lived here fearlessly.

For a minute I hung out in the driveway, leaning against the car, not yet ready to go inside. The air still smelled like fireworks, and I remembered the cheap dollar-store sparklers with which Rosie and I had always tried to write our names against the sky. I remembered Jake kneeling over a Roman candle, Dad calling cheerfully from the front porch, "Don't set your thumb on fire!" while Mom buried her face in her hands.

The truth was that no one ever worried about anything when she was around; we were confident she would worry enough for the rest of us.

The house was stuffy, retaining the day's heat. In order

to get past the entryway I had to kick aside a collection of Jake's shoes, avoid toppling a precarious tower of library books, and step over a crate of tangerines Dad had brought home from the farmer's market. I was mid–obstacle course when Jake came running at me, waving his phone in the air. "People are saying you saved a girl's life!"

His eyes were wide and frantic. Just meeting his gaze wore me out.

"I've been trying to call you," he said. "Did you turn off your phone?"

"It's dead," I answered.

We were joined by our father, whose gray hair was sticking straight up, like he'd been nervously massaging his head for a while. "Some Facebook users are under the impression that you're a hero." Dad spoke casually, as if relaying a theory he'd read about in the *New York Times*.

Jake babbled, "It's so weird, though, because they're saying it was Cameron Suzuki, and that she was with Ben O'Malley's little brother when it happened, and I didn't think you hung out with them. I didn't think you even knew those kids."

"She doesn't, I swear!" In striped socks pulled up to her knees, Rosie came slipping down the hallway. "She only knows, like, two people. It wasn't you, right, Audrey?"

Half the town had attended the Fourth of July festival;

of course everyone was posting about Cameron's collapse. Normally, I would have relished the chance to keep my family members in suspense before confirming the wildest rumor circulating Crescent Bay. But my sole ambition for tonight was to hole up in my room, maybe mess around on my phone until I fell asleep. If I was being honest, I wanted to check Mom's blog. Reading *Sprung Free in Italy!* had become my default Internet activity. It seemed, almost, like the responsible thing to do.

My dad and siblings were still staring at me, wanting to know if I'd returned home a hero.

"It was me," I said. "I mean, I was there." I tried to corral the three of them toward the living room, but they each took a step closer to me, Jake so he could continue his interrogation.

"You were there as a bystander? Or you were the person who performed CPR on Cameron Suzuki after she had a freaking *heart attack*?"

I pretended to think about it. "The second thing."

"How do you know CPR?" Dad asked.

"Um, from her job?" Rosie's tone implied a harsh *duh*. "Was it super hard?"

"We should celebrate," said Jake.

Dad mentioned the bottles of apple cider living in our garage.

"No, this calls for actual champagne," Jake insisted.

"That cider is really old," I said. "I think Mom bought it for my middle school graduation party."

Dad said, "Perfect. It practically *is* champagne."

My brother made a face. "I think we have some pizza bagels in the freezer. Audrey, would you like some celebratory pizza bagels?"

"What I would like is some celebratory personal space." I waved my arms until my family finally moved away from the front door. My hopes of hiding in my room had been dashed, but once I assumed my preferred position on the couch—my back against the armrest, legs stretched across the cushions—I felt more relaxed, ready to be interviewed.

"I learned CPR in night school," I told Dad. "And yeah, Ro, it was pretty hard."

My sister asked, "Is this Cameron person, like, a friend of yours? Or is it going to be super awkward next time you see her?"

Before I could think of how to answer, Jake cut me off. "Not everything is *awkward*, Rosie. Some things are more *life or death*."

Rosie wrinkled her nose. "Death is so awkward."

Dad was sitting, knees up, in his La-Z-Boy recliner. "Did this girl regain consciousness right in front of you?"

"No," I said. "They resuscitated her in the ambulance, with the defibrillator."

He looked thoughtfully toward the blur of the ceiling fan. "So maybe you didn't save her life."

"Maybe," I admitted, wishing he could just cop to being proud of me, like a regular dad.

"Is it fair to say you'll never know?"

"Sure. It's fair to say I'll never know."

Dad smiled, a fan of ambiguity.

My brother jumped to his feet and disappeared inside the kitchen. I heard the pop and hum of the freezer door opening. As he searched for pizza bagels, Jake called, "Hey, Aud, maybe you went into the right profession. Maybe you should be a doctor! You can save lives on the regular and make us all rich."

He sounded practically giddy with awe. I glanced at Dad, wanting to gauge his reaction to Jake describing my summer job as a *profession*. Dad may not have shared my brother's outward enthusiasm, but a ghost of a smile remained on his face. He was stunned, I realized.

"Can we call Mom?" Jake asked, re-entering the room. He had left the microwave whirring, and now a vaguely pizza-related smell wafted in from the kitchen. "This is going to astound her."

Panic flashed in Dad's eyes. "But we normally talk to Iris on Sundays," he said, his voice clipped.

Apparently their separation had rules. Rules that would be compromised if the four of us Skyped our mother without warning.

"We talk to her all the time," Jake said, confused. "She's our mother. . . ."

"Right," Dad said. "But, Aud, perhaps you want to talk to Iris privately? You must be overwhelmed."

I could have blurted it out. I could have forced Dad to come clean with my siblings, so I could stop wondering if keeping this secret from the two of them was right or unforgivably wrong.

In night school, we had learned to never, under any circumstances, treat or assist a patient if we weren't confident in our skills, sure the outcome would be favorable. The principle was "First, do no harm," a line I remembered from the summer Sara and I watched five seasons of *Grey's Anatomy* but also, evidently, a real thing. And I had no idea how to fix my parents' marriage. I didn't know if telling my siblings the truth would help or hurt. I didn't have the skill set, the training, the experience.

"That sounds good," I conceded, and neither Jake nor Rosie seemed suspicious. One-on-one time with Iris had always been a coveted commodity in our house.

Dad relaxed. "In the meantime, would you mind telling

us more about what happened? For instance, every detail that you can remember?" His relief had reverted quickly to enthusiasm.

Normally, Professor Nelson liked to be in control of all discussions. Your usual options were to ask him questions or to answer his, one after the other. As little kids, my siblings and I had learned that any unsolicited rambling about whatever had happened at school would cause Dad's eyes to glaze over, maybe even his back to turn. Only now that we were all various stages of grown-up did Dad sometimes invite our stories.

And when he did, none of us could ever resist.

So I told him about Seth and Cameron tossing the football into the sky. Cameron's knees buckling. Her lips turning blue. The ease with which a firefighter had flung me into the wet sand. The long hour in the waiting room, my bare feet, my impulse to ditch my friends the second I knew Cameron had made it. How everyone else, presumably, had stayed.

As I was talking, the microwave dinged, and Jake delivered to my lap a plate of steaming pizza bagels. Hungrier than I'd realized, I let the first bite sear the roof of my mouth.

"Well, Aud," Dad said, "this will be quite the story to share at freshman orientation."

"Oh my God, *don't*," Rosie advised me, as urgently as if I was about to press send on a campus-wide e-mail. "Everyone will think you're so much drama."

"No," Jake corrected her. "They'll think she's unique. That's the best thing about college. Everyone's so different."

Dad went, "Mmhm," which was the sound he made when he was unwilling to argue or agree.

It shouldn't have surprised me, but it always did—how no matter what happened on a given day in our lives, the Nelsons were always exactly themselves.

Keeping my eyes open had become an unrealistic goal. Rising from the couch, half stumbling out of the room, I told my family I was going to bed.

My phone rang, hours after I'd slipped into a deep sleep— but there was a reason I'd left it charging on my nightstand, volume up high. Not an assumption so much as a hope that Seth would call, even just to say something meaningless, like, *What a weird day.*

Instead, he said, "Hey. Audrey. I'm so sorry. You must be so tired. Please say no if you want to say no. But I'm still at the hospital. Everyone's gone. I don't have my Jeep, because—"

"Yeah," I whispered. On the top bunk, my sister rolled over. "I know."

"I called my dad, but he's . . . he's not feeling well. Do you think you could . . . ?"

"I'll be right there," I told him.

If Mom had been home she would have heard the front door creak open and click shut—would have confronted me in her striped pajama pants and Whedon College camisole before I'd even started the car—but the chances of Dad waking up were relatively slim. I left a note on the kitchen counter, just in case.

My hands were damp and they stuck to the steering wheel as I retraced my route back up the hill. At Steeds Memorial, I pulled into a parking space and texted Seth. He emerged from the building faster than I'd expected.

For a second he was outside of the car, his flannel midsection framed in the passenger-side window. A second later he was climbing inside, filling the MINI Cooper with his Seth-smell and his Seth-limbs.

His eyes appeared painfully bloodshot.

He said, "You didn't have to drive all the way out here, you know."

I ran my thumb along the bottom of the steering wheel, where the vinyl was cracked. "I know. It's cool, though. You can always call me for a ride."

"Always?"

"Yeah. Like when you're forty, and you get a flat tire, and you're stranded on the side of the road with your six children. Look me up. I'll come get you."

"We'll appreciate that. Me and the boys."

"All six of your children are boys?"

Seth sighed, like fatherhood had already taken its toll. "Boys run in my family."

"Your poor wife."

"Hey." Seth's tone veered toward serious. "You were amazing today. The whole thing was surreal. I'm sorry I wasn't any help."

He really did look sorry. I understood that being helpful was one of Seth's things, and that in his mind he hadn't just failed me and Cameron; he'd failed at being Seth.

"You didn't do anything wrong," I said.

"I was in your way."

"For, like, two seconds."

Seth blinked, and I could tell he was having trouble remembering the two seconds in question. For a long time after Cameron had collapsed, every second had been infinite.

"I didn't know that she . . . that you guys used to go out," I offered.

Seth raised his shoulders. "How could you have known?"

"Haven't most people in this town memorized your roster of ex-girlfriends?"

"No idea. I'm glad you haven't. Not that it's such an endless list."

I was certain that Seth's list would dwarf mine, but I felt no need to point this out. "You and Cameron are still friends?" I asked.

"Yes," he said. "Cameron's great."

I waited for him to provide some kind of explanation—of how they got together, or why they broke up—but Seth presented Cameron's greatness as an isolated fact.

"She is," I agreed, because it seemed appropriate, and because part of me was glad to learn that Seth wasn't the kind of guy who would diminish a girl he'd once liked, calling her unhinged or unreasonable, just to make his current crush feel less threatened.

Not that I was his current crush.

I needed to think of something more to say to him. Otherwise, there was nothing left to do but drive him home.

Seth beat me to it. "I have a question." With his head pressed back against the window, his long neck exposed, he looked so unguarded.

"Okay," I said, swallowing.

"Are you really going to Whedon?"

"Um." I was enrolled. I had attended my twenty-four hour preview and dutifully texted Vanessa a thank-you message. I had no intention of going to any other school. "Yes?"

"So you'll be here. In Crescent Bay. For the foreseeable future."

It wasn't the answer I wanted to give him, but it seemed like a safe answer—the probable truth. "Yup."

Seth went on. "So if I kissed you, is there a chance I could keep kissing you for a while? Say, into September and beyond?"

His last question took a moment to sink in. I stared through the windshield at the bright EMERGENCY sign outside the hospital entrance. Seth wanted to kiss me. And not just once, in this parking lot, or a few times post–night shift, but indefinitely.

I turned and met his eyes. He was watching me, hopeful and curious, as if he still thought I might do something other than reach for him.

My hands found his face, and we were finally kissing.

I had wondered if kissing Seth O'Malley would be weird. If, with the collision of our mouths, I would remember who he'd always been to me—some guy hugging some girl, their bodies fused together and blocking the hallway. Some cowboy. Some jock. No one I wanted to know.

It wasn't weird. Seth's lips were warm and eager, surrounded by a scruffy beard he'd most likely grown to hide what was, really, a minor amount of acne. His kisses weren't localized to the nerve endings in my lips and tongue; they only started there, before radiating through my belly, my thighs, my toes. Somehow, my whole body got involved, even as Seth's fingers stayed tangled in my hair.

It seemed as if the best course of action would be never coming up for air, never starting the car, never breathing a word of doubt or disbelief.

Time could pass as slowly as it wanted.

Around four in the morning I drove Seth back to his house. Behind the curtains in the front window, a bluish TV light flickered.

"Will you be at work?" I asked him.

I thought he might be planning to call in sick. If he wanted to spend another evening at Cameron's bedside, I wouldn't hold it against him. Kissing Seth didn't make him mine. Kissing Seth didn't change the fact that he had watched a girl whom he'd once liked—maybe loved, probably slept with—almost die.

But Seth just said, "That's where you'll be, right?"

"Obviously."

With his hand on the door, he flashed me a sleepy half smile. "From now on, my preference is to be where you are."

I was sure he had used that line before.

Probably because it worked.

TEN

The next afternoon, without getting out of bed, I called my mother. It was late at night in Italy, but Iris Cox Nelson answered on the first ring. I wasn't surprised. Answering on the first ring was one of her policies as a mother—along with memorizing our class schedules, meeting our friends' parents, and randomly pressing down on the tops of our shoes to see if they fit.

Her greeting was drowned out by a lot of background noise—people laughing, dishes clattering.

"Where are you?" I was aware of my tone, almost accusatory, like I expected her to stay locked inside her sublet, listing the pros and cons of remaining married to my father. If she was going to second-guess her entire life, the least she could do was focus.

"Just a faculty party. I'm dying to talk to you, though. Give me a second?" The noise of the party swelled as she, presumably, navigated a crowded room. I heard her say something to someone in upbeat Italian. It caught me off guard, how easily I recognized her voice in another language.

The din subsided. I heard a door clicking shut and Mom saying, "I understand you have a story to share."

"Jake told you already?" I asked, verging on crushed.

"Just the headline," she assured me. "Not the details."

I took a breath and, rapidly, as if someone might interrupt, began to describe the preceding day of my life. I stopped short of my first kiss with Seth, even though part of me was dying to tell her about it. Remembering the minutes I'd spent in the car with Seth was almost as good as the minutes themselves. But instead I included other details I hadn't divulged to Dad. How none of the boys at the scene had known what to do. How badly my arms had burned. How my mind had zeroed in on the technical procedure of pumping blood to Cameron's heart and I'd hardly registered the crowd forming around us.

I tried to avoid embellishments, but because I was talking to my mom and no one else, I said, "I think I might actually have saved her life."

"Wow," Mom exhaled. "Is it all over social media?"

"Haven't you checked Facebook?"

"You know I try to avoid the Internet."

For a second, I was speechless. It was almost like she knew I was *Sprung Free in Italy!*'s most loyal reader and was baiting me into admitting it. But there was no way Iris was savvy enough to track visitors to her blog. There was no way she knew the meaning of an IP address.

The truth was that the Internet was not as impressed by my life-saving skills as I had expected when I woke up and promptly Googled my name with Cameron's name. The only result was an old calendar of student birthdays, preserved in the archives of our fourth-grade teacher's website. Next I'd searched "heart attack" and "Crescent Bay" and set Google to show me only results from the last twenty-four hours. I tapped a link for *Word on the Beach,* a blog run by the long-time receptionist at our town's microscopic City Hall, who liked to keep everyone informed of small crimes and random rumors. Today, the word was that a recent graduate of the high school had suffered cardiac arrest at the Fourth of July festival. *It was a close call,* wrote the receptionist, *but witnesses say she will make a full recovery.*

That was it. My search had yielded no actual news stories.

It wasn't like I wanted a medal. But now that the shock had worn off, now that I knew the emergency had not nullified things between Seth and me, my mind was opening to the possibility that—even if I hadn't saved Cameron's life, exactly—I had probably helped. At least I'd kept her from slipping away before the firefighters and the paramedics got the chance to revive her.

"Maybe *I* should get certified in CPR," Mom said. "You never know. Weak hearts run in your father's family."

Annoyance crept into my voice. "It's not like it's easy. You really have to know what you're doing or you might make things worse."

My mother hummed her agreement. "True. They should teach basic First Aid in school. I don't think Whedon offers anything close."

"Probably not."

"Speaking of Whedon . . . are you getting excited? Only two more months."

School starting in two months meant Mom would be home even sooner. Her return flight was booked for the second week of August. Would she and Dad act like they were thrilled to be reunited? Would they immediately file for divorce?

The future had never been closer, and I had never been less sure what it looked like.

"Do you think it's, like, a problem that I have no idea what I want to study?" I asked her.

"Not at all."

I tried to picture her in some coat closet or spare bedroom. I couldn't imagine a University of Naples faculty party. Whedon College faculty parties were deafening, drunken affairs, often taking place in our own house. My mother always bought a surplus of cheap red wine and not enough vegetable trays or frozen pot stickers to go around—a formula, she assured me, followed by all the best parties. As a kid, elbowing my way through the professors crowding our kitchen, Whedon hadn't seemed to me like such a terrible place. More of a concept, synonymous with home, family, safety.

Now I tried to envision the school as something other than the manicured campus I'd toured a thousand times. Not the emblem of my parents' obsession with academics, but just a school. A series of classrooms in which I might learn something about the world, or about myself.

Mom was saying, "Honestly, I think it's *best* to approach your college years with an open mind. The whole point of a school like Whedon is that you can take courses across so many disciplines. You can figure out what you like. You don't even have to declare a major until the end of your sophomore year. Isn't that neat?"

"I really like nursing," I said.

Seamlessly, as if she'd prepared for this, my mother said, "Maybe you should study psychology."

If we were arguing, I had run out of counterpoints. "Maybe," I said.

We sank into the silence that usually precedes one person deciding to get off the phone. Not ready to let her go, I asked, "Are you excited to come home?"

She hesitated before saying, "Of course I am."

Her hesitation had neutralized her answer. "Really?"

"Absolutely. It's just . . ." I could hear her deliberating, trying to decide what she should tell me and what she should keep secret, oblivious to how much I already knew. "It's been a refreshing change of scenery. You know, a part of me still can't believe how many years I've spent in Crescent Bay. I know it probably sounds strange to you, but when the college hired Nelson and me, I never thought we'd stay there forever."

I could have pointed out that she'd been granted plenty of scenery changes over the years; she had traveled a ton. We all had. I could have asked her why, if Crescent Bay was such a drag, she had convinced me to apply early decision to Whedon. But I dismissed these obvious responses, pretty sure she was speaking in code.

Marriage was the thing she'd never imagined lasting forever.

Playing along, I said, "Then why'd you take the job?"

"It was an amazing offer to receive, fresh out of grad school. I figured Nelson and I would eventually move on to other opportunities. Your dad, though . . . He's very comfortable where he is."

"The kitchen," I said.

"Pardon?"

"He's in the kitchen. Working on his book." A minute earlier, I had heard him grinding beans for a second pot of coffee.

Mom laughed. "Of course he is."

"I thought you loved Crescent Bay," I said, although I had little evidence to support this assumption. Mom loved her job, and had the Whedon College logo-emblazoned wardrobe to prove it. She loved *us* with an intensity that verged on suffocating. But unlike Dad, she had never been openly enamored with the panoramic views from the highway. When we picnicked by the water, she winced each time she bit into her sandwich and crunched sand between her teeth.

"I do. But, Aud, do you remember how much you liked Seattle?"

"Yes." Just the word *Seattle* satisfied something in me, like when a friend, unprompted, mentions the name of your crush.

"Do you remember what you said?"

"Not really," I lied. "It was over two years ago."

"You said it felt like home and also like the opposite of home, all at once."

"Oh."

With a wistful sigh, she confessed, "That's how I'm starting to feel about Naples."

She had opened the door between the party and wherever she was hiding. The roar of fun in a foreign language crackled through the phone. Given my own nocturnal schedule, plus the nine-hour time difference, I wasn't sure if we should say good night or good-bye.

Instead, she told me to be safe.

Normally when I thought about that trip to Seattle, it was the city I remembered. The tall buildings on the edge of the ink-blue water. Slick sidewalks, steep hills, buses barreling down narrow streets. I'd loved the hectic, unpolished feel of Pike Place combined with the fresh scent coming off the Puget Sound. I'd loved the view of Mt. Rainier from our hotel room—how the city didn't force you to forget its wilder surroundings.

As I got ready for work that night, I remembered something else about our Seattle trip. It was on the interminable drive north, across the entire state of Oregon, that I had first heard Jackson Moon.

Mom's preference had actually been to fly. She was slated to present at a conference in Seattle and always got nervous before any public speaking event that took place outside of a classroom. "I don't want to stew in my own anxiety for the twelve hours it takes to drive," she'd told Dad. But, for our father, nothing could ever diminish the appeal of a family road trip.

He even chose the scenic route.

We were on Highway 97, bisecting the Willamette National Forest, when Dad began scanning the radio for something he could mock. He passed by classical, mariachi, and a man reading aloud from the New Testament without inflection. Then, two notes into a cheesy country song, Mom and Dad both hooted with surprise and began to sing along. At first, the singer—who sounded like Johnny Cash without the edge—seemed to be crooning a ballad about his one true love. But when I actually paid attention to the lyrics, I realized he was listing all the reasons his marriage was a disaster.

> When your dad got out his shotgun
> I didn't have a choice
> but I still can't stand
> the sound of your voice.

And,

> You're always hoping
> I'll fall down that well,
> but my wish for you
> is too gruesome to tell.

Our parents did not explain why they knew every clumsy word of that song, or why it delighted them so much. They didn't have to. In the backseat, Rosie and Jake and I were hysterical with laughter, our seat belts cutting into our necks as we doubled over. The song was funny because we'd been in the car for hours. It was funny because our coastal parents had adopted Southern twangs. It was funny because they were singing like they hated each other, when it was the opposite of the truth.

On our second day in Seattle, while Mom attended her conference, Dad allowed Jake and me to wander from the hotel and explore Capitol Hill. Rapidly, I fell in love with that neighborhood. I liked the sidewalks cracked by enormous tree roots, the restaurants and bars already crowded on a rainy afternoon. I liked the telephone poles plastered with flyers for upcoming shows and poetry readings. A neon sign flashing WASH! DRY! FOLD! above a Laundromat made me think that even laundry would be more exciting in the city.

To escape a sudden downpour, Jake and I ducked into a used record shop. The music playing through the speakers behind the counter was country. This time, the lyrics were conventionally sweet, but we recognized the guy's voice, which had the strange quality of being both scratchy and syrupy.

The girl manning the register wore dreadlocks twisted in a hive atop her head, and she beamed when we asked what she was listening to. "Jackson Moon," she said. "It's so retro."

She tossed us the empty CD case. In his photo, Jackson looked like James Dean if he'd been forced into a pair of overalls. The plastic case bore a five-dollar price sticker. We bought it, and presented it to our parents at dinner.

Their reaction had been more amused—less overjoyed, less stunned by the coincidence—than my brother and I had hoped. But they kept the disc in the minivan's glove compartment, and listening to "Shotgun Wedding" became a tradition. On long drives, when our collective mood began to slip—when Ro was on the verge of asking "How much longer?" and Jake mere moments from announcing he had to pee, again—Dad would slip Jackson Moon into the stereo and skip to track seven.

We would laugh, as a family, at the doomed country couple.

At work that night, I met the new resident in room 64. She was not happy. Earlier she had refused to eat in the dining room with everyone else, and now, because it was her first night, I was supposed to give her a second chance. But when I set down a tray, the woman just poked at the food, then let her fork fall into her mashed potatoes.

My supervisor hovered over the table while I pretended to be busy counting clean towels and rolls of toilet paper in the bathroom. After a few minutes had passed and the woman was still staring morosely out the window, Maureen cleared her throat.

I glanced at the clipboard dangling from the bedframe, craning my neck to read the patient's name. "Can you take a few more bites, please, Tamora?"

Unsure of how to pronounce *Tamora*, I had put the emphasis on the first syllable, which was wrong; I could tell by the way she glared at me. The lower half of Tamora's face was slack, not just with age, but maybe with an effort not to cry.

"No," she said.

I shrugged at Maureen, who crossed her arms and extended her neck, birdlike, as an alternative to scolding me. Tonight was my last shift as an unpaid trainee. To escape Maureen's constant supervision—to interact with my residents without her frequent scoffs, snorts, and interjections—was all I really wanted.

"Uh," I said, lacking conviction, "just try to take a few more bites."

"Or else . . ." Tamora rotated her hand in the air, reminding me of particular teachers from Crescent Bay High, to whom you could never speak quickly enough, whose time you always seemed to be wasting.

"Or else . . . nothing. But if you do, you can have two puddings!" This tactic always worked on Mr. Leary, down the hall.

Tamora narrowed her eyes, which were greenish blue, like sea glass. "You're going to be a terrible mother," she informed me. "You can't negotiate with your children. They have to understand that your word is final."

"Uh." I looked at Maureen, who was suddenly and conveniently captivated by something on TV. The volume was up way too high, which I somehow doubted was Tamora's preference. "You're not a child," I told her.

"Then stop treating me like one," she snapped.

For a moment, the three of us were silent. Tamora turned back toward the window and watched the waves crashing against the rocks.

Maureen gestured for me to try another strategy. When desperate for a resident's cooperation, we were encouraged to invoke their health directly and, less directly, their dwindling life expectancy. But before I could try, Tamora said, "Do you know what I had for dinner last night?"

"Nope," I said, relieved. "What'd you have?"

"Two In-N-Out Burgers, animal-style, and a chocolate milk shake. Which I consumed in the driver's seat of a Ford Thunderbird that no longer belongs to me. So—"

"Hold up." My voice lifted with excitement. "Isn't the closest In-N-Out Burger, like, a hundred miles away?"

"Yes, it is." She made withering eye contact. "So if you

don't mind, I'd like to preserve my memory of that meal a while longer, before I tarnish it with your—" She waved her hand above the untouched tray—"meat loaf."

Normally, residents who were admitted directly to the Assisted Living wing of the nursing home were not capable of driving, or of eating anything animal-style. I wondered why Tamora hadn't qualified for Independent Living, where she would have been allowed to park her car outside the private entrance to her own apartment. I gave Maureen a look, like, *Are you sure this lady's in the right place?*

Maureen stared meaningfully at Tamora's care plan. I grabbed the clipboard and skimmed the resident's long list of symptoms—dizzy spells, shortness of breath, migraines, blurred vision, decreased appetite—which, mysteriously, did not culminate in a diagnosis.

"All right," I said, dropping the clipboard and letting it swing from the bedpost. "You can wait until breakfast."

"Really?" Maureen asked. "That's your solution, Audrey?"

I shrugged. "I'm siding with Tamora on this one."

I was careful to pronounce her name correctly this time, earning me a glimmer of approval from Tamora herself.

Maureen rolled her blue-shadowed eyes and jerked her head toward the door, indicating that she wanted to yell at me in the hallway. That was when I heard a familiar name blasting from the TV speakers.

The first time I saw the video, I was impressed by its quality. Whoever had stood in the sand and filmed me performing CPR on Cameron had clearly just purchased a new phone. Maybe they'd even studied some cinematography. You could see my face, sweat-slicked and tense with concentration, and the muscles flexing beneath the soft flesh of my upper arms. The film proved that Cameron's lips were not blue, like I remembered, but practically purple—her mouth open and disturbingly slack. A wider shot revealed the crowd of people surrounding us, the water rolling toward the horizon, a sunset so vibrant it almost looked fake.

The newscaster managed to sound both vapid and alarmed. "Cameron Suzuki, an eighteen-year-old graduate of Crescent Bay High School who suffered sudden cardiac arrest at a Fourth of July picnic, was lucky to be in the company of fellow teen and Certified Nurse Assistant Audrey Nelson, whose expert administration of CPR saved Suzuki's life. The two girls were on a double date, looking forward to their town's annual fireworks show, when Nelson witnessed her friend's collapse. If not for Nelson's training and uncanny ability to stay calm under pressure, Suzuki would have died."

The footage was replaced by a trio of newscasters sitting

at a long desk in front of a generic beach background.

"Where is Cameron now?" asked the less bald of the two men.

The woman who had delivered the voice-over answered, "She's recuperating at Steeds Memorial."

"Holy smokes," said the unambiguously bald guy. "Imagine anyone, let alone a *teenage girl*, jumping into action like that. Do you think it was just a burst of adrenaline, telling her what to do?"

Here, I was vaguely aware of Tamora interjecting, "Imbecile."

"I'll tell you what I think, Don," said the female newscaster. "I think some of us are just natural caretakers. Some women excel at First Aid and keeping calm, no matter the emergency. This girl is a born nurse, is what I think."

In unison, both men repeated, "Wow."

One of them jerked his head toward the camera and made urgent eye contact with his viewers. "When we return . . . a grizzly bear at the Sacramento Zoo gives birth to not one, but *two* healthy cubs."

A commercial for orange juice filled the screen.

At my side, Maureen stood with her mouth agape. Tamora was frowning at the name tag hanging from my neck, as if not totally convinced that the teen godsend from the news and the awkward CNA who bartered with pudding cups were the same person.

"Maybe you won't be such a bad mother," Tamora said finally. "You'll keep the kids alive at least."

My first impulse was to wonder if my dad had seen the story. When I concluded that no, there was no way—the TV in our house was only ever used as a vehicle for Netflix—I wondered if I could call the station and ask them to send me a copy of the video. I wanted my family to see it. My brother had been class valedictorian; he had won essay contests, surfing competitions, scholarships. I had never won anything, but now, my expert CPR skills had been praised on the evening news. The story wasn't entirely factual—whose idea had it been to say we were on a double date?—but still.

"Just so we're clear," Tamora said, "if I go down, you can just let nature take its course."

I released the nervous laugh of someone trying to avoid chitchat at the gas station. The contrast between Tamora's amusement and Maureen's disbelief was a lot to handle.

"I'm taking my break," I announced. It was early, but I wanted to find Seth.

"Wait," Tamora demanded. "Did you decline to comment?"

I was already halfway out the door. "What?"

"When they called you," she explained.

"Nobody called me."

"Oh." She nodded grimly. "They will."

In that moment, it was easy to dismiss a vague projection from an old woman. I flashed her what I hoped was a warm smile and left the room.

I texted Seth and asked him to meet me by the Dumpsters outside the kitchen, a spot that had the best view during the day. As I pushed through the main doors and rounded the stucco corner of the building, the darkness exaggerated the sound of the waves smacking against the bluff.

Seth was already waiting. He stooped, slightly, as if to hug or kiss me hello—and I was so unprepared for a romantic greeting, I skidded to a halt, emitting a series of fractured sentences. "Someone filmed it. Cameron and me. Then sent it to the news. One of the anchors, bald, he thinks girls can't do CPR."

Seth stared at me, bewildered. "Someone *filmed* you?"

"Yeah. Performing CPR on Cameron Suzuki."

He frowned, and I regretted calling Cameron by her first and last name, like she was someone we barely knew.

"Wow." He heaved a colossal sigh. "That sucks."

I blinked. Seth had mistaken my excitement for panic. It was possible we didn't know each other all that well.

"But it'll be okay," he went on.

"It will?" I asked, cautious.

"Yeah. I mean, maybe they'll run the story a few more times. But then a whale will wash up on the beach, or someone will get themselves killed on the 101. . . . ." Seth's cheek twitched as he trailed off, formulating a question. "Does the video show Cameron's face?"

I nodded.

"Is it . . . bad?"

"A little," I said, shame washing over me. Anyone's face drained of blood and oxygen—let alone the face of someone you cared about—was bad. "It was the *Steeds County News*," I said. "She might have seen it."

"Nah," Seth said. "She's still recovering. She had her pacemaker put in today."

"Oh." Clearly he'd been in touch with Cameron, or her family. Of all the feelings to which I was not entitled, jealousy topped the list.

Seth was standing at a distance, tightening his ponytail. "I can't believe someone filmed it."

I shrugged. "People film things. It's like a reflex."

"Not for me."

"Never?"

From the pocket of his jeans, Seth produced a beat-up flip phone. "See? No video camera."

"Whoa." I grabbed it, grateful for the distraction. "This thing is sort of pathetic."

"It works fine."

"Does it, though?" The phone's outer shell had a small, cloudy screen that I assumed was supposed to tell the time, but didn't.

"It makes calls. What do you need that fancy one for?" He nodded at my iPhone, the shape of which was visible through the breast pocket of my scrubs. My phone, its face a spiderweb of cracks, was two years old. Mom and Dad had given it to me for my sixteenth birthday.

"Everything," I said. "Music, pictures, maps. What do you do if you get lost?"

"We live on the coast. How would you ever get lost?"

I thought of all the times I had entered Sara's address into my GPS app, just to see the familiar section of the road highlighted, the ocean a static blue mass on one side of the screen.

Seth had a point. "Okay," I said, "but what do you do if you need to know something fast? Like, how to pick a lock, or whether the spider in your shower is poisonous?"

"I'll just stick with you," he said. "You're full of unexpected skills."

"I am?"

"Yeah. CPR, late-night rescues . . . other types of things . . ."

This time, when Seth dipped his chin, I lifted mine in response. He aligned his fingertips against the base of my neck, and sensations from the night before—my whole body liquefying—came back to me as we kissed.

"We should have done this earlier," I mumbled. The weeks we'd spent working all the same shifts, never pausing to make out, suddenly seemed like a waste.

His lips curled into a smile. "Like, earlier tonight? Or earlier in our lives?"

"Both," I said, even as I considered how readily our younger selves would have laughed at the idea.

"Maybe if I'd known," Seth said.

"Known what?" I asked.

"That you weren't going anywhere."

By the end of our midnight lunch break, neither of us had eaten. We had barely come up for air. Seth promised to meet me in the parking lot at five a.m., armed with a feast of pilfered breakfast foods.

Before he went back inside the kitchen, he angled his face skyward and said, "Hey, Audrey. What was it like seeing yourself on TV?"

Somehow, being with Seth had caused me to forget all about the condescending anchors on the evening news. And the truth was that I hadn't looked my best on TV, with my face flushed, sizable circles of sweat spreading beneath the sleeves of my shirt. But, watching the clip, I had been transfixed by the determination in my own eyes. It was the same expression my dad wore when he was writing, scribbling words as fast as ideas entered his head.

I'd never known my eyes could look like that.

For Seth's benefit, I shrugged. "It was weird. It was like watching someone else."

And he nodded, satisfied.

ELEVEN

My phone buzzed beneath my pillow. Still half asleep, expecting Seth or one of my friends, I answered. There was a pause before a confused voice asked, "Is this Audrey Nelson?"

"Yeah." I lifted my head to see if Rosie was still around. She wasn't. A plate of half-eaten Eggo waffles rested precariously at the edge of her desk.

"This is Kristy Summers calling from the *Steeds County News*. Did I wake you?"

I hesitated. "You did."

The woman's laughter was high-pitched and hollow. "Good to know some things never change. Even the bravest teenager in northern California likes to sleep until noon, am I right?"

"Uh." I was mildly offended by the *northern* distinction. "I work nights?"

"Oh, of course. My bad. At the Crescent Bay Retirement Home, correct?"

"Sorry," I said, "but why are you calling?"

"Well, I'm hoping to learn more about you when I interview you and Cameron Suzuki for the *Steeds County News!*" She shouted the last three words, as if describing a prize I had won.

At first, my mind was blank.

"Cameron?" I sat up straight as the events of last night arranged themselves in my memory. "Cameron agreed to do an interview?"

"Well, no. We actually haven't been able to get in touch with Miss Suzuki, or her parents. We were hoping you could help us out with that."

My eagerness vanished. "Cameron's in the hospital."

"Oh no!" The reporter crooned. "I'm sorry to hear that. Is something wrong?"

"Uh, she had a heart attack." I was ready to get off the phone, but Kristy's rapid responses left no window through which I might make a graceful exit.

"But you successfully performed CPR. It says so here, in my notes."

"Cameron had surgery literally yesterday. I don't think we can come on your show. And actually, this isn't a great time to talk. I have to . . ." I trailed off, hoping she would take the hint, but Kristy was content to wait out the silence.

"When will Miss Suzuki be mobile, do you think?"

"I have no idea."

"We could certainly do the interview in the hospital."

I tried to imagine what Seth would say upon learning I'd brought a film crew to Cameron's hospital room. "I'm not going to bother her."

Kristy went "Hmm," conspiratorially, as if together we could brainstorm a new plan. "I suppose we'll just have to interview you by yourself! I think, in a way, your perspective is the most interesting. And then maybe you and your friend could come back on the show in a few months. Our viewers love a good follow-up story!"

I tried to picture myself on the news. My mind conjured some poised, well-groomed version of Audrey Nelson who would, with calm humility, explain the steps of CPR to the people watching at home. The fantasy was appealing, if not entirely realistic.

"You know, you might not get this opportunity again. . . ." Something like admonishment had seeped into Kristy's tone.

"This opportunity?" I echoed.

"To be recognized."

Did I even want to be recognized, again, by the *Steeds County News*? Most people I knew got their news from the Internet.

"I don't think I'm interested."

"No?" I could imagine Kristy Summers tilting her head, confused.

"No."

"Okay, I get it." She sighed good-naturedly. "Not a morning person. Fair enough. Why don't you get some coffee, think it over, and call me back?"

"It's not morning," I reminded her, before hanging up the phone. "It's noon."

I fell back against my pillows.

I couldn't let Kristy Summers interview me. There was no way Cameron would appreciate the news station continuing to air close-up shots of her lifeless face. Plus, Seth had so automatically disapproved of the video's existence, it hadn't even occurred to him that I might *not* resent the attention.

And, in reality, if I were to appear on our region's low-budget morning show, my mother would watch only reluctantly, through the cracks between her fingers. Dad and Jake would tune in and wait for me to do something mockable—to hiccup, or misuse an idiom—so that they could enter my humiliation into the Nelson family catalog of shame.

Hanging up on Kristy Summers had been my only choice.

Before I could commit to getting out of bed, Rosie came lurching into the room, holding out her phone like it was something thrilling and illicit. "Move over," she said, shoving on my shoulder until I made space.

She slid into bed with me and angled the screen so I could see the video—the one starring Cameron Suzuki as temporarily-but-not-officially dead. Someone had uploaded the clip to YouTube and given it the clunky title of *California Teen Hero Saves Life of a Friend.*

The video had been watched 7,034 times.

This was why Kristy Summers had called—not to offer me attention, but to capitalize on the attention I was already getting.

I should have known.

"You don't look so good," Rosie said, smirking at the screen. For a few seconds, I watched my arms flexing, my facial muscles straining as I endeavored to pump blood to Cameron's heart. Seth's shoes were visible in the background— not his boots, but the leather sandals he'd worn to the beach, two days ago.

I shut my eyes just before the video's single line of dialogue. I had sounded strangely calm when I'd announced to the crowd, *I need to stop.* No one had offered to take my place.

"There are a lot of comments," Rosie warned.

"Nice comments?" I asked.

She read aloud: "'Is it just me, or is this girl the spitting image of Emma Stone?'"

"That's nice. Emma Stone is cute."

"Emma Stone is a babe. Here's a not so nice one." My sister dropped her voice to portray the patronizing tone of a man on the Internet. "'Sorry to disappoint all of you but I'm a paramedic and Audrey Nelson clearly has no idea what she's doing. To be honest she's probably making things worse. Are we sure the victim even survived?'"

"All right," I said. "Next, please."

"'Holy shit, this girl is a superhero. Most girls her age would just start screaming and crying. LOL.'"

"Is that supposed to be a nice one?" I asked.

"They called you a superhero. . . ."

"They insulted our entire gender."

"Kind of like this one: 'Crescent Bay girls are hot. Anyone in Redding want to take a road trip for some tail?'"

Hearing these words exit my little sister's mouth made me feel impossibly dirty. "I don't like this," I said, skin crawling.

Rosie let her phone fall facedown into the blankets. Snuggling against my shoulder, a rare display of affection, she said, "The whole thing is kind of cool, though. It's like you're famous."

I smiled in spite of myself. Rosie actually sounded impressed. And even though it was embarrassing to realize that everyone had seen or would soon see this footage of me sweating, grunting, and pounding on another girl's chest—even though I was dreading Seth's reaction to the video's debut on the World Wide Web—a part of me thought, if I had to be slightly famous, at least it was for something unambiguously good.

"This woman just called and asked me to come on the news," I told Rosie.

My sister lifted her chin from my shoulder. "What'd you say?"

"I said no."

She fiddled with the frayed edge of my bedsheet. "No one else in our family has ever been on TV."

She was right. Occasionally, recordings of our mother ended up online, but panel discussions among bespectacled professors were not exactly the stuff of prime time.

"Maybe we're just not TV people," Rosie added, before changing the subject. "Hey, how'd you even know you could do it?"

"Do what? CPR?"

"Yeah."

"I didn't know for sure. I just had to try."

After a pause, Rosie asked, "Does everyone at your work know you're going to Whedon?"

"No," I admitted.

"They'll be sad when you quit," she informed me.

"You think so?"

"Yeah, now that you've gone viral."

I laughed, because Rosie was exaggerating. To qualify as viral, YouTube videos needed hundreds of thousands of hits. They needed to generate spin-offs and parodies and cheesy jokes delivered by talk show hosts. Ideally, they featured an animal doing something strangely human, or someone's grandma struggling to adjust to the new millennium.

But before work that night, when I checked my phone for any word from Seth, a text from Sara echoed Rosie's claim: **Are you aware that you've gone viral??**

I followed the link attached to my best friend's message. The view count had already tripled.

TWELVE

Tamora Sinclair was nocturnal. She had been nocturnal since her retirement ten years ago, and she was not going to change her ways just because the nursing home only served meals when the sun was up. According to Maureen, our newest resident had spent her first night watching public access television and proceeded to sleep through the next day. Now, in the middle of my first unsupervised shift, Tamora was wide awake and paging me.

When I entered her room, I found her sitting cross-legged on the bed she must have made herself—two more things of which residents in Assisted Living were not normally capable—and wearing a silk robe patterned with sunflowers. Her silvery blond hair, so straight it appeared flat-ironed, was tied at the nape of her neck.

"There you are," she said, as if it had taken me longer than two minutes to run to her room from the Health and Rehabilitation wing, where I worked the bulk of my hours.

Contrary to its optimistic name, Health and Rehabilitation was everyone's last stop. The opposite of health, if anything.

"How would I go about getting a midnight snack?" Tamora asked politely.

"I don't think midnight snacks are allowed, exactly."

Tamora blinked. Her eyes were eerily bright, and the lower half of her face hung from cheekbones you could tell had once been enviable. "Then how *exactly* do you expect me to get through the night?"

"Sleeping?" I suggested.

"I like to sleep during the day. Helps me avoid human interaction."

"Then I think your best bet is to wake up around six, go to the dining room long enough to slip some food into your pockets, and become a secret snack hoarder."

Tamora looked at me, one corner of her mouth turning south in amusement. "Like a child robbing the cookie jar?"

"Exactly."

"I'm seventy-eight years old."

"Around here, that's pretty young."

Rolling her eyes, Tamora changed the subject. "Did they call?"

I was on the verge of asking, *Did who call?* when I remembered our parting words from the night before. After the video's first appearance on the local news, Tamora had warned me that my phone would ring. "Yes," I admitted. "They called."

"Did you decline to comment?" she asked again.

"More or less. But I'm getting all these e-mails, mostly from people who write for different websites. They won't leave me alone."

Tamora's chin rotated in the air; I couldn't tell if she meant to shake her head or nod at me. "Let's strike a deal. You bring me food every night, and I'll teach you how to deal with the press."

In my pocket, my pager launched into a tinny version of "Pop Goes the Weasel." I still hadn't seen Seth tonight, and if I wanted our breaks to align I had to report to Maureen and find out what she needed from me now.

"That's a good deal," I said vaguely, already turning on my heel. "I have to catch up with my boss. I'll see what I can do about bringing you a snack, all right?"

Tamora looked hurt by my hasty good-bye, but I was used to sleepless residents trying to keep me in their rooms with various entrapments—stories, advice, photo albums, or what someone promised was an especially riveting *Law and Order* rerun. They were lonely. I was busy. Disappointing people, Maureen had assured me, was part of the job.

My lunch break did not align with Seth's. What my supervisor wanted was for me to change Mr. Leary's urine-soaked bedsheets without rousing Mr. Leary himself. Remaking an occupied bed was a skill I'd honed during my first week on the job—a skill of which I was weirdly proud, though I wasn't exactly sure how to phrase it for my résumé.

By the end of my shift, I was exhausted and convinced I would head straight home. But in the parking lot—the sunrise bleeding through the haze, rendering everything pinkish— Seth was, as usual, leaning against the trunk of his Jeep. With his stance wide, his arms crossed, he grinned at me.

"Long night?"

"Endless," I answered.

"Bedtime?"

"Not yet."

Something about Seth's perfect composure convinced me not to mention the video. The whole thing was out of our control. And maybe he was already over it, or maybe Cameron hadn't been as traumatized by the footage as Seth had predicted.

Maybe Cameron was just psyched to be alive.

Instead of driving down to the beach, we took the crooked, wooden staircase that led all the way from the nursing home to the sand. Few residents could still manage these stairs, left-over from the property's life as a summer camp for city kids.

"Question," said Seth, a step below me. "If you could be anywhere with anyone right now, where would you be and with who? And don't say right here with me, because that's cheating."

"What if it's true?" I asked.

"Still cheating." He had turned away from the beach. The backdrop of white sand put his features into high definition. The truth was that the only other place I wanted to be was in my bed, but that was a boring response. A conversation killer of a response.

"Okay. In a hotel room, overlooking a big city . . ."

Seth grabbed my hand to help me over a step that had rotted and caved in. "And who would be in this hotel room with you?"

"My brother and sister."

He laughed. "Really?"

"Yeah. My family travels a lot, and Whedon usually pays for my parents' room, so Jake and Rosie and I get our own. We always end up watching trash TV or joyriding the elevator in our pajamas or telling one another weird secrets. It's when my siblings seem most real to me. It's like we have to get out of Crescent Bay, and away from our parents, just to *see* each other."

"I know what you mean," Seth said. "Both of my brothers have already moved out, and when I visit Cory at his place with his wife and his kids, we're totally civilized. But when he comes home, especially if my dad's around, it takes

147

about ten minutes for us to start wrestling on the floor of the living room."

I jumped from the bottom step to the cold sand. "Seriously?"

"Last Sunday, my twenty-six-year-old brother tried to suffocate me with a couch cushion. Either of your siblings ever try to murder you?"

"Nah," I said. "We stick to verbal aggression."

"That makes sense."

"It does?"

"Yeah. You talk really fast."

In my family, if you didn't talk fast and loud, brandishing the biggest words in your vocabulary, no one would hear you at all.

I wanted to ask Seth an unexpected question, but not the same thing he'd asked me. Feeling wired and brave, before I could curb the impulse, I said, "If you had to marry one of your ex-girlfriends, who would you choose?"

Seth turned his palms toward the sky. "If I had to *marry* one of them?"

"Yes!" The question was ludicrous; we were eighteen years old, but I had a potentially self-destructive need to make Seth admit that he'd felt this way before. He'd already wanted multiple girls the way I wanted him now.

"Well, my preference would be to *avoid* making a lifetime commitment to *anyone* before, you know, puberty ends."

I was pretty sure puberty had finished its work on Seth O'Malley years ago. He could easily have passed for twenty-one.

"But if I had to pick . . . I'd pick you."

"That's cheating!"

"You never said I couldn't pick you!"

"But I'm not your ex. I'm not even your—" I stopped.

In school, the joke had always been that if you wanted to date Seth O'Malley, you could add your name to the waiting list.

Seth grinned. "You're not my girlfriend?"

I closed my eyes. Heat spilled across my cheeks and the ocean roared in my ears.

"Why is that, exactly?" he asked.

I could smell the laundry soap on his shirt, the wood smoke trapped in his hair. "I guess I didn't know it was an option," I said.

"Oh, believe me," Seth said, grabbing and swinging my hand through the air. "You've got nothing but options."

We were walking north along the edge of the ocean, stepping over driftwood and tangles of kelp. Ahead of us towered the dune that barricaded Crescent Bay's beach from the rest of the coastline. At the top was a sort of hollow in the rocks, a cave just big enough for two people—if the people didn't mind being horizontal.

I was about to ask if he felt like taking a hike, when Seth cleared his throat and announced, "I went to see Cameron yesterday morning. After work." Standing with his spine straight, he was half a foot taller than me. "The good news is that the surgery went well. Oh, and she never saw that video."

"Uh." I wondered if he could be joking. "Are you sure?"

"Positive. She was still in post-op when it aired on the news."

"But . . . she's going to see it eventually."

He frowned. "Why?"

My elation began to drain. Seth wasn't unconcerned about my accidental YouTube fame; he was just, somehow, unaware of it. "Seth," I said cautiously, "do you ever go on the Internet?"

"Yeah, I do e-mail."

"You *do* e-mail?"

"My house is outside of the cable company's boundaries, so we have this satellite thing? It's really slow."

Even so, it was impossible that none of Seth's friends from school had sent him the link. "Have you *done* your e-mail recently?" I asked.

"Actually, no. Not in a couple days." He shrugged. "I'm almost never home. And when I'm there, I'm asleep."

"Okay." No part of me wanted to tell him, but I had no choice. "The video's on the Internet. A hundred thousand people have seen it." Every time I'd checked, the view count had risen higher.

He blinked at me. "Who put it there?"

"The news station . . . it's kind of a big deal. A lot of reporters have asked me to do interviews. Cameron, too, probably."

Seth screwed up his face, disturbed. "People are the worst. As if you would want to talk publicly about something like that. As if *Cameron* would want to. Jesus."

"I'm sorry," I offered. The apology felt like a lie.

"Not your fault." But Seth's jaw was clenched. Searching his pocket for his flip phone, he mumbled, "I should call Cam. Make sure she's okay."

"She's probably asleep."

Seth directed a frustrated sigh toward the clouds. "Right."

I gave him a second to calm down, to stop seething at the sky. Soon he was smiling at me again. "I'll call her later. You're right—she's probably already seen it. And it's not like there's anything I can really do."

It was a fact that seemed to disappoint him. I pointed to the steep hill rising up behind us. "You feel like a hike?"

Seth hesitated, still mired in thoughts of his ex-girlfriend, and then he took my hand.

The dune was only about fifty yards high, but the incline was almost vertical, the sand so dry that our feet sank deeper with every step. My legs were burning by the time we reached the top, where we panted and surveyed our town. Steam rose from the Fish Shack. A neon sign blinked in the window of North Coast Outfitters, where I'd always followed Jake around as he bought wax for his board and tried to convince me I should learn to surf. At the far end of the beach was the playground with the jungle gym from which Rosie, age seven, had fallen and chipped her tooth.

I could remember standing in this exact spot while my parents waded into the ocean below. I had screamed at them to stop kissing each other so they could observe my fearless, flailing descent. They had, more often than not, taken their time.

This view was one of my favorites—sometimes but not always diminished by its achy familiarity. Currently, the landscape seemed as novel as Seth's fingers laced through mine.

I led him to the hollow in the rocks. We crawled inside on our hands and knees. With the top of his head pressing against the smooth ceiling of red stone, Seth said, "This feels a little like a coffin," and I teased him, saying, "Don't pretend you've never been here before."

He bit down a smile—not at the memory of his make out history, I hoped, but at the ease with which I'd delivered the joke.

In the cave, at the top of the dune, at six in the morning,

Seth O'Malley and I discovered that our bodies knew how to be together. His lips never moved against mine in a way I didn't like. His hands never roamed to a place where they weren't welcome.

As it turned out, his hands were welcome everywhere.

I'd never really been with a guy without feeling the need to memorize a play-by-play for Sara and me to analyze afterward—usually, immediately afterward, our legs swinging over the edge of her hayloft. But with Seth, I didn't want to detach. Didn't want to invite anyone else into this moment. I was too busy pulling his shirt over his head, running my hands across his chest and his warm, narrow stomach.

I knew that boys were not known for guarding their bodies, but part of me still couldn't believe I was allowed to touch him.

Seth's lips were close to my ear when he tugged on the waistband of the blue hospital scrubs I was still wearing, and said, "Do you want to . . . ?"

I pulled away, but only because I had been trying to answer the same question in my head for the last few minutes. "You've done it before, right?"

He smiled, like I'd questioned his ability to swim. "Yes."

"Recently?"

"Um." I couldn't tell if he was annoyed, ashamed, or both. "What do you mean, *recently?*"

"Like, this summer?"

"Audrey, no. Of course not."

"Sorry," I said quickly. "I just wasn't sure if we were, like . . ." Mortification swallowed the rest of my sentence.

"Exclusive?"

I hated the word, but said yes anyway.

"I told you." He kissed my throat. The combination of embarrassment and pleasure almost killed me. "You have nothing but options."

His words filled the small amount of space between us. The rocks above us smelled damp and salty, like the inside of an oyster. Seth asked, "Have *you* had sex before?"

I had forgotten the question could be applied to me. I wobbled my hand in the air. "I tried to, once, but it didn't exactly . . . work."

"Oh, really?" he said, faux-casual. "Who couldn't get it up?" His eyes contained a glimmer of competition—a side of Seth I hadn't seen, but couldn't hold against him.

"It's not nice to gossip."

"Just tell me." He spoke quickly, sounding exactly like Sara when she implored me to disregard human decency.

"Cole Hendrix," I admitted. "It wasn't that he couldn't get it up, necessarily. It was more of a mutual failure."

"Ah," Seth said, thumbing my cheek. Cole Hendrix and I had been together for the second half of eleventh grade.

Our dates had mainly consisted of driving up and down the highway, listening to songs that, at a certain volume, convinced us we felt much more than we did.

"I don't think we'll have the same problem," I told Seth.

"So . . . you do want to?"

"Yes."

"Now?"

I thought about the underwear I was wearing—green and white stripes with a hole beneath the elastic—and how long it had been since yesterday's shower. I thought about Sara's warning that sex in the sand wasn't as romantic as it seemed; everyone's body parts became extremely adhesive.

"Not now," I told Seth, aching.

"All right," he said. And still, there was something triumphant about the way he kissed me on the lips. "Just say when."

By the time I got home, the video had been on the Internet for almost twenty-four hours and my mother, so far, had declined to say a single word to me. She had definitely seen it, after following a link from Jake or Rosie or a nosy colleague, and I was getting anxious for her reaction. Not because I thought she'd be mad—accidentally going viral was not a punishable offense—but because I knew that, deep down, Iris had never wanted me to work as a nurse assistant, let alone get famous for skills I'd learned in night school.

The video might cause her to panic, the same way she'd panicked when Rosie got caught shoplifting with her weird friend Dana, or the one time Jake cut class because the waves off Point St. George were rumored to be epic. On both occasions, she'd shaken her head and sighed at her minimally rebellious offspring: "I just don't *recognize* you right now."

I didn't really expect Mom to blog her feelings about my YouTube stardom—to do so would defeat her halfhearted attempts at anonymity—but I checked the site, anyway. Reading *Sprung Free in Italy!* had become one of my pre-sleep rituals, along with brushing my teeth and also blowing a torrent of air into my still-slumbering sister's left ear, just to make her groan and roll over.

Lately I've been somewhat distracted by a development in my family life, but I just can't wait any longer before telling all of you about my Italian suitor!

Because my mother couldn't just say boyfriend or lover, something I could immediately interpret, I had to read this sentence a second time before its meaning sunk in.

My ears filled with the roar of imaginary engines. My eyes skimmed frantically over the post. I was afraid of missing a crucial detail, but I was equally afraid of encountering the kind of detail that would scar me for life.

. . . Realized I'd been in Italy three months without forging any real connections . . .

. . . locked my laptop in my desk and dragged myself to a faculty party . . .

. . . escaped the party and talked until sunrise, at an osteria by the sea . . .

. . . can't remember the last time I felt so fascinated and so fascinating, simultaneously.

And then my eyes landed on the worst part:

He's not, as my kids would say, "my type." He's not even an academic, was only at the party as the guest of a friend. He owns a vineyard and prefers old horror movies to books.

Then, there is the fact that my husband and I never agreed to see other people during our trial separation. Sometimes, I'm not even sure N fully agreed to separate at all. He was only humoring me, allowing me to think that my time in Italy could possibly clarify what each of us wants from the rest of our lives.

Well, if I'm being honest, this is what I want.

The post had twelve comments, half of which employed applause emojis.

I was very aware of the shape and weight of the phone in my hand. For the first time, it struck me as absurd that so much unwanted information had come from something so small and smooth and seemingly harmless.

I remembered being a kid, messing around with an old CD and asking my mom how the music got inside the disc. She had been unable to answer the question and reluctant to admit she had no idea. "There are grooves in the plastic. The grooves contain data. I'm not explaining it right, but I promise it makes sense."

Did it make sense that my mother could cheat on my father in Italy and, from my bottom bunk in northern California, I knew about it almost instantly?

My heart threatened to escape my chest.

I had been so careful, promising my parents that the retirement home was only a summer job. Doing my best to seem excited, or at least open-minded, about college in the fall. Not confronting Mom about her Internet activity, or demanding answers from Dad, or forcing my siblings to suffer along with me. As if, by sticking to my parents' plans for my own life, I could inspire them to stick to their wedding vows.

Being careful hadn't worked.

Buried in my in-box, beneath an ever-growing pile of messages from reporters and writers, was an e-mail from Kristy Summers. She had sent it as a follow-up to yesterday's call, on the basis that my uncertainty over the phone had been *palpable*. In her e-mail she'd referred to me as a hero twice.

I didn't think I was a hero. But I thought maybe I was a girl who was good at something that mattered—even if my life was straying, dramatically, from what the professors had envisioned.

Before I could change my mind, before I could dwell on anyone's disgust or disapproval, I wrote to Kristy Summers and agreed to go on TV.

If I was being honest, it was what I wanted.

THIRTEEN

A good idea would have been to get a full night's sleep before appearing on the *Steeds County News*. But in Kristy Summers's e-mail, she had asked me to arrive at the station at seven a.m. so that their in-house cosmetologist could do my hair and makeup before the live interview at eight. By the time I was sitting in a cracked leather salon chair, letting a pale girl in a baggy sweater fry my hair, I had been awake for seventeen hours.

At the end of our shift, Seth had given me a juice and a sticky cinnamon bun, kissed me, and said, "Just so you know, the other morning . . . I had a condom. I know you weren't ready. But I hope you don't think I wanted to have sex without, you know, having anything on me."

My expression must have been discouraging, because he continued. "I mean, without having a condom in my pocket. Which I did. And still do."

I didn't say anything, too busy trying to decide what it

meant that a condom lived permanently in Seth's pocket. He had laughed, mistaking my pensiveness for post–night shift fatigue. "Go home," he said, patting the striped hood of my dad's MINI Cooper. "Get some sleep."

I drove straight to the station instead.

When the cosmetologist knelt in front of my chair to do my makeup, she spent a lot of time frowning, dabbing flesh-toned gunk beneath my eyes. Later, having done "everything she could," she passed me off to an intern, who outfitted me with a microphone and escorted me to a low-budget set featuring a staged living room—two plush chairs, a floor lamp, and a coffee table covered in *Good Housekeeping* magazines. I waited in my assigned seat, palms sweating, while the surrounding cameramen messed with their equipment. Kristy Summers appeared. Her face was familiar.

I understood, then, that I had actually known her all my life—had seen Kristy's blond hair and red lipstick on a hundred different television sets without ever committing her name to memory.

"You ready?" she asked, offering me a tight, sterile smile and settling into the second chair.

"Uh." I leaned forward, thinking she might impart some advice, or brief me on the questions she intended to ask. Before I could say more, Kristy Summers nodded at a flashing light affixed to the far wall. A guy was using his fingers to count down from five. Kristy arranged her face into a creepy mask of charm and goodwill, and then, evidently, we were on TV.

"Hi," she said, crinkling her eyes toward the camera, as if acknowledging an old friend. "I'm here this morning with Audrey Nelson, the eighteen-year-old who saved her best friend's life. Audrey, can you tell us a little bit about what was running through your mind when you saw Cameron collapse on the beach?"

My tongue was stuck to the roof of my mouth. Who had ever said that Cameron was my best friend? Kristy's patient smile made it impossible to correct her. I would sound like such a jerk.

I cleared my throat. "Uh, well, I was hanging out on this log with my friends, and we were watching Cameron play catch down by the water with . . . one of our other friends. And the way she fell, it wasn't like she had tripped. It was pretty clear that something internal had happened. I had just taken a CPR class, so we'd watched all these videos where people experienced cardiac arrest."

"So you recognized the signs of a heart attack from those videos?"

"Yeah." I couldn't stop scratching at my thighs. I was wearing jeans, and nothing itched, but holding still was impossible.

"And would you say that instinct just took over? The next thing you knew you were at Cameron's side, performing CPR?"

"Well, no. I cleared her airways and made sure her spine was straight. That's what you're supposed to do. And, I mean, she wasn't breathing. Her lips were blue. I knew what had happened."

"Wow," Kristy said, with an almost imperceptible shake of her blond bob. "I think I speak for a lot of our viewers when I say, it's so rare to meet a young person with so much composure. Tell us a little about your job. You're a—" Her eyes darted to the wall behind me. "—a *Certified Nurse Assistant* at the Crescent Bay Retirement Home. What sorts of responsibilities do you have at work?"

"Uh." For the most part, Kristy Summers seemed to be ignoring the actual words leaving my mouth. Her loyalty was to her script. "I, like, change bedpans and sheets. Sometimes residents need help, like, showering. And I record everything they eat and drink."

Kristy arched a well-groomed eyebrow.

"I mean, that sounds weird, I know. But it's part of my job."

With a chuckle, Kristy moved on. "So, as I'm sure you're aware, other girls your age are out partying, joyriding, chasing boys. . . . How do you think you got so mature, by comparison?"

What was the connection between bedpans and maturity?

What did any of this have to do with saving Cameron's life?

"I'm not?" I guessed. "I mean, I think I'm pretty normal. I like . . . joyriding."

Kristy Summers was unfazed. "And you're planning to live at home, instead of running off to college? Is that correct? Because, and some people might disagree, but I think it's refreshing to meet a teenage girl who looks at the rising cost of a college education, and the national debt crisis, and says, 'No thanks, I'm going to come up with a more practical plan for my life.'"

My dad, brother, and sister were watching at home. I had told them about the interview, hoping I would come across as calm and competent—a girl who knew what she was doing with her life. Now I had to hope that my family members had slept through their alarms, or that the house had caught fire and they'd been forced to evacuate.

"I'm planning to live at home," I said, leaving Kristy's other assumptions unconfirmed. My mom would have wanted me to assure my audience that I was a freshman at Whedon; the nursing gig was temporary. But I couldn't. Not if I wanted to keep my job.

Kristy cringed playfully at the cameras, like, *isn't she*

adorable? "Your parents must be so proud of you. Is your mother a nurse?"

"She's a professor of political science."

Kristy stared deep into my eyes. "And your father?"

"He teaches English."

"Wow. So, is it safe to say that the apple falls pretty far from the tree?"

Nothing was safe to say. I attempted to smile and discovered I'd forgotten how.

"Well, thank you so much for taking the time to chat with us today. And let me tell you, if I'm ever in the hospital— knock on wood—I'm requesting Audrey Nelson at *my* bedside."

The red light on the wall blinked and went off. Kristy's face relaxed as she leaned forward, shook my hand, and hurried off the set like someone desperate to pee. A cameraman hollered in my direction: "That's it, sweetheart. You're free to go."

My palms had left damp streaks on my jeans.

Before leaving the parking lot, I opened the YouTube app on my phone, my gut already twisting with dread. Prior to my interview, the *Steeds County News* had aired a fifteen-second clip of me pounding on Cameron's chest. I knew I would find a fresh batch of comments beneath the original video, and I'd developed something of an addiction to the comments section. It felt like a version of myself was trapped on that page—doomed to suffer strangers' criticism from now through eternity, or until the Internet finally imploded. It was my job to check on that other Audrey, make sure things hadn't gotten out of hand.

Like reading my mother's blog, it was the responsible thing to do.

That Asian girl owes that white girl her life. Or at least her firstborn. LOL.

CPR Girl: 1

Heart Attack Girl: 0

Pretty sure this was staged. Females hardly ever have heart attacks, and never this young. + I don't think that's how you do compressions. imho this is FAKE.

They are both so hot I want them to take turns sucking my **.**

I don't get it. Any1 can do CPR??? I've done it and I'm 12.

Should we really be encouraging today's youth to seek attention in this way? What happened to living in the moment and enjoying the simpler things in life? This is sad, if you ask me.

Why is this chick so sweaty?

Audrey Nelson is an angel sent by God. Her parents must be so proud she's not whoring around like most skank-ass whores her age.

Some of the comments were irrelevant—links to websites selling weight loss supplements—or else only vaguely applicable; one user had posted the lyrics to "Wind Beneath My Wings" three different times. But most, especially those liked so many times they'd been bumped to the top of the page, were inexplicably crude. I tried to tell myself that the messages weren't really meant for me—that people had their own reasons for commenting, other than the hope that I would imagine their words being whispered in my ear.

Not that I had any idea what those other reasons would be. The occasional comment was actually nice.

Audrey is so cute!!!

This girl is going to be such a good nurse!

Can't believe she's only eighteen.

And, over and over again:

Audrey Nelson is a hero.

FOURTEEN

There were nights when Seth and I managed to take our lunch breaks at the same time, but sacrificed the meal itself in favor of hooking up inside a vacant room in the Health and Rehabilitation wing. Because the doors to those rooms didn't lock, we had agreed that our place of employment was not the best venue in which to go all the way. And because I knew that those horizontal, hospital bed kisses could under no circumstances lead to sex, it was those nights when I became singularly obsessed with the idea. The fluorescent lights would be buzzing. The air would smell strongly of antiseptic, faintly of sweat. The back of Seth's neck would be hot, but his fingers cold as they worked their way beneath the elastic of my scrubs. And all I wanted was to sleep with him.

But tonight—about a week after my live television appearance—Seth was preoccupied, mostly keeping his hands to himself as we kissed. Every time I asked him what was wrong, he repeated, "Nothing at all."

As far as I knew, Seth had no idea I'd gone on TV. He'd never mentioned it, and now my goal was to erase the whole ordeal from my memory. After a quick phase of teasing me for my alleged joyriding habit, my dad and siblings had dropped the subject, and whether or not Iris had seen the segment was unclear.

Recently, Mom had turned her blog into an episodic recap of a lengthy date she'd been on with her Italian suitor. References to the two of them wine-tasting and stripping the shells from grilled prawns with their sticky, bare hands were almost enough to make me quit reading, forever. During last Sunday's family video chat, I'd found it impossible to look directly into my mother's pixelated eyes. Luckily, Jake had commandeered the conversation with descriptions of his various summer adventures. A camping trip he took with his high school friends to Agate Beach. A night he stayed up reading Plato's *Republic* for the seventh time. A faded Justin Bieber T-shirt he found in a thrift shop in Eureka and was now wearing exclusively.

Without warning, Seth detached his mouth from mine and said, "Cameron wants to see you."

I sat up so fast, our heads nearly collided. "She does?"

"Yeah." He watched as I straightened my shirt, crossed my legs.

"But why?"

"Well. Remember that time you saved her life?" His smile was sweet, like always.

"Vaguely."

"I think she wants to thank you."

"Does she know—" The question began to leave my mouth before I could catch myself. Seth may have believed that Cameron wanted to thank me, but I suspected she had something else to convey, something other than gratitude.

"Know what?" Seth asked.

"That I went on TV."

In school, Seth O'Malley's grin had been constant. It was like every time you saw the guy he had just found five dollars. But now I was getting acquainted with the full range of his facial expressions, and some of them were devastating.

"You did? When?"

"About a week ago. It was a live interview on the *Steeds County News.*"

"You answered questions about Cam?"

"Not really. Most of the questions were about me. Or about some weird, selfless, heroic version of me. But they showed the video again, obviously."

Seth held perfectly still. "So . . . that morning we climbed the dune . . . you had already agreed to do this? And you didn't tell me?"

"No. I had no idea I was going to do it. It was a spontaneous decision."

Seth gave me a look, like my spontaneity was in no way comforting. "I didn't think you were interested in any of that."

"You just sort of assumed. And I didn't correct you."

"Okay . . ."

"Look, I've never really resembled anyone in my family. They're like this cult. This brainy, bookish cult. And all through high school I thought the only solution was to try to be more like them, not less. Now I'm thinking maybe it's less."

Slowly, Seth turned his palms toward the ceiling. "So . . . you're telling me you went on TV to prove a point to your parents? That doesn't make any sense, Aud."

I had gone on TV because I wanted to hear the host introduce me as *Audrey Nelson, Certified Nurse Assistant.* I wanted to test-drive a version of myself defined by what I did and who I helped—not by my grades, or which college had accepted me, or whose daughter I happened to be.

"Not to prove a point to my parents," I said, "but maybe to prove something to myself."

Seth was probably right; my split-second decision hadn't made any sense. Ultimately, the interview had mortified me.

"I just think you should have asked her permission," he said.

"Whose permission? Cameron's?"

"Yes."

"What happened on the beach happened to me, too."

"Cameron almost died. You didn't."

"Yeah, but—" I took a breath. The distinction felt so important. "She *didn't* die. No one died."

Seth was silent as his eyes roamed the room. The white medical carts and sterilized countertops seemed suddenly sinister. The overhead lights were buzzing like a warning. What the hell were we doing here?

He said, "I guess I don't understand why you would want *more* attention than you've already gotten." He was tranquil, even as he shamed me. It wasn't fair. If he wasn't going to smile and assure me everything was fine, the least he could do was get legitimately angry until we were both shouting things we regretted. Until we both owed each other an apology.

"I don't know, Seth. Maybe because I wasn't prom king."

"Excuse me?" Finally, an edge to his voice.

"This is the first thing I've ever been good at."

"Yeah, you're good at your job, Audrey. You'll be a good RN or doctor or paramedic or whatever you want to be when you grow up. But Cameron's heart attack isn't, like, a flashy addition to your résumé. You understand that, right?"

It felt like he was trying to take something away from

me, but I didn't know exactly what. If I could have traveled back in time and somehow ensured that Seth's ex-girlfriend was born with a heart that never failed her, obviously, that's what I would have done. I wasn't a monster. It was harder to know whether I'd delete the video from the Internet, given the chance. But I thought I probably would—if only to eliminate those few seconds of daily dread while I waited for the comments' section to load.

I would take it all back, if I could. So why did it feel like Seth was trying to negate some crucial part of the story?

"I do understand that," I said, sounding calmer than I felt. "But *you* have to understand that this is mostly out of my control. I can't stop people from watching that video, or talking about me and Cameron."

Seth nodded, but in slow motion, like he wasn't agreeing with me so much as agreeing to think it over. I touched his cheek. He turned his head and faced me, finally. Because he was Seth O'Malley, and I was a girl who believed she had him figured out, I attempted to fix the problem with my lips on his. Our fight hadn't had anything to do with our bodies, but I thought our bodies could probably erase it.

Gently, Seth grabbed my shoulders and pushed me away. "I've got to go," he said. "My boss gets pissed if I'm late."

He rose from the plastic-wrapped mattress and pushed

through the door that didn't lock. We had at least ten minutes to spare; Seth was nowhere near late.

Our argument had never really escalated. We'd used our indoor voices the entire time. I had no idea if I should chase after him and apologize profusely, or if he was the type to prefer space and silence to frantic pleas for forgiveness.

Not knowing was the worst part.

At the end of my shift, I was grabbing my bag from my locker in the break room when I sensed someone's eyes on my back. Assuming Seth had come looking for me, I turned, relieved.

It wasn't Seth. It was Maureen.

"You okay?" she asked, sticking out her bottom lip. "You looked upset earlier."

"I'm fine." To make up for my obvious disappointment upon seeing her, I admitted, "I got into a fight with my boyfriend."

"Oh?" Maureen cocked her head. "He's your boyfriend? That guy with the . . . ?" She fluttered her hand around her face, indicating Seth's general scruff.

The label had sort of slipped out. I wondered if being Seth's girlfriend was still an option. When I didn't say anything right away, Maureen asked, "You want to go to Dot's? My hubby's with the twins this morning."

Dot's was the local dingy tavern, separated from Highway 101 by a gravel parking lot and a stagnant collection of motorcycles. "I'm eighteen," I reminded her.

"Stick with me, and Dot won't even think of carding you."

I hadn't had a drink in months. Toward the end of the school year, I'd stopped going to the weekly bonfire parties up on Cape Defiance. All anyone ever talked about was graduation and what they were doing next. I'd been reasonably excited to become a legal adult. Excited, even, to test my parents' theory that college would change everything. But not excited enough to raise my can of PBR and toast the future, Friday after Friday night.

Part of me didn't want to step foot inside of Dot's Tavern. Part of me didn't want to go anywhere with Maureen. She was the kind of Crescent Bay local my parents had raised me not to be, the kind of girl Sara and I had defined ourselves against—because the two of us weren't doomed to work, breed, and die in this salt-eroded town. We were better than that.

Or maybe I wasn't better than anyone.

"Let's go," I told Maureen.

FIFTEEN

Seth's car was already missing from the parking lot. Climbing into Maureen's old Civic, I stared at the space normally occupied by the Jeep and had to swallow the lump forming fast in my throat. My hand reached for my phone.

"Don't text him!" Maureen screeched.

"Why not?" I asked, kicking aside fast-food wrappers. The back of the car was furnished with two car seats, a mountain of stuffed toys and cardboard picture books rising up between them.

"It's too soon," she said. "You say sorry now, you're claiming responsibility for the whole dispute. I always wait at least a day to see if I can get Chad to apologize first."

"How long have you been married?" I asked her.

Maureen waved her hand. "Oh. Forever."

She was, at most, about twenty-five.

Dot's Tavern was the kind of establishment most people I

knew only joked about patronizing. I assumed the barstools would be planted with drunk, grizzled seamen who hadn't moved in decades, the only lights filled with neon, and every surface sticky to the touch. As it turned out, my guesses weren't completely off base. Inside, a solitary customer had a white beard hanging to his lap. The place smelled like old popcorn, old carpet, and booze—but a row of windows against the back wall let in the early morning light, and Dot herself greeted us warmly before gesturing toward a cracked vinyl booth that appeared to be my supervisor's regular spot. Maureen ordered us two pints of Sam Adams. True to her promise, no one asked to see my ID.

"So," Maureen said, dipping her lips into the frothy head of her beer. "You like gossip?"

"Sure," I said, gulping my own drink. "Who doesn't?"

"Two of our new CNAs on day shift are already getting the boot. Both of them from your program."

"Seriously?" I asked, wondering who it was. Maybe the girl with the aquarium sweatshirt who had dreamed of taking her newly acquired skills to Los Angeles. I had never met any of the staff on day shift; I'd only learned to decipher their initials, scrawled along the edge of each resident's chart.

Maureen nodded. "They barely passed their clinicals, and now they're just not cutting it." She sighed. "You'd be surprised at how many CNAs pass through. The turnover rate is *high*. I don't know, it's like most of these girls think it's going to be a fun, easy job. Something they can do without going to college. I guess I don't have to tell you how misguided that is."

"It can be pretty fun, though." I hadn't eaten anything since before my shift, almost nine hours ago, and now my body was eagerly absorbing the beer. "So much more fun than watching the clock. You know, back in high school—"

"*Back* in high school?" Maureen interrupted. "You mean, like, two months ago?"

"Yeah, two months ago, I watched the clock like it was my job. It got to the point where I felt actual rage at the minute hand taking its sweet time moving over the numbers. I wanted to get up from my desk, smash the thing with my giant calculus textbook, and ask who among my peers had a clock that wasn't a lying a piece of shit."

"Language!" cried Maureen, but she was laughing into her pint glass.

"Being a CNA is way more fun than being a professional clock-watcher," I said.

"You're the best CNA I've trained, probably ever," said Maureen. The compliment was as surprising as it was abrupt. "The residents all adore you. And the director knows it. If you have any desire to switch to days, I'd check in with her."

Maureen had never been so nice to me for such a sustained period of time. The alcohol made me trust her faster than I normally would have.

"I like nights, personally, because I get to spend the afternoons with my kids. I used to work seven to seven, up at Steeds Memorial? Never even saw the twins awake. But obviously," Maureen said neutrally, "you don't have kids."

What I really needed was to cut my hours in half. Now might be the perfect time to tell my supervisor I was going to Whedon. And I tried to make myself do it, but the admission got stuck in my throat. That I would be a freshman at Whedon College in September had never felt less plausible.

"Are you thinking about nursing school, eventually?" Maureen asked.

"Um." I took a drink. "I'm not sure." Nursing school would mean going to college—but not a small liberal arts college like Whedon. Something more like the soulless state university of my parents' nightmares.

"You should. You'll make more money as an RN, have more options. And you'd be really good at it. You have that quality, that thing where the crazier stuff gets, the calmer you get? Like when you saved that girl. That was cool."

Maureen spoke casually, as if resuscitating Cameron

Suzuki was something I'd done on the job, in between combing what remained of Mrs. Lu's hair and arguing with Tamora over the availability of midnight snacks.

"Where'd you get your degree?" I asked Maureen, as it dawned on me that she could not have become a Registered Nurse without leaving Steeds County.

"Portland," she answered.

"You couldn't find a job up there?"

Maureen frowned. "I *had* a job up there. I wanted to come home."

"*Why?*" I was already too tipsy to rein in my disgust.

"What could be better than Crescent Bay?" She sounded almost sardonic. The jukebox was playing an old Steve Earle song, and now the man with the beard was swaying atop his barstool, in definite danger of capsizing. I wondered, dimly, whether it was even legal for Dot to serve alcohol at six in the morning. "Actually, though," Maureen continued, "Portland was fine, but I moved back home to be with my hubby. We've been together since high school."

Dot delivered two more beers to the table before I'd finished my first. Maureen challenged me to keep up, which—regretfully—I did, all the way through rounds two and three. Mostly my supervisor talked while I listened. She had a lot of complaints—about her fellow RNs, about the director of the nursing home, about the residents, including

Tamora, whom she considered to be a particular pain in the ass. At the high point of my drunkenness, Maureen struck me as entertaining. But gradually I grew tired and headachy, and her whole routine started to seem unnecessary.

Toward the bottom of her fourth beer, Maureen sensed my dwindling enthusiasm and changed the subject. "Did Mr. Leary give you any trouble tonight?"

Seconds after my argument with Seth, my pager had gone off. Maureen had been busy outfitting Mrs. Lu with an IV and needed me to assist Mr. Leary with the vicious symptoms of a stomach virus. I'd pushed through the door to Mr. Leary's room and found him curled like an apostrophe at the edge of his mattress. The smell of industrial strength disinfectant just barely masked the smell of vomit.

His eyes had opened and he'd looked at me warily, unsure if we knew each other. A lot of the residents in the Health and Rehabilitation wing had trouble remembering me from night to night; most of our interactions took place while they slept.

I smiled at him. At some point over the last few weeks, my on-the-job smiles had stopped feeling so fake. "Long night?" I asked him.

No answer. His eyes went glassy and he shifted his body even closer to the edge of the bed. In one movement I threw open a cabinet, grabbed a clean metal basin, and held it under Mr. Leary's chin.

When Mr. Leary had finished, he'd looked at me—more resigned than embarrassed—and replied, "Not as long as yours, I bet."

Now I assured Maureen that my patient and I had gotten along fine. "I changed his sheets and stayed with him until he fell asleep."

"It's a lot easier to clean up in that situation if you move them into the bathroom," she said.

"He wanted to stay where he was."

She raised her eyebrows. "So you let him?"

I shrugged. "Sure."

"Okay, but in the future, just make him move into the bathroom."

"Why?" I should have known better than to argue. "What difference does it make?"

"Trust me, it makes a world of difference. Wait until you're on day shift and you're trying to take care of seven people at once. You won't have time to change anyone's sheets for the hundredth time. Then again . . ." Maureen had a habit of staring pointedly at her own hands whenever she was about to insult me. "Maybe you're not ready for day shift. Not yet, anyway."

"Right," I mumbled, wondering at what point in this conversation I'd ceased to be the best CNA she'd ever trained.

"Anyway." She slammed down her empty glass, missing the cardboard coaster by about a mile. "Not all of us have tomorrow off." Maureen rummaged around in her oversized purse until she found her cell phone. I listened, somewhat incredulous, as she called her husband and baby-talked him into picking her up. When she rose from the booth, I arranged my features into a *what about me?* face, trying to salvage whatever camaraderie had formed between us and vanished so soon.

"Can't stay mad forever," she advised me, leaving a crumpled twenty on the table. "Time to call that boy, don't you think?"

I called a different boy. I called Elliot Slate. He arrived promptly enough, bright-eyed behind the wheel of his mom's car, puffy vest zipped straight to his throat. When I went to pull open the passenger-side door, I was surprised to find Sara already riding shotgun. She raised her eyebrows at me through the glass and gestured, patronizingly, toward the backseat.

"Thank you both for coming," I said, trying to sound dignified as I climbed inside the car and fastened my seat belt.

Apparently the effort was obvious. Elliot smirked at me in the rearview mirror. "Beer for breakfast?"

"It was a long night."

"Where's O'Malley? Facedown on the bar?"

"Seth had nothing to do with *any* of this." I waved my hand at the sloped, mossy structure of Dot's Tavern. Pulling a wide U-turn in the parking lot, Elliot grimaced—he didn't believe me, but wasn't going to argue—and Sara's silence struck me as increasingly suspect. What were they even doing together, so early in the morning?

"Did you guys hang out all night?" I asked.

"Yeah," Sara said. "Elliot stayed over."

"You *stayed over*?" I leaned forward, speaking obnoxiously close to Elliot's right ear.

"We sleep at Sara's all the time," he reminded me. "What's the big deal?"

"Usually it's the three of us. Not the two of you. *Alone.*"

Sara shuddered. "Stop accusing us of incest. Elliot slept in one of the guest rooms."

Now my voice contained a lilt of excitement; it had long been my dream to sleep in one of the guest rooms at Sara's house. "Did you use the eucalyptus shampoo?"

"Um," Elliot said. "I took a shower. . . ."

Sara leaned over the gearshift and sniffed Elliot's head. "He used the shampoo," she confirmed.

"I didn't know you guys were having sleepovers without me." I pouted.

"Well, we can't do anything *with* you," Sara said, revealing the reason behind her icy demeanor. "You're never around."

I was around. I could have done things aside from work and kiss Seth and sleep, if only I had kept conventional, sunlit hours. "Our schedules are opposite. That's all. You're asleep when I'm awake."

"Uh-huh," Sara intoned, unconvinced. And I wanted to remind her that she was the one leaving home at the end of the summer; I was the one staying exactly where I'd always been. I would, by default, miss her more than she missed me. But picking a fight—after the nonfight I'd had with Seth, plus the sudden tension that had tightened between Maureen and me when I'd stopped giggling at her beery diatribe—was the last thing I wanted to do.

"Hey, Elliot," I said abruptly. "Have you been to see Cameron at the hospital?"

"Yeah, I finally went the other night. I brought her some flowers."

I tried to say, "Chivalrous," but struggled with the second syllable.

"I mean, we were kind of on a date when it happened, so . . ."

"You should go on more dates with Cameron. A hundred more dates with Cameron."

Elliot looked over at Sara, who shrugged her shoulders. She was through with my antics. She was sober, superior. "I think, for now, I'm just going to leave Cameron to her recovery," Elliot said.

"But you *belong* together. You were *made* for each other." I had entered the phase of drunkenness wherein I could hear exactly how drunk I sounded—was, in fact, getting on my own nerves—but I was also powerless against my need to continue being an idiot.

Sara swiveled around, gripping the back of her seat so she could look me square in the eye. "Audrey. Even if Elliot thoroughly seduced Cameron Suzuki and they fell help-lessly, head-over-heels in love, nothing will change the fact that Cameron and Seth used to date."

"I know that," I said, petulant.

"Would you even *want* to be with a guy who felt indiffer-ent toward his hospitalized ex-girlfriend?" Sara demanded.

The correct response was *no*. My actual response was to groan and claim, "He cares more about her than me."

In a gentler tone than Sara had employed, Elliot asked, "Is it possible that it just *seems* that way? Because Cameron almost died a couple weeks ago?"

Heaving a dramatic sigh, I told them about Seth getting mad at me mid–make out session—about how, instead of actually yelling, he had gone stiff and silent and judgmental. How I'd tried to kiss him, and how he had pushed me away.

"Wait," Elliot said as I started to defend my right to appear on regional television. "You told him you weren't going to do the interview, and then you did?"

"I never told him anything. I told *myself* I wasn't going to go on the news, and then I changed my mind."

"Just because?" Sara asked.

"Just because."

"Maybe Seth finds you overwhelming," she theorized. "Not that I really know the guy, but he seems pretty . . . even-keeled."

"Are you saying I'm not even-keeled?"

Sara snorted.

"You can be kind of impulsive," Elliot said.

I endeavored to focus on this word, *impulsive*, to connect it to my recent behavior, to the infuriating nonfight I'd had with Seth. Was it a bad thing to be impulsive—to make quick, heart-pounding decisions? Was it really a problem I needed to solve?

Too wasted to solve any problems, big or small, I let my mind wander. Elliot was driving down a stretch of highway with an unencumbered view of the ocean. Early in the morning, the ocean always looked gray and foamy and miserable.

"I should get out," I announced.

"Do you feel sick?" Elliot glanced toward the road's shoulder.

"No, I mean I should get outta town."

"Get outta town . . ." Sara echoed my sloppy cadence as she fiddled with the heat settings on Ms. Slate's car. "What about Whedon?"

"Screw Whedon." I spoke with more conviction than I felt. I couldn't renounce Whedon College without renouncing the Professors Nelson, whom I still loved, even if my mother had recently lost her marbles.

"What about Seth?" she asked.

"He hates me. He thinks I'm a fame whore."

"Seth O'Malley did *not* call you a fame whore." Elliot nearly growled.

"Correct." I sighed. "He doesn't use bad words. Or degrade women."

Finally, my best friend threw a smile toward the backseat. "Maybe you should get some sleep before you drop out of college, break up with your boyfriend, and split town. You never know. You might change your mind, again."

Elliot had turned off the highway and onto the forested gravel road that wound its way to my house.

"How did you know?" I asked Sara. I had referred to Seth O'Malley as my boyfriend exactly once, in the break room with my supervisor, hours earlier.

"Know what?" Sara asked as we idled in my driveway.

"That he's my boyfriend?"

"Um." Sara and Elliot exchanged a look. And the way they sat up there, sharing eye rolls and shrugs, neither of them drunk or desperate—they might as well have been my parents. "Because he's all you ever talk about," she said.

Overturned in the hallway was a plum-colored suitcase.

At some point in the late nineteen-nineties my parents had dubbed this particular piece of luggage "Old Purple," and in my mind it had always been the emblem of both family vacations and those unsettling periods of time when Mom traveled alone, abandoning the rest of us.

Old Purple had flown to Italy in March. Most likely, the suitcase had not returned by itself.

I crept down the hall and through the kitchen, on high alert for further evidence. The empty coffee cup in the sink could have been Dad's, or Jake's. The crumpled paper towel containing the uneaten, unfrosted corners of a strawberry Pop-Tart had definitely been left behind by Rosie, a big believer in midnight snacks. But the sound I could now detect coming from the living room—the asthmatic snore of a woman who had forbidden all pets, even gerbils, from crossing the threshold of the Nelson family home—had only one possible source.

I didn't know whether I should feel relieved that she had come back, or upset that she was sleeping on the couch.

But because I was still in unwashed hospital scrubs—with beer on my breath, Seth on my mind, the potential for impulsivity coursing through my veins—I tiptoed past her and went to bed.

SIXTEEN

Lately, my little sister only ever wore two facial expressions: complete indifference or alarm. When she woke me up a few hours later—the noon sun filling every corner of our room—her eyes were wide.

"You need to report to the kitchen," she said.

I squinted at Rosie through the film of my hangover. "Says who? Mom?"

"You already know?"

"She was sleeping—" I stopped short of revealing that our mother had entered our house in the dead of night and chosen to crash on the couch rather than join her spouse in their bed. "She was asleep when I got home from work, but I saw her suitcase."

"She says it's time for you to get up." Rosie tugged on my arm, and I pretended her efforts had sent me spinning out of bed, onto the floor. I was maybe still a little drunk.

"Any idea why she came home early?" I asked, as if I

had no special insight into our mother's personal life.

Rosie nudged my rib cage with her bare foot. Her toenails were painted to resemble watermelons. "She says she got lonely."

I laughed.

"Why is that funny?"

"No reason." I rose from the carpet and followed her out of the room.

In the kitchen, the two of them occupied their old places at the table, twin cups of coffee resting on loose sheets of Dad's manuscript. Dad was leaning forward, on the edge of his seat, looking at Mom like she was responsible for everything beautiful in the world. He did that sometimes. It always made me feel squeamish, and safe.

"Look who it is," Jake said. "Our resident vampire." He was perched on the counter, cheerfully eating a banana and swinging his heels against a cabinet door. Too distracted by my entrance to reprimand my brother, Mom pushed back her chair and wrapped me in her arms. She was tan, but otherwise unchanged—same gray, androgynous hairstyle. Same khaki shorts and T-shirt advertising Yale University, where she'd gone to grad school and met Dad.

"Audrey," she exhaled. "I missed you so much."

I let myself enjoy her embrace for a count of three before disentangling my arms and moving toward the coffeepot.

"Missed you, too," I said quickly.

It wasn't my intention to be mean, but Mom wasn't just Mom, anymore. She was the sole author of *Sprung Free in Italy!* She had let some guy gaze at her the way Dad was gazing at her now. They had eaten shellfish with their hands, like semiaquatic mammals in love.

"You can always count on your offspring for an enthused greeting," Dad said.

"I'm overwhelmed," Mom agreed. "I would never have expected such a warm reception after a mere *four months* abroad."

"And why would you? What would give you the right?"

"Not carrying her in my womb for two hundred and eighty-nine days—that's for sure." Suddenly swept up in nostalgia, Mom cut the performance short. "God, remember how big I got with Audrey? It was practically obscene."

Dad's sigh was much too deep. "I remember."

The two of them made lingering eye contact.

"Get a room," Jake said.

"Please," Rosie whimpered.

I was hiding my face behind a Whedon College mug, concentrating on the delivery of caffeine to my bloodstream. It felt like someone had cinched a wire around my skull and was pulling it tighter and tighter. I needed to go back to bed, or else I needed to call Seth and make things right. Anything but this Nelson family kitchen theater.

Mom had crossed her arms and was appraising me from a distance now. I could feel her scrutinizing the shadows beneath my eyes, the way my hands—wrapped tight around the mug—trembled slightly.

My mother was known for her sweetness—for bringing doughnuts and coffee to her students, for hosting other people's retirement parties, delivering speeches that made her guests laugh and weep in equal measure. Within our family, she was the first to notice when someone looked nice, or seemed sad. A part of me was always surprised when other people's moms were awkward or preoccupied or cold.

But occasionally, Mom changed her mind about being nice. When she transitioned to a side of her personality Rosie called "Officer Mom," the switch was absolute. She did not waver.

"You're hungover," she announced.

"Nah," was my halfhearted protest. "You're mistaken."

"I am *not* mistaken." Mom turned to Dad. "Is this the new norm? Our daughter comes home drunk, sleeps until noon?"

Bewildered, Dad turned up his hands. "Audrey works nights!"

"Apparently she *drinks* nights, too."

"How is me getting drunk Dad's fault?" I asked.

"I left your father in charge," Mom said. "I thought he could handle three reasonably well-behaved adolescents by himself for a summer."

"He handles us fine," Rosie said. She had joined Jake on the countertop and was resting her head against his shoulder. With each other, my siblings had an uncomplicated relationship that both annoyed me and filled me with envy.

"He doesn't really handle Audrey," Jake said. "She's spiraling out of control."

"I'm tempted to agree," Mom said.

Before I could choose between defending myself and walking out of the room, the five of us were simultaneously distracted by the sound of car wheels on the gravel road. Our house was the second to last on our street, our neighbors an elderly couple who rarely freed their rusted Cadillac from its weedy parking spot. Car wheels, more often than not, meant visitors.

The engine grew louder, then shut off. We heard a door slam, followed by the thump of someone's shoes on our front porch.

Not just shoes. Cowboy boots.

"Seth," I whispered.

"Who?" Mom asked.

Rosie's eyes nearly escaped their sockets. My brother was already sliding across the floor in his tube socks. Madly, he scampered down the hall, making a beeline for the entryway. I listened, frozen with panic, as he threw open the front door.

"Seth O'Malley! What a perfect time for you to drop by! Come in, come in."

I cringed, picturing my brother's Justin Bieber T-shirt on proud display, the fear that must have been flashing in Seth's eyes as he asked, "Are you sure? Can I just—is Audrey here?"

"Let's go find her!" Jake bellowed.

I was dressed in an old pair of boxers and the tank top I'd been wearing beneath my scrubs all night. Before falling asleep I had twisted my hair into a bun, but now the bun felt sort of like a wild animal clinging desperately to the top of my head. I wanted to dart inside my room, but it felt imperative to stand guard between Seth and my deranged relatives.

He entered the kitchen, trailing behind my brother. Upon seeing me, Seth smiled with one corner of his mouth.

Our nonfight suddenly seemed abstract and inconsequential. Was I allowed to kiss him in front of my entire family?

"Hi," I said. Embarrassed, elated.

"Hi." Seth sounded almost shy.

"Hello," Dad interrupted, as if some great injustice was taking place under his roof.

"Sorry, Mr. Nelson." Seth turned to my father and stuck out his hand. "I'm Seth. I'm Audrey's . . . we work together."

Without getting up from the table, Dad shook Seth's hand. "You can just call me Nelson."

"Um, sure," said Seth. I'd never explained the deal with my father's name, having never actually intended to introduce the two of them.

"You work together?" Mom looked Seth up and down. "You're a nurse assistant?"

"He's janitorial," I said.

"You're a janitor?" Mom asked.

"My official title is janitorial slash kitchen aide," Seth said.

My parents were frowning at him like he'd spoken a foreign language—one in which neither of them was fluent. In the chaos of Seth's arrival, Rosie had slid off the counter and was now hanging monkey-like from the doorframe, a pose Mom always insisted would *weaken the integrity of the house.*

Jake was leaning against the pantry, shoveling dry Cheerios from the box into his mouth.

"It's a good job," Seth said.

"Sounds like it." Mom smiled, her sense of decorum gradually returning to her. "Sit down, Seth. Would you like some coffee?"

"No, thank you." He sank obediently into one of our rickety chairs. He looked tall and cramped and captured sitting there. Several strands of hair had escaped his ponytail, and I wanted to tuck them behind his ears.

I could have explained to my family that Seth and I had been in the same grade all through school. I could sense my mother trying to figure out how old he was—if he was some rough-handed laborer I'd picked up at my grubby summer job, or just a kid, like me. But I wasn't ready to give her the peace of mind. She would have to earn it.

Dad, as far as I could tell, was more concerned with Seth's physique than with his age. His effort to visually measure the width of Seth's shoulders was obvious; his eyes kept darting from side to side.

"Do you play a sport?" Dad asked.

Seth swallowed. "I played some football."

Nelson looked at me like I had crushed his every dream.

"Audrey is going to Whedon College in September," Mom said.

"I know," Seth said.

"Whedon's a good school," Jake piped up, his mouth full of cereal. "Very hard to get into."

I glared at my brother. "No one here believes I got into Whedon on my own merits, Jake."

"I do," Jake said. "I believe in you."

I rolled my eyes, hating him for making me play the little sister role.

"Seth, what are your college plans?" Mom asked.

"I don't actually have any. Not yet."

When Mom tilted her head in confusion, I noticed the ballpoint pen stuck behind her ear. I wondered how long the pen had been there—if she'd spent the plane ride marking up her latest article, or jotting notes into the margins of a book.

"I'm going to keep working for a while," Seth explained. "Save some money."

"Responsible," my father said.

"It's a good job," Seth repeated. "I wouldn't do it if I didn't like it."

Mom's smile contained a trace of condescension. I didn't think Seth would detect it, but I was painfully aware of it. In fact, I was painfully aware of a lot of things: my mother's arrogance, my brother's eagerness to emulate her attitude, Dad's discomfort with a perfectly disarming teenage boy—one whose only error had been to drop by unannounced, today of all days—and Rosie, with her Popsicle-stained lips, her California board shorts. My sister was unwilling to utter a single word in front of Seth; she was equally unwilling to leave the room.

"I like my job, too," I announced.

"I'm glad," Mom said. "I knew it would be a rewarding experience."

My heart raced as I said, "I'm not quitting in September."

Jake froze with his hand buried in the Cheerios box. Dad lowered his glasses so he could massage his eyelids, aggressively, and Rosie made a humming noise in her throat, like a toy airplane about to take flight.

Mom was cautious, calculating. "Well . . . maybe you can keep a couple of shifts after school starts. Or else you could stay on as a volunteer. But I have to be honest, sweetheart, I think freshman year is a full-time job."

There was something funny about this moment, when my mother seemed to believe—against all evidence—that my life was still under her control.

I could let her believe it. I could cling to the small, dimming part of me that still thought Whedon College might turn me into a true Nelson; all it would take was the right class or the right book to draw me into my parents' world. And then I would understand the rush of the all-nighter, the satisfaction of crawling into bed at dawn, my mind exhausted.

I looked at Seth, imprisoned in the center of the kitchen.

He looked back at me with tired, patient eyes. We already understood the rush of the all-nighter.

"I'm not going to Whedon," I said.

And whatever had been knotted tight in my chest all year—some combination of dread and anxiety—came loose.

"Excuse me?" Mom said.

I was eighteen years old. If I didn't start college in the fall, it wouldn't be the end of the world. It would just be the end of a bad idea.

"I'm not going," I repeated.

"You know it's too late to apply elsewhere," Dad said.

"It's too late for this year," I said. "There will be other years."

"And what *about* this year?" Mom's voice verged on distraught. "How do you imagine spending your time?"

"Working. Figuring out where I might go to nursing school."

Seth was tugging on the end of his ponytail, staring at the spaghetti-sauced linoleum. Mom had yet to comment on the state of the house, but a tirade was forthcoming; I had caught her eyeing the grease-streaked microwave, the full-grown dust rabbits lurking beneath the table. My siblings were watching Seth in awe, as if he alone had set today's events in motion. As if he had managed to lure me away from our parents' careful plans—with his four-wheel drive and rugged good looks—and was here now to oversee the fallout.

I remembered, too late, the question Seth had asked me just before we kissed the first time. Heat flared across my cheeks. I needed to get him out of this house. I had so much explaining to do.

"Audrey, I don't know if I want that for you," Mom said.

"Want what?" I asked, preoccupied by Seth, who wouldn't look at me.

She took a breath. "I don't know if I want you to spend your life taking care of other people."

At first, what she had said seemed harmless, a routine concern. In another second the concern gained weight and her words, as they echoed in my head, were as jarring as if she'd called me by the wrong name.

I faced my mother. "Why not?"

We were all watching, waiting. Nelson appeared especially rapt. If Iris didn't want me to spend my life taking care of other people, why had she spent hers taking care of us?

Most of her life, anyway. Everything up until the last four months.

Mom tore her gaze away from me and, briefly, met Dad's eyes. She blushed. I couldn't stand the silence anymore. Seth had gone from uncomfortable to miserable, and my priorities realigned themselves. We needed to get out of here.

With an exaggerated sigh, I said, "Let it go, Mom. I've sprung free."

"Pardon?"

"It's over. My mind's made up. I've sprung free."

She squeezed her eyes shut. "Why do you keep saying that, Audrey?"

"You know why."

"I don't understand."

She was pinching the bridge of her nose, breathing deeply. Of course she didn't understand. She had believed her blog anonymous, and it had probably felt anonymous—sitting in her rented apartment in a foreign country, typing about places her family had never been, people we'd never met.

"Mom," Rosie squeaked, "are you okay?"

Our mother opened her eyes. Silently, she pleaded with me, terrified I would keep talking, would reveal—recklessly, unceremoniously—that she'd had an affair with some European winemaker, some horror movie buff.

And despite everything I'd already said, it killed me that she thought I would do that to her.

"She's fine," I said. "We're fine. Everybody's fine. Seth?" He stared at my outstretched hand as if it were on fire. "Want to get out of here?"

Seth stood, gingerly, taking pains not to elbow my

father—who was still seated at his side—or bump into my mother, who hovered above his chair. "It was nice to meet you all," he said.

Jake was the only Nelson who responded, securing the cardboard flaps of the Cheerios box and suggesting, in a neutral tone of voice, "Come back soon."

SEVENTEEN

Wordlessly, Seth and I sank to the porch steps. We were side by side but staring straight ahead at the overgrown grass of the front yard, at all the dandelions gone to seed. I stretched out my bare legs, absorbing the warmth of the sun. A thin layer of hair covered my calves and reflected light. I couldn't remember the last time I'd shaved.

I couldn't remember the last time I'd been so unsure of what to say to him.

Seth appeared deep in thought, leaning over his knees and compulsively picking at the stitching on his boots. The Jeep was parked in my usual spot, its nose nearly touching our garage.

"Nursing school?" he said finally.

"It's just something I'm thinking about." I wanted to inch my thigh closer to his, until there was no space between us, but I couldn't tell how Seth felt about the space.

"Makes sense," he said.

"I think so. It feels like a solid plan. Going to Whedon felt like a bad plan, from the start."

He nodded, processing this information. "So . . . where's the closest place to get a nursing degree?"

I threw a look back toward the house, where I'd abandoned my entire family. "To be honest, I think I'd be more interested in the farthest place."

Playfully, Seth clamped a hand over his heart. "You lied to me, Audrey. You said I could kiss you into September and beyond."

"You can. You will." I shifted, closing the gap between our legs. "I'm not going anywhere before September. And I didn't lie to you about Whedon. At least, not intentionally. Dropping out was—"

"A spontaneous decision?"

Seth forced a smile, but I could see the hurt behind it. I remembered Sara theorizing that I overwhelmed him. Lately, I overwhelmed myself.

"I'm sorry," I said, and then the apologies just kept unfurling. "I'm sorry my brother dragged you into the kitchen. I'm sorry I let you sit in the one chair that's about to break. I'm sorry my little sister ogled you, and that everyone was so—"

"Hey." Seth took my face in his hands. We kissed, and I was so relieved that I forgot about my unbrushed teeth.

Nothing mattered except the warmth of the sun, the warmth of his lips. The fact that, after everything Seth had witnessed, he was still interested in kissing me.

Then, remembering how three pints of beer had turned my mouth into a desert, I pulled away.

"What's wrong?" Seth asked.

"Nothing," I said. "Just my breath. I got drunk after work." It was an awkward confession, but I was done keeping secrets from Seth.

"You got drunk? With who?" Concern edged his voice.

"With my supervisor. She took me to Dot's Tavern."

"Oh." Seth relaxed. "My dad loves that place."

"Everyone's dad loves that place," I lied, knowing Nelson wouldn't be caught dead in Dot's. Nelson would sooner be buried at sea.

"You didn't get carded?" Seth asked.

"Nope."

"How drunk did you get?"

"Drunk enough to drown my regrets."

"Ah. I have some of those."

"Yeah?" I asked, a little bit hopeful.

"That's why I came over. To apologize." Seth pulled my hands into his lap and started playing with my fingers. "I shouldn't have acted like you committed some grave sin, going on the news. It's just . . ."

His face was tense as he searched for the right words. More than anyone else I knew, Seth spoke carefully. Deliberately. "Cam's not ecstatic about the video being all over the Internet. She's tired of the attention. She's tired of being *that girl who almost died*. But I get that it's your story, too. You're allowed to be proud. You're allowed to be . . ."

He trailed off, unsure of my rights.

I said, "Audrey Nelson, Certified Nurse Assistant."

Seth laughed, nervous. "Um, what?"

"That's how I thought they would introduce me on the news. All fast and professional-sounding, like when they introduce a politician, or some kind of expert."

"Kristy Summers didn't make you feel like an expert?"

My cheeks warmed. I'd never told Seth that my interview had been with Kristy, meaning that someone else had told him. "Kristy Summers made me feel like a Crescent Bay townie," I admitted.

"You are," Seth said.

"Yeah, but I'm *your* townie, right?"

With his arm around my shoulders, Seth squeezed. "Right. Beer breath and all."

"So I'm guessing you didn't get wasted last night?"

He shook his head. "Nah. I don't drink."

And then I remembered—I already knew that about Seth. Or at least, I'd known it a long time ago. In tenth grade, when Rusty Tillman had called her boyfriend to come pick us up from that party, she told me not to worry; her boyfriend didn't drink.

Fresh memories of Seth had a way of stunning me. It was hard to fathom exactly how I'd overlooked him, year after year.

"Were you always so good?" I asked him, knowing the question was too vague. Knowing he wouldn't be able to answer unless I came much closer to saying what I meant. But after a second of bemused, uncertain stammering, Seth sat up straight. He frowned at the Jeep.

"Hey. Why am I parked in your spot?"

Seth was right; the driveway should have been occupied by the MINI. Mentally I retraced my steps—from work, to the front seat of Maureen's car, to the backseat of Elliot's.

I groaned. "It's possible I need a ride."

I had left my dad's car at the retirement home, and then—in the chaos of this interminable morning—forgotten all about it.

"Hurry up and get dressed." Seth nudged my knee with his. "I'll take you wherever you need to go."

EIGHTEEN

"Still courting fame, I see."

In room 64, Tamora Sinclair remained nocturnal. Tonight she was propped up in bed, dressed in polka-dot pajamas. To explain her comment, she handed me a section of the *Sacramento Bee*.

The reporter had called a few days ago. Her voice was warm, containing none of Kristy Summers's syrupy-sweet condescension. Still, I might not have agreed to answer the woman's questions on the spot if my mother hadn't been following me from room to room, shooting me tight-lipped looks and mouthing, anxiously, "Who is it?"

I'd tried to tame her with a cold, hard stare—a stare that meant I remembered every word of the blog she'd hastily deleted, the day she arrived home. Since that day, my stare had lost its potency. She knew she had me. I wouldn't say the words *Italian suitor* to Dad, or *trial separation* in front of my siblings. Iris was in charge of her own life; all I wanted in return were the keys to mine.

But Mom was having trouble with the trade. She hovered over my shoulder for the duration of the phone interview. Consequently, my answers had been less than eloquent.

HEROIC TEEN SAVES FRIEND'S LIFE BY PERFORMING CPR

The small, scenic town of Crescent Bay is particularly proud of one of its citizens after recent high school graduate Audrey Nelson jumped into action and saved the life of her friend and classmate Cameron Suzuki.

Nelson (18) and Suzuki (18) were enjoying an Independence Day picnic when Suzuki suffered sudden cardiac arrest at the ocean's edge. Nelson, a Certified Nurse Assistant trained in First Aid and CPR, rushed to Suzuki's side and began chest compressions. Nelson's efforts led to the successful resuscitation of Suzuki, whose arrhythmia had gone undiagnosed all her life.

"I just thought we were going to go down to the beach and hang out until the fireworks started," said Nelson. "My boyfriend wanted to build a sand castle, but I told him no."

After witnessing her friend's collapse, Nelson knew Suzuki wasn't playing a joke. "I could just tell, the way she fell down, it wasn't normal. It wasn't like she'd tripped or collapsed for fun. It was just like her heart had stopped working."

Authorities have confirmed that Suzuki will make a full recovery. The victim's mother, Violet Suzuki, wants parents to be aware that "a cardiac rhythm disturbance like Cameron's is not likely to be caught by your child's pediatrician during a routine checkup. Cam had told us the day before that it felt like her heart was fluttering. We assumed she was too young for it to indicate anything serious."

Dr. Terrance Dashwood, a cardiac surgeon at Steeds Memorial, confirmed that if your child complains of a similar "fluttering" sensation, "it wouldn't be a bad idea to bring him in for some tests."

Violet Suzuki also added that she is "so, so grateful that someone was there who knew what she was doing."

Nelson herself admitted that CPR is not something just anyone can do. "Most people who haven't had a lot of experience doing it get it wrong. You have to have a lot of upper arm strength."

When asked about the future of her friendship with Suzuki, Nelson said, "She doesn't really owe me anything. I wouldn't call myself a hero."

But the community of Crescent Bay, California, is calling her just that.

I dropped the newspaper on the nightstand. Tamora's room was free of clutter—no framed photographs or glass grapes or jars of potpourri.

"Upper arm strength, huh?" she said.

"Shut up."

"Let's see those guns."

"Only if you show me yours first."

Tamora's smile was subtle, one edge of her lips tugging downward. "No."

"Oh, in that case," I jerked my thumb toward the door, "maybe I should go? Let you get some sleep?"

She ignored me. "What's a girl like you doing with a boyfriend?"

Normally people wanted to know what a girl like me—or a girl like Sara, or any girl with limbs and teeth—was doing *without* a boyfriend. "What do you mean?"

"You seem smart. Good at what you do. Trying to save money to get the hell out of Dodge, am I right?"

I hesitated. "Something like that."

"Why waste your time with this . . . sand castle–building buffoon?"

"He's not a buffoon! The reporter asked me about our Fourth of July plans, and I was trying to explain that we hadn't really made any. Seth had floated the idea of entering the sand-sculpting contest. I didn't think the woman would *quote* me on that."

Tamora considered my defense of Seth before concluding, "You don't need a boyfriend. Trust me. And also, they never quote what you think they'll quote. If you'd come to me for some media training, I could have prepared you."

"Media training?"

"Mmm." Tamora examined her fingernails, which were perfectly manicured. I could imagine her at the age I was now—popular, proud, quick on her feet.

"Okay, I'll bite. What are you, some kind of expert in Internet fame?"

"Internet fame?" Tamora scoffed. "Not Internet fame. Real fame. I was a talent manager in Los Angeles for forty-five years."

"Oh yeah?" I perched on the foot of her bed. "Did you ever meet anyone famous?"

Tamora narrowed her sea glass eyes at me. "You think I might have sustained a career in the entertainment industry for half a century without meeting anyone famous?"

I shrugged. "Okay, so tell me."

"Tell you what?"

"About your famous clients."

"You've never heard of my clients. You're a fetus."

"Try me."

Folding her arms, Tamora looked toward the darkened window. "Milan Lorca, Blake Dunne." She paused. "Jackson Moon. I managed his career from start to finish."

"Jackson Moon?" Excitement lifted my voice. "The 'Shotgun Wedding' guy?"

Tamora looked skeptical. "You're a country music fan?"

"My parents really liked that song." I refrained from adding *ironically*.

"Your parents really liked a song about two hillbillies in a mutually abusive relationship?"

"Yup."

Tamora accepted this. "Everyone did. Well, almost everyone. Jackson hated it."

"Didn't he write it?"

"We wrote it together."

I tried, but was unable to imagine Tamora penning lyrics like: *I saw you in town, girl / lips stuck on a scoundrel.*

"Jackson never meant for that song to define him," Tamora went on. "But really, the boy has nothing to complain about. We made out like bandits. 'Shotgun Wedding' paid for all of this." She gestured sweepingly to the contents of her room, and I couldn't tell to what extent she was kidding.

"So did you, like, discover him?"

"Of course. I was new to the game and so was Jackson. He sent me his head shot, his résumé. What he wanted originally was to be an actor. He thought he was going to play the preppy romantic lead. The Lothario. But then I met with him. Heard him sing in this gentle, Floridian accent. We came up with a new concept."

"You made him change what he wanted to be?"

She wrinkled her nose. "Just the details."

"So, how does a Florida prep become a cowboy overnight?"

Tamora looked at me like it was a stupid question, but one she'd been asked a hundred times before. "By changing his shoes."

In the minutes we spent talking, before my pager finally interrupted us, Tamora gave me the lowdown on Jackson Moon's career. She told me about booking his first gigs in dingy Los Angeles bars, where no matter how many Townes Van Zandt covers he played, people still scream-requested "Stairway to Heaven" and chucked peanuts onto the stage. She described staying up all night in a rented recording studio off Ventura Boulevard, telling Jackson over and over that he needed to sound more like Johnny Cash and less like Johnny Rivers. Later, they had gone to every awards show and industry party arm in arm. They'd vacationed together. For the past ten years—since their mutual retirement—Tamora and Jackson had even been living together, down in Sacramento.

"Until he fell in love and finally kicked me out," she told me, glossing over the part where she became elderly and, by some measure, sick.

"He kicked you out?"

Tamora waved a hand, dismissing her own exaggeration. "It was time. Letting him move on with his life was the least I could do, after . . . after everything. At least if I'm stuck in here, Jackson doesn't have to worry."

I looked around the unadorned room. "Do you have any pictures of him?"

"Get out your pocket watch."

I studied her face. As a nurse assistant, I was trained to identify the first signs of dementia, but Tamora was inscrutable. "My what?"

She rolled her eyes. "Your iPhone."

Relieved, I produced my phone and searched the Internet for Jackson Moon. Perusing his Wikipedia page, my real-life surroundings were temporarily blurred by Jackson's past. The article confirmed Tamora's account of his humble beginnings, referencing the seedy bars and the Ventura Boulevard recording studio. The article also revealed details Tamora had omitted—Jackson's struggle with cocaine during the late eighties, and the long list of country music starlets he had dated.

And then, toward the bottom of the page, under "personal life": *While linked to dozens of women over the course of his career, Moon never married. For many years he cohabitated with his manager, Tamora Sinclair, who was twenty-five years his senior and known for managing several major acts in the 1970s.*

There was a picture of the two of them on some red carpet. Tamora stood with her arm draped through the crook of Jackson's elbow. His Stetson looked weird with his tux, and her dress resembled the kind of overly ornate Christmas tree you'd find in the lobby of a cheap motel.

She had been beautiful, though. With long, stick-straight hair, high cheekbones, a strong jaw. The differences between then and now were striking—but it wasn't just that her hair had turned to a dull white. On the red carpet, she looked happy, thrilled. The way my friends and I looked in the self-ies we took, messing around on the beach.

Lately, Tamora never seemed thrilled. Whenever I entered her room, I found her staring out the window, or up at the muted television screen, looking sleepless and sad and—above all—bored.

Putting away my phone, I refocused on present-day Tamora.

"What are you doing here?"

If she found the question invasive, her expression didn't show it. "It was Jackson's idea. What choice did I have?"

"You're seventy-eight years old. You can do whatever you want."

Tamora smirked at me. "Says the girl with her whole life ahead of her."

NINETEEN

After surprising us with her early return from Italy, Mom spent a week cleaning every inch of the house. Aggressively, she pushed the vacuum into previously cluttered corners, vanquishing tumbleweeds of dust. When I passed her in the mornings—still in my scrubs, on my way to bed—she would be crouched in the kitchen, scouring the inside of the oven or polishing a cabinet door until it gleamed. And she would be muttering. Some refrain or admonishment I could never quite catch, because the moment she sensed my presence she would crane her neck and give me a beatific smile.

She was scaring me.

Because I worked nights, I had no idea if she and Nelson were sharing a bed, or if Iris had been sneaking downstairs and curling up on the couch after my siblings were asleep. Maybe she stayed up late, texting sweet nothings to her Italian suitor, or maybe she had started a brand-new password-protected blog.

I was almost relieved, one afternoon, when she asked me to set aside my next night off for a family dinner. Either she and Dad would reveal their plans to resume their separation, or else the dinner was purely symbolic, an effort to restore their marriage to factory settings.

I hoped for the latter, until Mom informed me that we were going to Beachcomber Bill's.

"What?" I asked. "*Why?* You hate it there."

At Beachcomber Bill's, families who were waiting for tables were corralled through the labyrinth of the gift shop. Little kids squealed over pale pink conch shells and dehydrated starfish—assorted ocean paraphernalia you could find in the sand, or for which you could pay $6.99 plus tax. We had last been there on Rosie's ninth birthday. After our bread bowls of clam chowder and our flaming Baked Alaska, Mom had heaved a sigh of relief. Beachcomber Bill's wasn't a place you would choose for your birthday celebration once your age hit double digits.

"Yes," Mom acknowledged. "I do."

"So, why would we go there?"

She leaned back against the counter, a blue-striped dishtowel draped over her shoulder. "Nelson agreed to a family dinner . . . he agreed to *come clean* . . . on the condition that we go to Beachcomber Bill's."

In her faded Whedon College T-shirt, she appeared exhausted.

There were about a thousand questions I could have asked.

On our way to the restaurant, Friday night, I endeavored to set a mood that would make my parents change their minds about *coming clean*. I didn't want Jake and Rosie to know about the separation. I was dreading pretending to be as blindsided by the news as everyone else. Part of me knew it was childish to imagine that the right combination of inside jokes would inspire Mom and Dad to fall back in love. But another part of me thought, *why not?* Whatever had come between them couldn't have been all that profound. I hadn't even noticed it happening.

"Guess who I've been talking to?" I began, wedged between my siblings on the middle bench seat of the minivan. The seat farthest back was folded down to accommodate two surfboards Jake had meant to sell on eBay before leaving for college a year ago.

"Everyone," Rosie said, referring to the frequency with which my phone buzzed in my pocket. Whenever the video was posted anew by an online magazine or person with a lot of Facebook friends, I received a fresh batch of notifications.

So far, I had been glad to hear from Joan—the instructor of my CNA training course, who complimented my *flawlessly executed* chest compressions—and then baffled to hear from Vanessa, the freshman who had shown me around Whedon and was now *really pumped* to see me in the fall.

"Besides everyone," I said.

"Oh, call on me." Jake raised his hand, flattening his palm against the ceiling of the van. "I have a guess."

"Jacob," I allowed.

"My guess is you've been talking nonstop to your improbably handsome boyfriend, Seth O'Malley."

I ignored him. "Jackson Moon's manager. That's who I've been talking to."

Everyone sank into perplexed silence. Only my brother caught on fast. "Jackson Moon's manager is a resident at the nursing home?"

"Yes," I replied. "Her name is Tamora Sinclair and she's awesome."

"Jackson Moon was popular decades ago," Mom said.

"We know that," I said. "He's incredibly famous. Tamora managed a bunch of other people, too. Milan Lorca. Blake Dunne."

"Those people are actors," Dad said. "I've heard of them."

"Um, yes. Everyone on earth has heard of them." Jake

was exaggerating. Most of Tamora's clients had ceased to be stars a long time ago, but Jake's knowledge of pop culture was encyclopedic. He turned to me. "Do you think this lady knows if Jackson Moon truly had an extramarital affair with Dolly Parton?"

This time, Mom remained sitting forward in her seat, her eyes on the highway.

"Probably. Jackson is like a son to her."

Rosie mused. "If Jackson is like her son, why doesn't she live with him instead of in a nursing home?"

"Sometimes relationships change over time," Mom said sagely—as if we might contemplate this wisdom and conclude that it would be refreshing if our parents filed for divorce.

"Can I meet this lady?" my brother asked. "Please, Audrey? Please?"

"Maybe," I said, not even knowing how that would work.

"Why do you want to meet her so bad?" asked Rosie. "It's not like *she's* famous. She just knows a bunch of famous people."

"Even better," said Jake. "She'll tell me all their secrets."

"Can we listen to that song?" Rosie asked. "The one about the shotgun?"

Nelson flashed Iris a look. I couldn't tell if it was anxious or hopeful.

Mom pressed on the glove compartment, letting the door fall open. "The CD's not in here," she said, slamming the door shut before any of us could see for ourselves. "I must have accidentally thrown it away."

Judging by the number of napkins that fluttered to the floor, no one had cleaned out the glove compartment in years.

As we approached Beachcomber Bill's, Mom and Dad grew quiet. Dad thrummed his knuckles against the steering wheel while Mom tugged on the short locks of hair at the nape of her neck. By the time we turned into the parking lot, their faces were ashen.

My insides flipped. Suddenly, my stomach did not seem like a vessel I should fill with large amounts of chowder.

After our mandatory tour of the gift shop, our server—a boy whose face I dimly recognized from the halls of Crescent Bay High—led us to a varnished picnic table. On the wall above the window hung a life preserver. The restaurant had been built on stilts at the edge of the bay; our view was of seagulls perched on the bows of fishing boats bobbing in the murky, agitated water.

Our server returned with Cokes for me and Rosie, an iced tea for Jake, and two Heinekens for our parents. Dad took a long swig of his beer and nodded toward the tank of live Dungeness crabs stationed outside the kitchen. "Hey,

Jakey, remember when you realized what goes into your crab burger?"

Nelson family legend had it that Jake reached the ripe age of seven before connecting the crustaceans behind the glass to the food on his plate. He'd wept. As a kid, my brother had been a prolific crier.

Jake looked at Dad and shrugged. Clearly, Nelson was trying the same trick I'd pulled in the car—delaying the inevitable with references to the past—but Iris still refused to engage, and my brother and sister could tell something was up. They were both sitting with their shoulders slumped, their stares hollow.

Probably, I realized, they thought this dinner was about me. Damage control for my unmapped life.

"I think we should talk," Mom said.

"I think we should order first." Dad flagged down our server. He'd been a grade or two below me in school—the sort of kid who kept his raincoat on all the time, even during lunch. Without consulting anyone else, Dad asked him for the exorbitantly priced Pirate's Platter. Mom exhaled through her nostrils and locked eyes with me.

She wanted me on her team. And while I understood that Dad's behavior was infantile, I couldn't take her side. She'd cheated. The experience had left her *fascinated*.

"Time to talk," Mom said firmly.

"About what?" Rosie asked.

Dad held his drink with the bottleneck already angled toward his lips. "Your mother is having a midlife crisis, I'm afraid."

I expected Mom to object to this diagnosis, but she remained placid as she said, "That's one way of putting it. The truth, guys, is that my trip to Naples wasn't just for work. It was also designed to give your father and me some time apart."

"Apart?" Jake echoed.

"A trial separation," Mom explained.

"Your words, not mine," Dad said.

"*Why?*" Rosie squeaked, her tiny face crumpling.

"Good question," Dad said.

The four of us looked to Mom for the answer.

"I've been feeling . . . trapped," she said. "Trapped and tired."

"Maybe you should get more sleep," was Dad's helpful suggestion.

The kid from school deposited a basket of bread on the table. By the time he scurried off, our mother had abandoned her calm. Pointing a finger at our father, she said, "Don't make me play the villain. We both agreed a long time ago that we'd always present a united front."

"Darling, we agreed to a lot of things a long time ago."

Dad began buttering a slice of the complimentary bread. He appeared to be casually losing his mind.

"This is the message you want to send to our kids? That I've been miserable and you've been perfectly satisfied?"

"I *have* been perfectly satisfied. Everything was fine before you left."

"Oh, really? Then why didn't you go with me?"

Dad almost choked on the wad of sourdough in his mouth. Wordlessly, Rosie nudged his water glass toward him. He took a long drink, recovered, and said, "Why didn't I go with you to *Italy*?"

"Yes." Mom fumed.

"I don't know, Iris! Don't you think it would have been too much—with the kids, and my book?"

She rolled her eyes. "You haven't finished a book in eight years."

Jake and I shared a look of confusion. Was that true? Had Dad really been working on the same novel since I was ten?

"And it's not just Italy," Mom continued. "You didn't come to Berlin three years ago when I was invited to speak at the Free University. And you refused to move to New York when Columbia offered me the visiting position."

My brother's jaw dropped.

"New York gives me anxiety!" Dad protested. "You know that!"

Rosie burst into tears. She was always doing that—repressing her emotions until they conquered her so fully, she couldn't breathe.

Mom leaned across the table and took Rosie's trembling hand. "Sweetie, the plan right now is to continue our separation. We haven't made any final decisions yet. One of my colleagues, Professor Hale, has offered to let me stay at his beach cottage for the rest of the summer. I'll just be a short drive away."

"You're moving out?" I asked, just as Jake asserted, "I'm going with you."

Mom didn't argue with either of us.

"I can't believe you told Bernie Hale about our personal problems," Dad said.

"I didn't tell Bernie Hale anything," Mom snapped. "I said I needed a quiet place to work on my manuscript."

Even though I hadn't forgiven my mother for her affair, the last thing I wanted was to resume living alone with Dad and Rosie. It was obvious that Mom was essential. Her presence translated our jokes into affection, our insults into intimacy. Without her, our house wasn't home; it was just a dumping ground for the flotsam of our separate lives.

"If you went to Italy to get away from Dad . . ." Rosie sniffled. "Then why'd you come back early?"

Mom hesitated. She looked to me, like maybe I would

supply her with a convenient explanation. *Mom came home because I embarrassed her on the* Steeds County News. *Mom came home because I took my stunt of a summer job a step too far.*

Or maybe: *Mom came home because she was tormented by guilt.*

Mom came home because adultery isn't all it's cracked up to be.

Before anyone could answer Rosie's question, our server returned, weighed down by the enormous Pirate's Platter. The fifty-dollar appetizer included crab cakes, calamari rings, baked oysters, Tater Tots, clam strips, and grilled prawns with their coral-colored shells and beady eyes still intact.

Everything smelled delicious and nauseating at the same time. The way, I imagined, food smelled when you were dying.

I needed to get out of here.

As my family—all of them despondent, but apparently ravenous—loaded up their plates, I texted Seth beneath the table: **Hey, can you pick me up from Beachcomber Bill's?**

I knew he had the night off; we always requested all the same shifts from our respective supervisors. Maybe he was on the beach with his high school buddies—the jocks and the cowboys about whom I never, ever asked. Maybe he was playing poker with his dad. Maybe he was with Cameron at the hospital.

Wherever he was, his reply was an instant **Sure!**

In the language of texts composed on Seth's dumbphone, an exclamation point indicated pure joy.

I leaned over and whispered my plan in my little sister's ear. And then, as if only headed as far as the restrooms marked BUOYS and GULLS, I made my way across the restaurant, back through the gift shop, and out the door.

TWENTY

"I love this place," Seth said, gazing fondly at the entrance to Beachcomber Bill's.

I shuddered as I buckled my seat belt. "I wish you hadn't told me that."

"Haven't you ever been there on your birthday? They sing to you."

"I'll remember that. Maybe for my twenty-first." I tried to smile at him, but the idea of living in Crescent Bay three years from now was, frankly, devastating.

"What's wrong?" Seth asked as we turned south on the highway.

"Nothing," I claimed.

"You seem down."

"Not anymore. What'd you do today?"

Seth kept his eyes on the road. "Not much. Had lunch with my dad. Saw Cameron."

"That's great." I could hear a slightly manic quality in

my own voice, and I hoped Seth wouldn't notice. I had to force myself to ask, "How is she?"

"Good," he said, calm and careful. "She's back home now."

"That's great," I said again, meaning it more this time. Cameron at home seemed like less of a threat than Cameron hospitalized. Now, instead of an ex-girlfriend in mortal danger, she would be merely an ex-girlfriend. Everybody had one of those.

"Where are we headed?" Seth asked me.

"Can we go to your house?"

Seth looked at me for as long as the curves of the highway allowed. "My house?"

"Will your dad care?"

"If you come over? Of course not."

"Will he care if we . . . ?"

I wanted to feel like my life was mine, my family a footnote. I wanted to feel like the adult I technically was. More than anything else, I wanted Seth.

"Uh." I appreciated his nerves. Seth's usual confidence was charming, but it was nice to overwhelm him, sometimes. "Are you saying . . . ?"

"I'm saying when."

Part of me worried he'd try to talk me out of it. Sara had warned me, years ago, that guys were psychologically fragile and liked to maintain control over a relationship's milestones. Lines like *But you're upset!* and *It just doesn't feel right* were usually boy-code for *This wasn't my idea.*

Seth didn't say anything like that. His eyes were bright, the skin around them slightly creased by the suggestion of a smile. The smile—had he given into it—would have said exactly what I wanted to hear.

Outside Seth's house, two Labradors chased the Jeep into its parking spot. We got out of the car and the dogs stopped barking, pressing their noses into our knees, tails moving back and forth like rudders. Seth greeted them by name—Faith and Tim—prompting me to wonder which member of Seth's family was such a devoted fan of country radio. I was too nervous to ask. Seth was already taking my hand, leading me up the porch steps. We pushed through the front door, and then—because the house had no entryway—we were standing in a dim living room. On a faded gray couch, Seth's dad sat drinking a beer and watching a baseball game. A bowl of popcorn rested between his knees.

Mr. O'Malley looked at me, and I immediately stopped touching his son. I was painfully aware, in that moment, of Seth being someone's son.

"Hey!" said Mr. O'Malley, evicting the bowl of popcorn from his lap and standing to greet us. His tone and his body language suggested he might try to hug me; I was glad when he didn't. It could have been the contrast of the lamp-lit corner of the couch with the darkened rest of the room, but there was a glint in his eyes that didn't match his grin, and my heart raced in response.

"You must be Ashley," he said, reaching to shake my hand. His palm was dry.

"Audrey," I said.

"Audrey, sorry. You guys want to hang out? Have a beer?"

"No thanks, Dad." Seth didn't sound half as wary as I felt. "We'll be in my room, okay?"

"Ah," said his dad, disappointed, sinking back into the couch. "Okay. The offer stands, if you kids change your mind."

"Thanks," Seth repeated, reclaiming my hand and pulling me down a carpeted hallway.

"Is your dad all right?" I whispered to Seth as he flipped the light switch in his own room.

"Yeah, yeah," Seth said. "He's fine. He's just lonely."

I knew that Seth's mom lived in southern California with her second husband, and also that he had two older brothers who had already moved out.

"Doesn't your dad know you don't drink?" I asked.

Seth hesitated. "I drink with him sometimes."

"Why?"

"Because it makes him feel bad if I don't."

236

"But that makes no sense. You're eighteen."

"He's weird." Seth took a breath. He cupped my face in his hands. "Hey," he said.

I was dizzy, confused—but who cared if Seth sometimes had a beer with his dad?

"Hey." I looked into his eyes, which were damp, but focused.

"I missed you," he said. It had been about fourteen hours since we'd last seen each other, but I knew exactly what he meant.

"Me too." I pressed on his chest so that he moved backward and flopped against the bed. A cat meowed, vacated Seth's pillow and then the room. Neither of us mentioned the cat as I straddled Seth's hips. My hair fell everywhere, and I thought he might offer me a rubber band from the permanent collection on his wrist. Instead, he just swept my hair aside and kissed me with a kind of urgency that made me ache between the legs, but also felt partially born of nerves, or fear—something less than sexy.

I could feel him getting hard, and even though the same thing had happened every time we'd ever made out, tonight the tension in his jeans took me by complete surprise.

"You okay?" Seth said, separating his lips from mine.

"Yup," I said, and tried to cover up my alarm by tugging on his shirt. Seth wore his clothes fairly tight for a boy, and the T-shirt got stuck around his shoulders, forcing him to finish the job himself.

Somehow, despite looking the way he did and living by the ocean, Seth was not the kind of guy who seized every opportunity to be gratuitously shirtless. I had only seen his bare chest in the context of the two of us hooking up, and I normally took a not-so-subtle second to stare at the perfect boyness of him. But tonight, he seemed panicked to be the only one half undressed, and he fumbled for the edges of my tank top, and then the back of my bra.

"There's no clasp," I said. It was the sort of lacy, glorified sports bra I had to peel from my boobs, one by one, and then pull over my head. Having made no plans to lose my virginity tonight, it hadn't occurred to me to put on my favorite underwear. I hadn't perfumed my neck or applied more than a few cursory strokes of deodorant after getting out of the shower. My only plan for the night had been to endure a semicivilized dinner with my family—but that plan had fallen through.

Now, I willed myself to forget about the Nelsons. They were my blood relations, but I hadn't chosen them; they were basically roommates to whom I'd been randomly assigned at birth. Seth was different. Seth and I had picked each other.

We were sitting up on the bed. He had one hand on my hip, guiding me into his lap, and one hand moving somewhat frantically from my neck to my left breast. From the living room, we heard his dad wail "Nooooooo!" in the despairing way of men watching sports.

Laughing, we fell onto our backs. The interruption was both a relief and a disappointment.

"I'm sorry," said Seth. "I can't stop shaking. I swear I've done this before."

"Thanks for the reminder."

"Sorry." He repositioned his body over mine. Only now, as my heart rate regulated, did I realize how fast it had been racing. Looking into Seth's eyes, I felt certain.

I had felt a lot of things this summer, but not always certain.

"You still want to have sex with me?" he asked.

"Yeah. I think we just need to calm down."

So we did, with deep breaths. And then we kissed for a half hour, or maybe longer—however long it took for our pants to seem superfluous and for our hands to explore every region of each other. Our nervous laughter returned during Seth's unwrapping and graceless application of the condom—but by then, the stakes felt somehow lower. Like maybe we had the rest of our lives to get this right. Like maybe beneath all the awkwardness and the embarrass- ment was a tough layer of love that could survive an infinite amount of both.

At first, he tried to push inside of me and he slipped, pushing against the mattress instead. I said something romantic, like, "Uh, that's not me."

A wave of discouragement threatened to pull me under, just because I didn't think I could bear a repeat performance of my attempt to sleep with Cole Hendrix—I would have to seriously wonder if there was something wrong with my anatomy—but Seth just winced, and tried again. This time there was a flash of pain that vanished almost immediately, replaced by a feeling that wasn't at all bad.

I was struck by a memory of my sister trying a raw oyster for the first time. She had been six, and after placing the empty shell back on the ice she announced, "I don't know if I like this now, but I can tell I'm *really* going to like it someday."

I laughed out loud. Seth said, "What's so funny?" his breath hot against my cheek.

"Nothing. I'm just happy."

"Same," he whispered.

Afterward, we lay sprawled and sticky across a tangle of sheets. On Seth's nightstand, an electric fan twisted from side to side, blowing stray pieces of our hair into our faces every few seconds.

"You okay?" he asked, kissing my sweaty temple.

"I'm good," I said. "Are you good?"

"I'm great."

An hour earlier, I hadn't been able to think about anything but putting distance between the Nelsons and me. Hundreds or maybe thousands of miles were required to mute the sound of my family splitting in two. Now I had to wonder if any city would ever make me feel as free as I felt in Seth O'Malley's bed. He may have been ponytailed and much too friendly—he may have been Crescent Bay incarnate—but he was mine.

Pressing my cheek against a Seth-scented pillow, I said to him, "Hey, did you win one of those senior superlatives? Like Most Likely to Succeed, or Class Clown?"

He rested his hand on my bare stomach. Pleasure pooled beneath the surface of my skin. "You mean you didn't vote for me?"

"I didn't vote for anyone."

"Yes." He sighed. "I won."

"For what?"

Struggling and failing to keep it in check, Seth said, "Best smile."

TWENTY-ONE

I had promised Seth I would introduce him to Tamora, warning him that, by Crescent Bay standards, Tamora was not exactly friendly. Seth dismissed my concern, confident that he and Tamora would get along the same way he got along with everyone.

If there was one thing Seth took for granted, it was his own popularity.

On our lunch break one night, toward the end of July, Seth showed up in Tamora's room right on schedule. He delivered to the foot of her bed a tray heaped with breakfast food—slices of quiche, Tony's famous muffins, sausage links, and three mugs of reheated coffee.

I gave Tamora a look: *impressed yet?*

Without breaking eye contact, she shrugged and popped a sausage link into her mouth.

"Sit, both of you," she ordered, gesturing to the chairs by the darkened window. I grabbed two and pulled them to her bedside. Next to me, Seth smelled like the kitchen—like cooked vegetables glazed with cleaning supplies.

"I've heard a lot about you," Seth said to Tamora, reaching for a cup of coffee. I was already devouring a muffin. Working at the nursing home every night meant I never realized how hungry I was until food was literally under my nose.

"How strange," Tamora said. Her voice became extra husky with someone new in the room. "Because I've heard almost nothing about you."

Turning to me, Seth clutched his heart. "You don't brag about me to your friends?"

"Just to the press," Tamora said.

Seth rearranged his mock-offended expression into one of actual confusion.

"It was just an article," I rushed to explain. "I made a joke about how you wanted to enter the sand-sculpting contest and I wouldn't let you. It was dumb, but the journalist printed it anyway. They always do."

"Huh." Seth gulped his coffee. "I'm sorry I missed that one."

Slicing a fork through her quiche, Tamora asked him, "You were there that day, yes? But not in the video?"

"I think my feet are in the frame," Seth said.

Until now, I wasn't sure if Seth had ever seen the clip. The

Wi-Fi signal at his house was too weak for video-streaming.

"And have you also been indulging the media?" Tamora wanted to know. "Granting interviews left and right?"

Seth answered with a firm "No."

"Good boy," Tamora said. "So then, what's your story?"

"My story?" The pocket of his jeans vibrated, and the sound took me by surprise; Seth hardly ever used his phone when we were together. Most of his friends didn't even have the number.

Tamora chose to ignore the interruption. "You heard me."

"Well." He swallowed a bite of muffin and offered up a piece of information I had never heard. "My parents got divorced when I was seven because my mom fell in love with her boss."

"Where did she work?" Tamora asked.

"Bureau of Land Management. They counted wild horses together."

"Romantic." Tamora nodded her approval. "Good for her. Go on."

"She and her boyfriend eventually moved out to Twenty-nine Palms, and my brothers grew up and got married, and now I live with my dad."

The food I had practically inhaled became a rock in my stomach. I didn't want my mother to move to Twentynine

Palms, let alone to Italy's version of Twentynine Palms—if Italy even had deserts, or trailer parks. When I had finally gone home, the night of the disastrous dinner at Beachcomber Bill's, Mom and Jake had already transferred their prized possessions to Professor Hale's beach house. Rosie had strewn a collection of books, clothes, and sweat-stained flip-flops across the floor of our brother's room and was sound asleep in his bed.

I had found my father in the kitchen, nursing another beer.

"Hey, Dad," I said gently.

Iris would have yelled at me for skipping out on dinner. Nelson, I knew, could only focus on one conflict at a time. "I'm sorry," he said right away. "I'm sorry I was so fantastically hostile to your mother. She doesn't deserve that."

It was possible Mom deserved much worse, but I wasn't going to tell him. I felt overly self-conscious; my clothes were slightly loose from having been pulled off and put back on. Remembering Seth's body against mine induced a rush of vertigo, and I bit down hard on the inside of my cheek.

"She never asked me to go to Italy," Dad said, then waited for me to confirm.

"I have no idea," I said.

"She didn't. I mean, how would that have worked?" Locking eyes with his reflection in the door of the microwave, he released a note of high-pitched laughter. After a few more awkward exchanges, I had gone to bed.

"Plans for the future?" Tamora was asking Seth.

"You don't have to answer that," I said, horrified. Bringing Seth to Tamora's room was almost as bad as introducing him to my parents.

Seth frowned at me, like I was the one being rude. "Just saving money for now," he told her. "My dad and I have some . . . debts. Next year I might start at the community college, but I'm not in any rush."

"You're happy here?" Tamora asked. "By the seaside?"

"I love the seaside," Seth said.

"Uh-oh."

Tamora shot me a look, and I felt my eyelids close, as if in response to a sudden headache. "What?" I argued. "I like the seaside." My hometown had its charms. Besides, Crescent Bay was a temporary affliction; someday I would sleep between sheets that were not always, no matter how recently laundered, gritty with sand.

"I thought you were plotting your escape," Tamora said.

Seth furrowed his eyebrows and stared into his coffee. Tamora had made it sound like she knew something he didn't. Desperately, I wanted to assure him that she was making stuff up—just a crazy old lady, taking a stab in the dark. But the truth was that I *had* begun to plot, a little. At least I'd sent an e-mail to my instructor from night school, asking if she had any connections to retirement homes in bigger cities. Just out of curiosity.

Just so I could consider my options.

"Not necessarily," I said, reaching for Seth's hand. I was relieved when he laced his fingers through mine, and even more relieved when he changed the subject.

"So what's *your* story?" he asked Tamora.

"I fainted twice," was her blunt response.

"What?" I dropped Seth's hand and sat up straight. "When?"

"Relax, Nurse Nelson. It was a while ago. Before I arrived. Once on the couch and once on the stairs. When it happened the second time, I bruised my tailbone, which became Jackson's excuse for enrolling me in this preschool. That's my whole story. The part that ended up mattering, anyway."

Carefully, I said, "Falling can be really serious as you get—"

Tamora arched an eyebrow.

"As your bones lose density," I finished.

She asked, "Are you people too young to know Joni Mitchell?"

We shook our heads, Joni Mitchell being the preferred songstress of every mom in the state of California. Again,

Seth's phone buzzed in his pocket. Again, he ignored it.

"Jackson always said he was *gonna make a lot of money* and *quit this crazy scene.* I didn't realize he considered me part of the scene, but there you have it. He met someone, and I agreed to move into a facility so long as he found me someplace nice, with an ocean view. No bingo, no karaoke."

Folding his arms across his chest, Seth studied her. "That can't be the whole story."

Tamora—who, I realized, had applied lipstick and blush for this occasion—leaned toward us and said, "You're right. Here's how it ends: I die. And then Jackson and his lover are left to deal with the mess I leave behind. Currently I'm paying eighty dollars a month to store everything I've ever owned in a garage in Arcata. Or else I'm paying eighty dollars a month to ensure my revenge, depending on how you look at it."

She chuckled.

Tamora's was the most sterile room in the Assisted Living wing. Everyone else had their own bedding, their own vases and chess sets and bowls of polished rocks. The only thing mounted to Tamora's wall was a dispenser of hand sanitizer.

"I can't believe he kicked you out just because he met someone," I said.

She rolled her eyes. "Would you want to spend your prime years shacking up with an old woman?"

"You were his best friend!" I protested.

"I suppose. For a while. But you have to understand, back then, it was hard for Jackson to be close to people. He was so famous. Everyone wanted him to be Jackson Moon, country legend, every second of the day. By the time he finally hung up the Stetson for good, he craved real intimacy. Not a stand-in." Tamora heaved a sigh. "Anyway, there's a point at which even your best friend gets a free pass, don't you think?"

Seth wrinkled his nose. "A pass on abandoning you?"

"No." Tamora stared at the smoke detector on the ceiling, as if she'd grown bored with this conversation. "On selfishness."

Outside of room 64, with a few minutes of our break to spare, I meant to tell Seth about the e-mail I'd sent to my old teacher. If the message amounted to anything—an application, or an interview—I didn't want to blindside him with the news. But Seth was preoccupied, holding on to the heavy tray of dishes, struggling not to tip our half-drunk cups of coffee.

His jeans vibrated again.

Seth winced. "A little help?"

I took the overloaded tray. The screen of his phone was so clouded with water damage, I couldn't even sneak a look at who was calling.

A male voice erupted from the speaker.

"Um," Seth said, a moment later. "I'm kind of busy right now. I'm at work."

I could hear the octave of the other guy's frustration.

"How much did he drink?" Seth asked. "Can't he just stay with you and Sophie tonight?"

Sophie was his brother's wife, I remembered.

"Okay, okay. Chill. I'll be there in a second." Seth hung up, exhaling through his nose. He was more agitated than I'd ever seen him.

"I'm sorry, Aud, but do you mind taking that stuff back to the kitchen and telling Tony I'm going to be late? Say it's a family emergency. He'll be a dick about it, but you can just run away afterward. Do you mind?"

"No, I don't mind, but—"

"Thanks." He was already turning from me. The heels of his boots squeaked against the freshly mopped floor.

"Seth, what's up? Where are you going?"

Begrudgingly, he spun back around. "My dad spent all day at my brother's, and I guess he's wasted. They got into a fight about something. Not sure what. Now Cory doesn't want him there, but my dad's too drunk to drive himself home."

"Can't your dad just, like, crash on your brother's couch?"

"You would think. But Cory has little kids, and . . . I don't know. I need to run."

"Seriously? You're ditching work?"

It shouldn't have bothered me. If Seth wanted to piss off his boss, that was his own business. But I had never known my boyfriend to be frantic, or distracted, or stressed. A phone call had undone his essential Sethness, and I didn't like it.

"I'm sorry, Aud," he said again, "but I don't have a choice."

TWENTY-TWO

In the first week of August, my instructor from night school sent me links to a handful of jobs on the West Coast. It was easy enough to pass up positions in Fresno, or Bakersfield—medium-size cities in California, neither of which had ever entered my fantasies. But a listing for a job in Seattle caught my attention. Full time, day shift. The list of required skills matched everything I already knew how to do. *Shoot them your résumé*, Joan wrote. *Drop my name and a certain video, and I'm guessing you have a good shot!*

The job would start on the first Tuesday in September, at an assisted living center in Capitol Hill—the downtown neighborhood with which I'd fallen in love when I was fourteen. I did not, as Joan had suggested, include the viral video with my résumé, but I submitted an application before I could think twice.

Around the same time, Tamora started feeling sick. Her symptoms matched those already listed on her chart—

her head ached; she had no energy; she didn't feel like eating. The dizzy spells that had worried Jackson were worse than ever. Now she could hardly stand long enough to wash her hair without blackness encroaching on her field of vision and, still, she wouldn't let me help her in the shower. But despite her complaints, Tamora's vitals were fine. Every night I asked her what was wrong, and she just kept repeating, "I don't feel well," until, it was clear, the question was getting on her nerves.

One night, after I had made her a cup of chamomile tea, I pressed her: "Just tell me what's *really* wrong and then I'll stop asking."

"I don't *know*," she said, beyond irritated.

"Then just tell me the truest thing you know."

It was a tactic Sara's mother always used on her and that, over the years, Sara had also used on me. The demand always lessened the pressure to come up with the correct answer, leaving you with something that usually came close.

It worked on Tamora, too. "I screwed up," she said. "I wanted to die in my house. I let Jackson convince me this place isn't about dying—it's about *living*. But I was being moronic."

"You're not going to die anytime soon," I told her.

Her face was half hidden behind her mug of tea. "*You're* not going to die soon. I'm going to die *quite* soon."

I had no argument. Tamora held my gaze until a sigh broke her focus. "I miss Jackson," she admitted.

"Do you want to watch him on YouTube?"

"I try to stop myself from looking up old friends on there."

"Why?" If my friends had been famous, I was sure I would have searched their names all the time.

"It's never really them. Just some show they put on a long time ago, for an audience of strangers. Turns out that when people kick the bucket, you don't miss the famous parts of them; you miss the parts nobody bothered recording."

"That's very profound," I told her, "except that Jackson's not dead."

Tamora examined her nails impassively. The one nursing home luxury of which she took advantage was the weekly visits from a professional manicurist named Maxine. "Fine," she said. "Put him on."

Pulling up the YouTube app on my phone meant bypassing a screen full of my mother's texts. She had sent me Professor Hale's address, begging me to stop by after work—**sweetie, you know we need to talk**—and then, for good measure, she'd attached a photo of the view from her new backyard, as if I would find the prime beach access irresistible.

YouTube recommended a lot of videos based on my personal taste. YouTube was under the impression that I was obsessed with both California teens and small town heroes. Ignoring the array of sensational thumbnails, I searched for Jackson Moon and tapped the first link that came up.

Tamora's eyes were wide as she repositioned my phone for a better view of Jackson's 1983 appearance on *Late Night with David Letterman.*

The band played a raucous, mocking cover of "Oh Susannah!" as Jackson made his way across the set. A still-brown-haired Letterman rose from his desk to shake the country star's hand. Jackson formed a gun with his fingers and pretended to shoot Letterman, who, in turn, pantomimed being mortally wounded. The whole thing was hard to watch.

After Jackson sank into one of two leather armchairs, the audience's applause died down. Behind the host's desk was a shelf of reference books leaning in all directions, plus a framed photograph of a German shepherd, as if Letterman had invited Jackson into his pleasantly disorganized home office.

TV had been weird back then.

Letterman proceeded to quiz Jackson about the success of his latest album, his house in Beverly Hills, the Golden Globe he'd won for writing a song that played over the ending credits of a biopic about Waylon Jennings, and then, naturally, his love life.

"So you've had an incredible amount of success . . . winning awards, selling millions of records. Answer me this, Jackson—the question I think we're all wondering—do you have someone to share it with?"

Sheepishly, Jackson lowered his hat, as if to cover up the blush spreading across his face. "I can't really be tied down, if you know what I mean, Dave."

Inexplicably, the audience cheered again.

"You must have friends, though. Are you one of those celebrities with a collection of pals, each more famous than the last? Or is your loyalty with the folks you left behind in Chattanooga?"

To Tamora, I said, "I thought he was from Orlando."

"A technicality," she mumbled, entranced.

Jackson drawled, "To be perfectly honest with you"—he paused like he was about to reveal a great secret—"my best friend is my manager."

The audience was quick to hoot and holler in response. When I turned up a hand, confused, Tamora admitted, "Our relationship, while *strictly* professional, had become somewhat . . . notorious."

On-screen, Jackson protested, "Nah, it's not like that! She's old! Ancient! She's the same age as my ma!" He winked at the camera. The scruffy beard growing down his neck made me think of Seth.

"Well, both your *ma* and your manager must be so excited," was Letterman's final line.

Tamora was silent for a second. Then she asked, "Are there more?"

"Sure. You want to watch another?" I was already navigating back to the search results, hoping to find something in which Jackson actually performed. I wondered if anyone had ever uploaded a live version of "Shotgun Wedding."

Tamora surprised me, asking, "Can we watch the one of you?"

"Uh, sure." I hardly ever watched *California Teen Hero Saves Life of a Friend*—mostly, I just obsessed over the comments—and still I'd managed to become more or less desensitized to the video. The footage felt disconnected from the event itself. On-screen, Cameron and I might as well have been actors performing in one of the many instructional movies I'd seen in night school.

Tamora interrupted my line of dialogue—*I have to stop*—to point at my phone and say, "What's this number here?"

"The number of times people have viewed it," I said.

"You're telling me *two million* people have seen this movie of you?"

"Well, some people have probably watched it more than once. Like me. Or my mother."

"Jackson's number was only thirty thousand!" Tamora was dismayed.

"Well . . . it was kind of a boring interview."

I had said the wrong thing. Tamora lifted her chin and informed me, "Jackson was a real talent. He was a *celebrity*."

Her implication being that I was a talentless hack. Not wanting to upset her, I tried to explain the difference. "First of all, we watched one of a hundred Jackson Moon videos. Second, the clip of me and Cameron went viral. Like the flu. Everyone gets it and then everyone forgets about it."

Tamora was narrowing her eyes at me.

"People will be listening to Jackson's music for the rest of time," was my bold promise.

"Have any of Jackson's movies gone viral?"

I sighed. "Not unless he has an adorably deformed cat or something."

"*What?*"

"Nothing." I looked out the window. It was so dark, I couldn't tell where the ocean ended and the sky started. "Did Jackson even like going on those talk shows?"

Tamora frowned. "I don't think I ever asked him."

"It seems like he'd get tired of answering the same questions over and over."

"They flew us out to New York for that interview . . ." She spoke slowly, her words decelerated by nostalgia, and maybe sleep deprivation. "Afterward, we had to catch another flight to London, but it was delayed. There was a problem with the windshield."

I could imagine her and Jackson soaring over the Atlantic, sipping champagne and discussing the details of his world tour. Eventually Tamora would get tired and pull one of those silk sleep masks over her eyes. The fantasy was appealing, so I included myself in the scene. I could hear the roar of the engines, taste the bubbles on my tongue.

I wondered if Seth had ever been on a plane. Was it possible he'd never left the state of California?

Tamora's eyelids were sinking shut. "Ready to sleep?" I asked her.

With a jolt of surprise, and a sigh of relief, she admitted that she was.

Before the end of my shift, I logged onto the desktop computer in the break room and pulled up Tamora's file. As I'd hoped, Jackson Moon was listed as her emergency contact. My pulse raced much faster than it would have, had I been listening to the automated voice-mail greeting of a non-famous person.

"Uh, hi," I said after the tone. "Mr. Moon? This is

Audrey Nelson calling from the Crescent Bay Retirement Home about Tamora Sinclair. She's having kind of a tough time adjusting, and I thought it might help if she had some of her stuff from home. Like, a lot of our residents bring pictures, artwork, bedding, or kitchen stuff . . . whatever makes their apartment here feel familiar. So, um, call me back if you can maybe help with that."

I was still sitting dumbly in front of the computer, waiting for my heart rate to return to normal, when Maureen entered the break room.

"Hmm. Okay. What are you doing right now?"

It was never a good sign when Maureen began her sentences with *okay*, or when she clasped her hands together, just beneath her chin.

"Uh, I'm just—" The phone on the desk started ringing. I lunged for the receiver before Maureen could beat me to it.

Jackson Moon's voice bore absolutely no resemblance to the drawl that had distinguished him as a country music star. "Hi, Audrey. I just got your message and yes, of course, I think it's a great idea. I tried to talk her into packing some of her personal effects from the very beginning, but she's stubborn, as you've probably noticed by now."

His accent—breathy, fast, with every sentence ending like a question he never wanted answered—was strictly

Californian. Jackson continued talking over my nervous laughter. "Listen, I can't make it all the way up to Crescent Beach this weekend. I'm in Redding, visiting my partner's parents. But the storage unit is in Arcata. It's about halfway between you and me. Do you mind meeting me there?"

I glanced at Maureen, who was standing over me, hands on her hips. Arcata was about ninety miles south on Highway 101. Road trips were not part of my job description, but neither was my friendship with Tamora.

"Sure," I said into the phone. "I could do that."

As we made a plan, I tried to keep my responses vague enough that Maureen wouldn't guess my intentions to meet a resident's emergency contact at a faraway storage facility. Easily done, since Jackson only paused long enough for me to confirm that yes, this Friday at seven p.m. would work fine.

When I hung up, Maureen lifted a freshly plucked eyebrow.

"Just confirming a resident's nut allergy," I improvised.

"At four in the morning?"

My eyes flew to the time on the computer screen. I had somehow managed to forget that my entire life now took place in the middle of the night. But Jackson Moon hadn't sounded half asleep. He had sounded alert, caffeinated.

I relaxed, realizing that even though Jackson Moon was famous, he was also Tamora's family—her next of kin, her fellow insomniac. And I was excited to meet him.

After work, I told Seth I had a plan. Maybe I imagined it, but I thought I saw him flinch.

"What is it?" He reached behind his head to tug on his ponytail. The sky above the parking lot was the exact color of cotton candy. I was pretty sure that, no matter what happened, I was going to associate the sunrise with Seth O'Malley for the rest of my life. It seemed sort of extreme. Most boyfriends were allowed to ruin a song or two; was I really going to give Seth the dawn?

"On Friday I'm driving down to Arcata to get Tamora's stuff out of storage."

Seth relaxed. He put his hands on my waist, tightening the fabric of my scrubs until it became clear I had an actual body beneath the shapeless uniform. "Arcata's not that far. I'll go with you."

"Yeah?" It was what I'd wanted him to say. "Should we take your car?"

"Nah. I like it when you drive." Seth pulled me closer. My hip bones were pressed against his thighs.

"You do?"

"Yeah. I like being able to watch you when you have to

watch the road. And I like the way you always take your sunglasses on and off. And I like it when you pull your left foot onto the seat, and drive with one knee bent."

I'd never realized he found my mindless habits so fascinating.

"Okay," I said, the word catching as he kissed my throat. "I'll drive."

TWENTY-THREE

Before sliding into the passenger seat Friday afternoon, Seth opened the back door of the MINI Cooper and loaded in a small mountain of supplies—a Frisbee, a football, a package of jerky, a blanket, an umbrella, a six-pack of Dr Pepper, a long-stemmed lighter, a bundle of firewood, and a Duraflame log.

I couldn't stop staring at the Duraflame log.

"What's all this?" I asked, slowly facing Seth.

"Snacks, toys, and stuff for a campfire on the way home."

My friends and I built fires on the beach all the time, but we never used a starter log. That would have been cheating. Seth noticed my eyes darting to and from the supplies. Sensing my judgment, he said, "It might be dark by the time we get Tamora's stuff. Could be hard to find enough kindling."

I took a breath, wanting to ask whether he'd purchased the Duraflame log fresh from the Qwick Mart, or if he had taken one from his ex-girlfriend's stash. Cameron must have had extras, left over from her awkward attempt to flirt with Elliot.

Seth kissed me. "You have the best ideas," he said, convincingly unaware of my obsession with the log and its provenance.

"I do?"

"Yeah." He pressed his back to the seat and regarded me. "Surprising Tamora with her stuff? It's nice of you. You're nice."

I wasn't sure anyone had ever called me nice. It wasn't a trait Sara, Elliot, or I had ever aspired to possess. Crescent Bay was full of kindness, but we had set ourselves apart from our smiling, surf-happy peers. We had wanted something more than something nice.

But now, I wondered, what the hell was wrong with nice? I would be good, generous—even *sweet*—if it meant that Seth O'Malley would look at me like I had hung the moon. Like I didn't have all this jealousy poisoning my blood, fighting my urge to smile back at him.

Jealousy lost. I started the car.

Halfway between Crescent Bay and Arcata, Seth unmasked my darkest secret. He pulled my phone out of my bag and asked if he could put on some tunes.

"You think you can operate my *fancy* smartphone?" I teased him.

"I can probably figure it out." He sounded adorably unsure.

Distracted by the switchbacks of the highway, I had forgotten that no one ever scrolled through my music. It wasn't a problem I normally encountered; Sara commandeered the speakers wherever she went.

I glanced over at Seth. A look of astonishment spread across his face at the exact moment I realized my error.

"Give me that." I lunged sideways for the phone. Seth held it just beyond my reach.

"Gosh," he said, "you really love country."

I had everything, ranging from the relatively sophisticated—Gillian Welch, Patty Griffin—to the truly, truly embarrassing: Tim McGraw, Kenny Chesney, Lady Antebellum. Songs about pickup trucks, trailer parks, and going to church. Songs about *the road.* Songs about *the bar.* Songs that referred to our country as *The U.S. of A.*

"This is incredible," Seth said, scrolling. "You have every single that's ever been considered for a Country Music Award, and about ten thousand that haven't."

"I'm aware." I didn't need a mirror to confirm my cheeks were on fire.

"Am I the last to know about this?" Seth asked.

"You're the *only* one who knows." If my parents had ever suspected that our family's ironic appreciation of Jackson

Moon had instilled in me a sincere love of lyrics about dads with shotguns and moms with tears glistening in their uniformly blue eyes, the professors would have given me up for adoption long ago.

"Amazing," Seth said. "If we ever get married"—as if we might casually wed someday between night shifts—"you're walking down the aisle to Lyle Lovett."

I laughed. "Deal."

"How come you don't have any Jackson Moon songs?"

I had only ever listened to Jackson Moon in the minivan, wedged between my siblings, Mom and Dad singing along. It would never have occurred to me to listen to "Shotgun Wedding" by myself.

I just shrugged. "He's so corny."

"Cornier than Faith Hill?"

Seth pressed play, and "This Kiss" blasted from the speakers, as cloyingly nonsensical as ever. The song was one of my secret favorites. I especially liked the part where Snow White and Cinderella discussed the relative shortage of knights with fast horses.

Over the next three minutes and fifteen seconds, Seth proved he knew every word.

After exiting the highway, we drove through residential streets, passing houses that looked like mine, then houses that looked more like Seth's. Beyond a field full of cows, mud puddles, and gutted school buses we found the turn-off for Humboldt County's premiere self-storage facility.

We parked and got out of the car. Hand in hand we traveled a long, concrete corridor lined with garage doors painted bright orange, searching for Tamora's unit, number 247. Standing up ahead was a guy clad in neon running gear, his chin dipped toward the phone in his hand. As we approached, I saw he was wearing those amphibious shoes that outlined each toe.

We had arrived at Unit 247, but Jackson Moon was nowhere to be found.

Our shadows fell over the runner, prompting him to look up.

"Hi," he said, extending his hand. "Are you guys from the nursing home?" His hair was peppered with gray, but he had the lean, ropy body of a teenager.

"Yes," I said, confused.

"I'm Jackson Ross."

"Ross?"

"I took my husband's name when we got married. As for why Tammy's so attached to my *maiden* name, it's a long story."

"Tammy?" I echoed.

"I know, I know. We call each other by our least preferred identifiers. What can I say? We're spiteful."

Same as on the phone, his voice was devoid of any country twang. He wore no Stetson. He didn't look like someone who had ever done a shot of Jack Daniel's or fired a rifle in his whole life.

Jackson Moon, if he'd ever existed, had definitely retired. Mr. Ross beckoned us into the storage unit, which was crammed with furniture—a green velvet couch, a set of suede chairs, a hat rack—and lifted one box after another from a tower against the wall.

"I put these together when we were packing up our house," he said. "I had a feeling she'd send for her stuff eventually. I put in some pictures, her favorite teapot, a Pendleton blanket she always had on her bed, some books, some odds and ends." He shrugged.

Seth bent his knees, wrapped his arms around several boxes, and stood like the weight was nothing.

Jackson cocked his head. "You lift?"

"Uh, yes," Seth replied. "You?"

Jackson smirked. "I just wanted to see if you'd answer that question in earnest."

Now Seth looked offended. For some reason, it was me to whom Jackson winked an apology. Taking my hand again, he said, "Thanks for driving all this way. Thinking of her depressed up there, without her favorite things . . . It was beginning to get to me. I'm glad she finally came to her senses."

"She didn't," I said, following Seth back into the alley. "It's a surprise."

"Ah, good luck with that. She hates surprises."

"I'm not worried."

Jackson gave me a tight smile and reached to secure the storage unit's door.

"So when are you coming to visit?" I asked him.

"Soon," he said unconvincingly. "It's complicated. You probably think she's my mother, right? That I'm, like, the world's worst son. But no. Tammy's an old friend. I helped her transition to assisted living because she doesn't have any family of her own."

Seth and I shared a look, acknowledging Jackson's assumption that we had no idea who he was, or who he had been. Did he think we were too young?

"You know," I said experimentally, "my whole family really loves that album you made in the eighties. *Shotgun Wedding*? We always listen to it on long drives."

Jackson Moon's face darkened. Now, in his sharp sun-tanned features, I could see the brooding country star Tamora had made of him.

"That album is trash," he said, as if reasserting the verdict of an argument he'd won years ago. Dramatically, he turned on the heels of his high-tech running shoes. Seth and I watched as Jackson moved west down the shadowed alleyway. The sun was sinking into the square of sky framed by two rows of storage units.

"I guess he probably didn't have an affair with Dolly Parton," I said.

Still gripping the boxes, Seth looked at me, confused.

I shook my head. "Sorry. Inside joke with my brother." For a second, I missed Jake as much as I did when he was away at school. Since moving in with Mom, my brother had kept his distance from the rest of us, as if participating in a trial separation of his own.

"You think Jackson will ever visit the nursing home?" Seth asked.

It was an obvious question, but my heart sank anyway. Tamora knew full well that Jackson was no cowboy—she had assigned him to the role herself, coached him on his country twang and swagger—but she believed in their friendship. She believed she knew the real Jackson Moon beneath his award-winning performance.

"Yeah," I said, "he'll come."

For Tamora's sake, I had to believe it, too.

TWENTY-FOUR

We were still about eighty miles from home when we followed an exit sign for a beach to which neither of us had ever been. Seth gathered all his supplies in his arms and went stumbling fast over the dunes, toward the almost deserted shore. By the time I had locked the car and caught up with him, he was poised to send the Frisbee slicing through the air, straight at my chest, so that I had no choice but to catch it.

Framed between the white sand and the sky on fire, he grinned at me, hands raised. I threw the Frisbee, forgetting about the horrors of phys ed—the gymful of boys scowling at every girl who had not spent her entire childhood hurtling objects across the backyard. The disc veered a good forty-five degrees from my target, but Seth didn't mind; he just sprinted to intercept its path. Effortlessly, he snatched the thing from the air.

As we played, I took subtle steps toward Seth, slowly closing the gap between us until we were just passing the toy back and forth. I pressed it flat against his chest. He seized both my wrists. The Frisbee fell.

Years ago, Sara had warned me that once I started sleeping with someone, kissing that person would fail to hold its original appeal. Sara had been mistaken. The list of things I loved about kissing Seth was long. His skin smelled like cheap soap, and vaguely woodsy. He never shoved his tongue inside my mouth without first, gently and wordlessly, making the request. And as his hands moved from my face to my waist to the small of my back, they warmed the places they touched, until I was compelled to push him to the ground.

We stopped short of anything that could be described as sex, because the sun disappeared and the sand became extremely cold. Seth went back to the rocks where he had deposited our campfire supplies and returned with the wood, the lighter, the Duraflame log.

He built the fire fast. Soon the blaze was hot on my cheeks and bare feet, while cold air gnawed on the back of my neck. Leaning against Seth, I checked my phone. Before we'd left Arcata, I'd taken a second to text my brother, *Surprising twist: Jackson Moon has extremely questionable taste in running gear. Also, he's gay.*

So far, silence.

"Waiting to hear from your other boyfriend?" Seth asked.

In his mind, jealousy was just a joke.

"My brother," I said.

Responding to the disappointment in my voice, Seth pressed his lips against my forehead.

"Hey," I said, "what was it like when your parents split up?"

He hesitated. "I was seven."

"You don't remember being seven? When I was seven, Rosie was two. She used to bite my cheek so hard she'd leave teeth marks. Then, before I could run and tell Mom, she'd stroke my face and say, *No worries, Audrey*."

Seth smiled. "You're right. I remember being seven."

"And?"

"And my mom's boyfriend tried to sell me on the divorce by promising I'd get two of everything. Two toothbrushes— one at home and one to keep in the bathroom of their trailer. Two Spider-Man night-lights. Two stuffed SpongeBobs. Two bikes."

"Couldn't you just have unplugged your night-light and taken it with you on the plane?"

"In the car," Seth corrected me. "I've never been on a plane. And anyway, it didn't end up mattering. Guess how many times I've seen my mom since I was seven."

"I don't know. Fifty."

Shadows leaped across his face. "Five. My brothers and I drive down every other Christmas."

I could not imagine a single scenario in which my mother would tolerate seeing me every other year. She had attempted to leave me for a mere six months and had failed. Probably I could join a cult, or the army, or the Peace Corps, or the circus—and still Iris Cox Nelson would find me, if only to ensure that my teeth were brushed and my shoelaces tied.

Seth read my mind. "If your parents end up getting divorced, it will be completely different."

"I won't get two SpongeBobs," I said.

"But you'll get to keep both parents."

"How do you know?" I challenged him, even though he was so obviously correct. "The one time you met my family, we were a train wreck."

"Only because you randomly decided to cancel your college plans and threatened to expose your mom's anonymous blog."

"Exactly! It was a disaster."

"It wasn't." Seth shook his head. "Somehow, it wasn't."

I didn't know how to explain to him that I required something more than tolerance from my family. That I needed both of my parents, not just individually, but as a unit. Because I had never belonged in Crescent Bay—trapped between the Pacific and the redwoods, nowhere to go but a long way north or a long way south—but I was convinced I'd belonged with the Nelsons, safe within our inside jokes and worn-out routines.

My phone vibrated in my pocket. Instead of a new message, the screen flashed a number with a 206 area code. I answered, half expecting another reporter, already knowing there was no way I could discuss Cameron's heart attack in front of Seth.

"Audrey Nelson?" The voice belonged to an overly cheerful stranger.

"Yeah," I confirmed. Seth looked at me, and I made a show of rolling my eyes.

"Sorry to call you on a Friday night. It's been a crazy week over here."

"Um, over where, exactly?"

He chuckled. "This is Greg, calling from the Capitol Hill Assisted Living Center. We're wondering if you'd be available to swing by for an interview next week."

Seth's shoulder remained pressed against mine as I said, dumbly, "I live in California."

"Yes," Greg agreed. "I remember reading that on your application." He didn't bother to verify that I was the teen hero who had saved my friend's life, but it was obvious he had called for no other reason.

"Next week is really soon," I pointed out.

"The position doesn't start for a month, but we're eager to get someone lined up. We received a lot of résumés." When I didn't say anything—too conscious of Seth, so close he could probably hear both sides of the call—Greg added, "Of course, we were most impressed by yours."

My résumé was not impressive. My résumé said I had graduated from high school in June and worked as a CNA for less than a summer. Only my name, printed in all caps at the top of the document, could have inspired this guy to dial the number listed underneath.

Finally, Seth shifted his weight away from me, and I could focus on what was happening. A stranger in Seattle was offering me a chance to get out of town. Just because he recognized my name from the news, my face from You-Tube. In this moment, I couldn't have cared less *why* Greg had called. I wanted the job. I wanted September to bring changes—a new address, a new view, a new city's smells and sounds and weather patterns.

I was eighteen. What else was I supposed to want?

Beside me, Seth had gone rigid. He was sitting with his elbows on his knees, staring blankly at the fire.

"How's Wednesday?" I said into the phone. I had a night off in the middle of the week. If I needed more time, I could call in sick—something I'd never done before.

"Wednesday's great!" Greg chirped. "I can't wait to meet you in person!" He laughed, suddenly embarrassed by what he'd said, which implied we'd met previously—not in person, but in the glow of a screen.

By the time we hung up, my mind was racing. In a matter of days I would need to transport myself to Washington. I would need to find something to wear—something other than hospital scrubs or my frayed, sun-faded jeans. I would need to find a hotel where I could spend the night. I would need to rehearse my answers to Greg's probable questions, and to explain the trip to my parents.

Sparks flew up from the flames and died in the sand. Right now, I needed to explain myself to Seth.

"I applied for a job in Seattle," I confessed.

His gaze still fixed on the fire, Seth said, "And now you have an interview."

"I'm sure I won't get it. They probably want to meet me as, like, a joke. I'm the girl from the viral video, right?"

I was talking way too fast, and Seth knew I was bullshitting. "It's not a joke, Audrey. They wouldn't ask you to travel so far if they weren't serious about hiring you."

I couldn't keep the elation out of my voice as my thoughts unfurled, out loud. "I guess you're right. I mean, of course you're right. Oh my God, Seth, I wonder if I'll have to fly up there? Do you think there's a bus? I need to talk to Sara, like, tonight. She knows how to plan this kind of stuff."

"Are you actually . . . ?"

Seth trailed off, looking at me like the rest of his question should have been evident. I stared back at him, no idea what he was trying to ask. Seth swallowed. "Would you really move to Seattle if they made you an offer?"

My excitement—which had been close to boiling over—cooled immediately. I remembered, again, how I had promised we would be together through September and beyond. Already I had renewed the promise more than once. "I—I don't know," I stammered. "Maybe I just want to see if being Internet famous can *actually* get me a job in a big city. Maybe it's like an experiment."

Seth frowned. "Maybe?"

"I'm not sure."

His response came out uncharacteristically fast. "Are you ever sure of anything?"

Despite having snapped at me, he forced a smile now. Like he was giving me permission to pretend he wasn't mad, that my actions hadn't hurt him. Denial remained an option.

Or maybe smiling at me was just a reflex, a habit Seth couldn't break.

"How can anyone ever be sure of anything? I mean, how do you know you're making the right choice until you've found out what happens next? Maybe no one should be permitted to say they're one hundred percent certain of something unless they have, like, a Master's or a PhD in decision-making."

I was rambling. For the first time ever, Seth's expression contained a trace of disdain. Frustrated, I threw the question back in his face.

"Are *you* sure of anything?" I sounded petulant, like a little kid. And I knew he would say yes; he was sure he wanted to stay in Crescent Bay, with his dad and his brothers, nestled high in the hills. He was sure that our hometown was enough; he had nothing to prove.

"Yeah," Seth said, as predictable as ever. And then, catching me off guard, "I'm sure that I love you."

The first thing I felt, after Seth O'Malley declared his love, was a hot wave of shame. It didn't seem like a fair move on his part, telling me he loved me when I had just finished spewing a lot of defensive nonsense, when I had just finished fantasizing about a new life far from Seth and everything that mattered to him. Why couldn't he have said it earlier, when we were in the car singing along to a song about perpetual bliss? Why couldn't he have said it weeks ago, as I'd laughed into his pillow and he'd rested his hand on my stomach?

Seth had stopped searching my eyes for a reaction. Now he was watching the waves, which were barely discernible in the dark.

His shoulders shook with silent laughter.

"What's funny?" I asked, a confused giggle rising up my own throat.

He spoke into the sleeve of his flannel shirt. "I've never said that to anyone before. I had no idea it would be so awkward."

That I was Seth's first—at least in this particular, consequential way—was the best news I'd ever heard. "It's only awkward because I haven't said anything back," I informed him.

The tension left his limbs, and he leaned into me. "Oh, is that the problem?"

"Yup. I'm making this way harder than it needs to be."

"Maybe you could show a guy some mercy?"

"You don't want to be kept in suspense? I could text you later—or I could send you an e-mail! You love doing your e-mail."

Seth slid his hand against the back of my neck. "Audrey," he warned.

Someone loved me. Someone who wasn't even legally obligated to love me. Someone like Seth O'Malley.

"Fine." I shrugged. "I love you, too."

With his mouth mere inches from mine, Seth grinned. "Thank God."

The firelight perfected the rougher details of his face—his minimal acne, his patchy beard. I had been wrong about certainty requiring a PhD.

"Did you really think I might not say it back?" I asked.

"Honestly? I never have any idea what you're going to say."

With the same line, Seth could have been pointing out a flaw, or even making an accusation—but his tone, right now, was all reverence. It was like he loved me for all the same reasons I sometimes drove him crazy.

I texted my dad and told him I'd been asked, last minute, to cover someone else's shift. Seth delivered the same story to his own dad, and then—as I listened, baffled—called his brother and told Ben the truth, reciting the exact address of the Paradise Cove Motel. When he hung up and saw my stare, he said, "O'Malley brother code. We keep each other informed."

And then I envied the straightforwardness of their policy. My siblings and I could have used a code.

I was worried about leaving Tamora's stuff inside the car. Seth promised we'd bring the boxes up to our room once we got the key. I said, "What if she can tell that her prized possessions spent a night in a seedy, highway-side motel?" and Seth said, "Is that worse than a garage in Arcata?"

I figured that, for Tamora, the answer would be yes; the motel hadn't been her idea. But I also figured that she would, in some subtle way, approve of what Seth and I were doing.

Getting a room had been my idea.

On the ground floor, a dimly lit office smelled like pipe tobacco and water-damaged carpet. A cocker spaniel was lounging on a recycled couch cushion beneath a display of dated pamphlets advertising various coastal attractions. The moment the spaniel locked eyes with Seth, it came padding over to him. Seth knelt to converse with the elderly dog, while I approached the elderly man behind the counter and announced—in my calmest, most grown-up tone—"We'd like a room for the night."

The man peered through thick glasses at Seth. At me. Back to Seth. Embarrassed, Seth remained hunched over the dog, asking, "Who's a good girl?" and answering, "That's right! It's you!"

"You would like a room," the old man repeated. His T-shirt commemorated a 2003 county-wide clambake. "You and your . . . companion."

"That's right."

"ID, please."

I didn't know if it was normal for a motel manager to check a guest's ID, but I took out my wallet and produced my driver's license, proving I was eighteen. Old enough to do most anything.

Dryly, the man asked, "King, queen, or two singles?"

I could see, on a chart beneath the glass countertop, that the price difference between each option was a mere eight dollars. "King," I said, staring the guy down.

After I paid for the room in cash—my bank account activity was still, for now, accessible to my parents—the man reluctantly gave me a room key and directions to the ice machine down the hall.

"Don't worry," I told him, accepting the key. "We won't do anything bad."

Seth chose this moment to bid farewell to the spaniel, standing and revealing his full height, his strong arms and overgrown hair.

"It's already bad," the man said.

Thinking I detected a trace of humor, I argued, "But we're in love!"

Behind me, Seth blushed. The old man's look of disgust surrendered to a slight smile. "Congratulations," he dead-panned.

We got Tamora's stuff out of the car and carried the boxes up an exterior staircase to a long balcony lined with numbered doors. The Paradise Cove Motel did not look especially distinct from the storage facility where we'd met Jackson Moon. The room itself featured heavy curtains blocking an ocean view; a two-cup coffeemaker; a bible; a boxy television set; and, on the nightstand, an old phone, instructions to run for the hills in the event of an earthquake, and a tide table.

Seth and I stood at the foot of the mattress. For a second, I was paralyzed by indecision. The possibilities seemed endless. We could watch TV, or jump on the bed, or read about the moon's effects on the waves, or sleep. All ordinary activities—none of which we'd ever done together. But in another second I made up my mind and pulled my tank top over my head, undid my topknot, and shook a lot of sand out of my camp-firey hair. I was unzipping my jeans and Seth was laughing, shedding his own grimy clothes, following me into the bathroom. With his hands reaching for my waist I forgot how showers worked; I led us into the tub before turning on the spray. The water was pressurized and ice cold. My scream bounced off the tiled walls and Seth, cracking up, reached around me for the knob. And then we were warm and wet and kissing. Like the world would end if we stopped.

Shower sex proved to be beyond our range of skills, and we moved to the bed. It was comforting to realize that sex was not like certain sports—tennis, for instance—where one person's years of practice prevented him from playing with an amateur. We each had a body, and we each knew things about our own bodies that were embarrassing to try to communicate. There was a lot of needless apologizing. A lot of giggling.

A lot of trial and error.

Afterward, we took another shower, involving soap and shampoo this time, and spent the rest of the night asking each other weirdly specific questions. "Have you ever owned a pair of Crocs?" and "When did you realize Santa was a fake?" and "What's the worst thing that's ever happened to you at a rest stop?"

We lay sprawled across the plasticky bedspread, clean and calm and wide-awake. That night, time moved faster than I'd realized it could. Seth kept telling me he loved me. He kept saying it at random intervals—when I shifted positions on the mattress, or got up to peek through the heavy curtains, or lifted the ancient phone from the nightstand, pressed the receiver to Seth's ear, and said, urgently, "Listen to this. It's like a sound effect from an old movie."

He was like someone who had been suppressing a crucial element of himself—a Southern accent, or a weakness for puns—and was finally allowed to relax, to let his weakness show.

He said it like he'd been wanting to say it all summer.

TWENTY-FIVE

On my lunch break, I carried Tamora's boxes from my car
to the hallway just outside her room. Rehearsing my lines in
my head, I knocked and went inside. She was still wearing
the pajamas she'd had on since Thursday night. She was sitting on the bed with her legs sticking straight out, like one
of those old-fashioned dolls with soft bodies and porcelain
limbs.

"When did you last shower?" I asked her.

"Nice to see you, too."

"Are you sick? Should I get you a nurse?"

"You're a nurse."

I didn't correct her, because I liked the way it sounded.
"Do you want my help getting cleaned up?" I was bluffing.
Helping her in the shower would ruin my plan; I needed the
room to myself.

Tamora blinked, pausing with her eyes squeezed shut.
"Did you just offer me a sponge bath?"

"It's in my job description," I said, keeping my face as straight as possible.

Swinging her legs over the side of the bed, Tamora gave me a strident "No, thank you," and disappeared inside the bathroom.

I was alone.

Unpacking the boxes, my hands shook a little, from nerves or maybe just fatigue. I had slept that afternoon but even my dreams had been tiring, set in the Paradise Cove Motel, where Seth and I were still wrapped in threadbare, bleach-scented towels, still laughing and kissing ourselves delirious. Since waking up I'd felt a heavy, waterlogged sadness for a simple reason: We had not been able to stay in that motel room forever.

Seth and I had agreed to spend the next twenty-four hours apart. "It will be good for us," he'd told me, my car idling in his driveway, the morning sun low in the sky. "We'll get some rest. Some space."

He was right, even if I wanted him to be wrong. With our eyes bloodshot and our voices hoarse, it had become hard to believe we weren't doing something destructive to our bodies—something more destructive than falling in love.

At some point between the motel and Seth's house we'd come to another agreement, unspoken this time: We weren't going to talk about my interview in Seattle. Not yet.

When Tamora emerged from the shower, her hair wet and dripping onto the floor, I watched, anxious, as she took in the fresh additions to the room—the copper kettle on the stove, the mugs on the shelves, the wool blanket folded at the foot of her bed, and the photo albums stacked atop her nightstand. I'd already peeked at a random page and discovered the pictures had never been arranged in chronological order; a colorless portrait of Tamora as a gap-toothed little kid overlapped with a shot of her and Jackson, in full cowboy regalia, at the Country Music Awards. Guilt, followed by the sound of the shower shutting off, prevented me from snooping further.

"He was here?" She sounded confused, hopeful, and hurt. All at the same time.

"No," I said carefully. "I met him at the storage unit."

"In Arcata?" She chewed her bottom lip as her gaze darted from the blanket to the kettle. From the leather-bound albums to the collection of mismatched mugs. One said *Together we make beautiful music!* and featured two cartoon raisins singing into microphones.

She had planned to die without seeing that California Raisins mug again. I wondered if I had made a mistake, reuniting her with that mug.

"He called you? He made you drive all that way?" She

covered her mouth with her hand and looked at me. "Whose idea was this?"

Tamora's stare was so intense. She was willing me to give the right answer.

"It was Jackson's idea. Obviously."

"Good," she said, moving toward the stove. Removing the lid, she peered inside the kettle and carried it to the sink.

"You want some tea? Let me do that."

A frown creased her brow. Tamora ignored me. "He doesn't want to visit me here. Not with all these old ladies roaming the halls. He's afraid they'll recognize him."

"Have you asked him to come?"

"He knows he's always welcome."

"But have you told him you need him to come?"

She grimaced, heaving the full kettle from the sink to the stovetop. "I don't *need* Jackson to do anything."

Except that her need had been all over her face, the moment she'd stepped out of the bathroom and seen the artifacts from their life together. "You never told me he was gay," I said, sitting at the table by the window.

"Oh." With her back to me, she shrugged. "I guess I'm used to hiding it for him."

"That's a pretty big thing to hide."

I couldn't help thinking of my brother, who had always

refused to be closeted. To anyone who veered toward homophobia—not remotely uncommon in this town—he would announce he was gay before the person could finish whatever joke or adjective their lips had started to form. It was exhausting, Jake admitted, to take a moment through which he could have smiled and nodded and instead make it awkward as hell. But the polite smiles would have been exhausting in a deeper way.

"I suppose it's a pretty big thing to hide," Tamora said. The way she sank into her chair looked a little too sudden; I wondered if she was having one of her dizzy spells, and I waited for her to grip her head. She didn't. "That's not how I saw it, at the time. Everyone in Los Angeles was hiding something. Nobody *hides* things anymore. They go online and disclose their most banal thoughts, their deepest desires."

Between my parents and their crew of academic pals, I had been subjected to about one thousand speeches bemoaning my generation and our addiction to the Internet. The lecture was so boring, I always had to physically restrain myself from reaching for my phone.

"We still hide things," I said. The kettle began to whistle, and I jumped up before Tamora had a chance.

"Not like we did," she said with a hint of pride. "We knew how to keep a secret."

Reaching for two mugs—the one with the California Raisins and another celebrating the fifty-year anniversary of the Grand Ole Opry in Nashville, Tennessee—I almost laughed at her. "I don't know if you're as mysterious as you think you are," I said.

"Oh? You think you can read my banal thoughts?"

"And your deepest desires."

At the end of my shift I almost gave into my urge to find Seth and break our daylong vow of separateness. But then I thought about my bed—its twist of sheets and rumpled pillows—and I practically sprinted to the parking lot, worried Seth would renege on his own proposal, try to lure me into his Jeep Cherokee for another sleepless morning.

The Jeep was still in its spot. The back window was covered in dirt from the O'Malleys' unpaved driveway. I used my index finger to draw a heart on the glass, then made my escape.

My house was quiet except for the hum of the refrigerator, the click of the ceiling fan. For a minute I hovered over the kitchen sink, draining a glass of water. The dead silence of these mornings at home still felt weird to me, especially when contrasted against all the hectic weekday mornings of my previous life. Before school, Rosie and I had been prone to fighting over the last bowl of sugar-dusted cereal. Jake often needed to yell at whichever insomniac professor had embossed his term paper with coffee-cup rings. Mom had pushed nutritious brown-bagged lunches into our hands, and if any one of us peered inside and frowned at the bag's organic contents, Dad would slip us each a few bucks. Enough for a soda, or a grease-streaked sleeve of Tater Tots from the school cafeteria.

Abandoning the empty glass in the sink, I drifted toward my room. The top bunk was unoccupied. I didn't like sleeping alone as much as I'd always thought I would, and sometimes found myself straining to hear Rosie across the hall, turning pages or creaking the springs of Jake's bed.

The moment I was horizontal, I remembered Seth's lips against my throat. I remembered his dramatic reading of the motel's evacuation instructions.

When you hear the tsunami warning, get into your car and drive to higher ground, at least one hundred feet above sea level.

If you do not have a car, run.

In another moment, I was blissfully unconscious.

Sara was mad at me. It was obvious when I entered the barn that afternoon and the sound of my footsteps on the long, sawdusted floorboards didn't prompt her to look up. She kept her back turned as she brushed the neck of a gray mare whose name, I knew, was Isobel Stevens. In junior high Sara had gone through a phase of naming her pets after characters from whatever TV show she was binge-watching at the time.

I'd meant to tell her about the interview first thing, but now I found myself asking, "How have you been?"

I cringed as soon as the words had left my mouth. It was such an awkward question for one of us to ask the other, but I hadn't seen Sara in over two weeks. In the scheme of our friendship, two weeks might as well have been two years.

"Good," she answered, no intention of divulging any details. Over the back of the horse, Sara finally met my eyes. "And you?"

I crossed my arms, covering the CNA badge clipped to my scrubs. "Work's been crazy. My parents *are* crazy, it turns out, but we already suspected that."

Her lips formed a distant smirk. She didn't know anything about the professors' trial separation or my mom's affair; I had only told Seth.

I tried again. "What've you been up to?"

Sara shrugged. I held my hand up to the mare's nostrils and she snorted, wetly. Isobel's lead was secured to a wooden post, but she was patiently enduring the brushing, neither shaking her head nor stamping her hooves.

"Just tell me one thing," I said. "Anything."

"Elliot and I went to a party at Chelsea Hamilton's two nights ago."

Chelsea Hamilton still worked the day shift at the nursing home. The Sunday morning on which I'd caught her and Seth O'Malley flirting outside the main entrance felt like an eternity ago. I wondered if Seth had known about the party—if, as we'd fooled around in our room at the Paradise Cove Motel, he'd given any thought to the predictable summer we had both forfeited in favor of this summer with each other.

"Have fun?" I asked.

She shrugged again. "Elliot and I holed up in a corner and played that drinking game you invented sophomore year."

The game was simple. A group of people—or in our case, exactly three people—sat in a circle and passed around a bottle, or a can, or a commemorative stein of something alcoholic. When the beverage was in your possession, the person to your left tried to guess something that you wanted. The person might theorize that you wanted a puppy, or a McDonald's milk shake, or to get into Berkeley, or to make out with the girl who sat beside you in physics, or for your phone to ring. If they were correct—if even a small part of you wanted it—you drank. If they were wrong, then the other person drank. Over the years, I had sniffed out Elliot's crush on a ponytailed 4-H enthusiast named Jenny

Kincaid; Elliot had guessed Sara's desire to graduate first in our class; and once, Sara had said to me, "You secretly long for the Professors Nelson to praise you like they praise your brother."

Was it such a secret? Either way, I drank.

"The two of you played alone?" I asked.

"Yup. Elliot guessed that I want you to break up with Seth."

I blinked at Sara, stunned. If she loved me at all she wouldn't want me to break up with Seth. He was the best thing Crescent Bay had going for it.

"I told him he was wrong. I made him throw back a shot of Fireball just for having the audacity to suggest I'm such a coldhearted bitch."

"Good," I said.

"But later—" Sara paused with the brush halfway down Isobel's velvety hip. "Later he guessed that I wish you would hang out with us as much as you used to, before you got an all-consuming job and boyfriend combo."

"And?"

Sara took a step back and surveyed the horse, whose coat gleamed. "I think I'm still hungover."

"I'm sorry." I took a breath, ready to offer an explanation, but Sara cut me off.

"It's okay. I kind of get it. For us, this summer is the

end of everything. It's fun for us to get wasted at Chelsea's because we're never going to see any of those people again. We're never going to listen to Marcus Kramer talk about jacking up his rig or watch as Sloane Anderson finishes her third beer and announces that it would be *completely hilarious* if we all played strip poker. But for you . . . this summer must feel more like a beginning."

Even if Sara wasn't aiming to offend me, she'd failed at hiding an undercurrent of judgment. The way her gaze dropped to the floor and landed on the waterproof sneakers I'd started wearing to work revealed exactly what she thought of my life's new chapter. But I wasn't really bothered by her judgment. What got to me was the way she had referred to *us*, including herself and Elliot but not including me.

"I have an interview in Seattle," I said.

Sara's eyes widened. "You do? When?"

"Wednesday."

The interview felt real, now that I'd told her about it.

"How are you going to get there? What are you going to tell your parents? Your boss?"

"No idea."

I watched my best friend absorb my news. Maybe, in just a few weeks, I would move to Seattle. I would get my own studio apartment with a fire escape and a view. And maybe the view would be of a nondescript office building or a

Laundromat's neon sign, but during Sara's reading week she would fly up from Davis and we'd explore the city together.

"What's in Seattle, anyway?" she asked.

"Rain. Kurt Cobain's ghost. A space needle."

"And you, maybe?"

I smiled. "And me, maybe."

Sara unknotted the horse's lead and walked Isobel back into her stall. "I'll help you plan your trip," she offered, as I'd hoped she would. Sara was the competent kind of person who had been ordering her own food in restaurants since she was four, scheduling her own dentist's appointments since middle school.

"Will you go with me?" I asked.

"I could do that." Sara sounded casual, but she was grinning as she secured the metal gate. "Elliot, too, or just us?"

Officially, Sara and Elliot and I were a trio. Unofficially, there was a layer of my friendship with Sara to which a boy could never be granted access.

"Just us," I said, relieved that we'd restored the word to its rightful meaning.

TWENTY-SIX

On Monday morning I exited the nursing home and discovered Seth, as usual, leaning against the rear of his Jeep. Our promise to take a break from each other had outlasted its initial expiration date; I'd worked another busy shift without seeing him once, and now I was almost nervous, my heart thumping as we locked eyes. But as I approached, Seth nodded meaningfully at a fixed point across the lot. I followed his gaze to the rickety staircase leading down to the beach.

My mother stood at the top—one hand on the hip of her yoga pants, the other thumbing through messages on her phone.

It would have been easy enough to pretend I hadn't seen her, to duck inside of the Jeep and ditch her, but I was helpless against whatever magnetic pull governed the airspace between us. As I moved toward my mother, Seth saluted me. He climbed behind the wheel of his car and started the engine.

Mom looked up.

"Hello, Audrey," she called cheerfully. As if we often encountered each other in deserted parking lots at dawn.

"What are you doing here?" I asked.

She frowned. "You know I'm always up by five."

"Yes. What I'm wondering is how you ended up outside my place of employment, with no car, by five."

"I walked on the beach," she explained.

I had forgotten about the beach access from her borrowed cottage. In Crescent Bay, certain places were connected by miles of inconveniently crooked roads, or, if you knew exactly where you were going, a much shorter stretch of sand.

Mom and I watched as Seth's taillights disappeared over the edge of the bluff. From his car we could hear the faint scratches of a country radio station, until we couldn't anymore.

"You wouldn't answer my texts," Mom said finally.

"I'm always asleep when you text."

"I figured. That's why I'm here now. On your schedule."

I wondered if, in fact, she was here to confront me about the flight I'd booked to Seattle without her permission, without even using her frequent flyer miles. There was no way for her to know about the trip; yesterday, Sara had shown me how to hack the airline's advertised fare by buying a string of one-way tickets from Steeds County to Portland to

Seattle and back again. We had charged the flights to Sara's debit card. Still, part of me believed in my mother's ability to intuit my plans. It was the same childish part of me that had always worried she could read my mind.

I waited her out.

"Do you want to walk back with me?" Mom asked, stalling.

"I can't." I gestured to the MINI Cooper, the lone car left in the lot. Since my mother and brother had absconded to Professor Hale's beach house with the minivan, Dad rarely had access to a vehicle—which suited his desire to spend each night anguishing over his manuscript, occasionally heating up a can of soup or asking Rosie to produce a good synonym for *heartbreak*.

She tilted her face skyward. Abruptly, she said, "It was a mistake."

"What was?"

"Italy."

I felt myself bristle. "You loved Italy."

She squeezed her eyes shut and shook her head. "What makes you say that?"

"Um, your anonymous account of your trial separation from your husband of twenty-five years."

She cringed again. "Not a very catchy subheading, is it?"

I was annoyed, almost offended. By going to Italy, my

mother had—at least temporarily—gotten everything she wanted. To suddenly claim she'd been as upset by the distance as the rest of us seemed awfully convenient. "I thought you were living it up in Naples," I said.

"Not really. It was a story I was telling myself about an experience I wanted to be having."

I crossed my arms, challenging her. "So the sleazy Italian suitor wasn't real?"

Mom's sigh was all remorse. "No. He was real."

If I was grateful for one thing, it was not knowing the guy's name.

"So which part was made up?" I asked.

"The part where I got off the plane and spent a single moment thereafter thinking about anything aside from you, your brother, your sister, and your infuriating father."

And yet, she had reported making progress on her Machiavelli book. She had reported dreaming in Italian, falling in love with the Mediterranean. "You weren't sprung free?"

Mom looked me in the eye. She rarely wore makeup and never shaped her brows. Consequently, my mother's face was never a surprise; she always looked exactly the same. "Audrey, I was miserable."

She was telling the truth.

And I was glad to hear her say it, even as I knew how little it mattered, whether or not she had enjoyed her Italy experiment. That she had been willing to leave us, and willing to cheat on Dad, meant that everything I'd always taken for granted had already unraveled, a long time ago.

"I'm going to Seattle," I announced. Like a child, I added, "I don't need your permission."

Mom frowned, but only slightly. The wind rearranged her no-nonsense haircut. "Seattle? What's in Seattle?"

"Potentially a job."

Her shoulders relaxed. "You have an interview?"

"Yeah. In a couple of days. And the thing is . . . I think I might get it? Because it seems like they're looking for a Certified Nurse Assistant who doubles as a viral video star?"

"Sounds like you've got a shot," Mom conceded.

"Seth doesn't want me to go."

"Did he ask you to stay?"

"No," I said, defensive. I knew she believed that a boy like Seth could only hold me back, could only keep me rooted in this town. But Seth would never ask me to stay if what I wanted was to go. We had to choose each other willingly or not at all.

Her smile was distant, as if in response to some joke I wasn't in on.

"Do *you* want me to stay?" I asked her.

Mom looked west, toward the water. Crescent Bay's portion of the Pacific was the most violent stretch of ocean I had ever seen. Our waves were loud and whitecapped, and I was pretty sure they towered over the gentle surf in Los Angeles, the benign breakers in Florida. "You know I wanted you to live at home," she said. "I wanted you to go to Whedon during the year and travel with me during the summers. I thought we'd drink wine at sidewalk cafés in Paris. I'd show you the catacombs, the Louvre. And every September I'd bring you right back to California with me."

My mother, I was beginning to realize, was susceptible to detailed fantasies. "You never mentioned the part about the wine."

She ignored me. "I still want those things for you, Audrey. But I also want you to move to Seattle and start your career. I want you to have everything."

It was both touching and intolerable, the sincerity with which my mother expressed her love. I wanted to mark her love as FACT and file it in a drawer for safekeeping; I did not particularly want to offer her a response.

She didn't even balk when all I offered her was a ride.

We drove in comfortable silence toward Mom's temporary home. She refrained from remarking on the state of the MINI, which was just shy of squalid. The flattened Styrofoam cups, empty except for the dried dregs of old coffee, were mine, but Dad was to blame for the library books littering the backseat, the gum wrappers filling the cup holders.

Professor Hale's cottage had brown shingles and bright red trim. Above the front door hung a varnished piece of driftwood inscribed with the assertion LIFE IS BETTER AT THE BEACH! There was something disorienting about seeing my brother's sandals abandoned on a stranger's porch.

I told my mother I would talk to her soon.

She asked me to promise that I would pick up my phone every time she called from now until the day she died.

I said I would do my best.

With her hand on the door, Mom hesitated. "Audrey, how did you find my blog?"

I looked at her. Not for the first time this summer, I marveled at the innocence of old people. "So, when you sign up for a blog and you use your real e-mail address, it doesn't matter what you call yourself in your profile. Unless you specifically tell it not to, the host site still matches you with all of your contacts who have ever registered for the same kind of blog. Then it sends out a message announcing your new blogging habit to all those people."

Mom appeared stricken.

"Some of them might be your relatives," I added.

She was shaking her head. "I don't understand. *Sprung Free in Italy!* was supposed to be private."

"It's the Internet. There's no such thing."

She threw a hand over her eyes and groaned. "I can't believe you read that part about—"

"Mom." I cut her off. "Could we never talk about your blog again? Like, ever?"

Iris squared her shoulders. Finally, she pushed open the car door and stepped into the crisp morning air. Her voice was sharp with professorial authority—no shame, no apologies—as she concluded, "I think that would be ideal."

TWENTY-SEVEN

Like most places in Crescent Bay, the Steeds County Regional Airport was always nearly deserted. After Sara's father dropped us off outside the terminal, Tuesday morning, it took us all of five minutes to get our boarding passes, shove our backpacks through security's lone scanner, and claim window-facing seats at the gate.

Beyond the edge of the runway was the ocean. Waves thrashed against a jagged sea stack, half submerged at high tide. That the sky was, for once, clear and blue struck me as a good sign. I wasn't scared of flying, but I generally appreciated being able to see the distance between the belly of the plane and the ground.

As we waited, Sara fed me Skittles and asked me practice questions for tomorrow's interview.

"What's your proudest accomplishment?"

"Skipping every single pep rally in high school."

"What do you hope to accomplish in the next year?"

"I wouldn't mind another growth spurt."

"What's the best part about working with the elderly?"

"Showing them how to send selfies to their grandchildren."

Sara laughed. "Does that really happen?"

"Constantly," I said.

When it was time to board, a flight attendant led us and approximately twelve other passengers through a set of glass doors and across the tarmac. We climbed a short set of stairs onto the tiny propeller plane that would take us to Portland for our connecting flight. Sara whispered to me that she felt like the president. The flight attendant overheard and chirped, "We strive to make all our customers feel presidential!"

Sara had to struggle to keep it together.

Twenty minutes later, as the plane was gathering speed, I leaned into her and said, "Did you know that Seth has never flown anywhere?"

Sara was white-knuckling the armrest and seemed grateful for the distraction. "Makes sense," she said. "O'Malley is so *born and raised*."

The plane lifted its nose. For a second, the wheels were still grazing the ground, and then we were aloft. "What does that even mean?" I asked. My best friend was in the habit of inventing idioms and inserting them casually into conversations, no disclaimer. Outside our window the runway and the water receded fast, until our view resembled a map of the coast.

"You know when, like, someone asks your grandpa if he's always lived in Crescent Bay? And your grandpa thumps his chest and says, *born and raised?*"

"My grandpa lives in Washington, DC," I told her.

Sara half rolled her eyes. "Well, the rest of us have chest-thumping grandpas. And someday, Seth O'Malley will be someone's chest-thumping grandpa."

I thought that Sara was probably right. And at first I smiled, imagining Seth all wrinkled and gray ponytailed, proud of his seaside roots. But soon I became irrationally jealous of whatever local girl had turned him into a dad, then a grandpa. Jealous of the whole O'Malley brood—the kids and the grandkids and the dogs who would unambiguously belong to Seth.

It wasn't healthy, feeling jealous of my boyfriend's future dog.

The plane dipped dramatically to one side as we turned north. Sara took a sharp breath and I took her hand. For the first time all summer, I made an honest effort to forget about Seth.

* * *

After our layover in Portland, we touched down at the Seattle-Tacoma International Airport just after sunset. We took a light-rail train into downtown, then a bus all the way up Broadway Avenue toward Capitol Hill, where Sara had booked us a room in a hostel. The darkened windows of the bus mostly reflected our own faces, but we caught glimpses of the city's broad brick buildings and steep, tree-lined hills.

Still, it wasn't until Sara unlocked the door to our room—on the fourth floor of an old house—that I really saw it. The city. The landscape of traffic lights and fire escapes and power lines easing into the dark expanse of the Puget Sound. The Space Needle, all lit up and looming.

I hadn't been here since I was fourteen, but I still loved it. Some things were instinctual. If I got the job, and if I gathered the nerve, moving to Seattle would be like walking into Mr. Longo's classroom that morning in April and choosing to sit next to Seth—something I would do just because it felt right. Just because the notion made my heart pound while a voice in my head whispered, *Excellent idea.*

"Am I a good planner, or what?"

Sara flopped backward on the bed, which was covered in the ugliest duvet I'd ever seen—brown moths flying between green and yellow stripes.

"You are," I told her. She'd figured everything out,

including the transportation from the airport and our plan for tomorrow.

She threw her arms above her head. Her shirt rode up and exposed her soft stomach. I remembered an afternoon in ninth grade when Sara and I had been killing time at the Fish Shack with a bunch of kids from school. Some comment of Sara's about feeling bloated had launched the two of us into one of those arguments over whose body was preferable, more desirable—each of us advocating for the other's.

A boy named Julian had tried to judiciously end our spat by declaring, "The truth is that Sara has the nicest legs, but Audrey's stomach is flatter."

Sara and I had regarded him silently—this boy with pockmarks cratering his cheeks and a perpetual aroma of AXE body spray—before erupting with laughter. Because Julian didn't get it. The boy was clueless. Our fight had not really been about our bodies; our fight had not even been a real fight. It had been more of a time-honored ritual, a way for Sara and me to assure each other: *you are mine, and I love you.*

Now, I flopped beside my friend. "Thanks for bringing me here."

"Any time," she said.

We were quiet for a minute or two. Sara's eyes were closed, and I was wondering if she'd fallen asleep when she finally asked, "So, how many times have you slept with him?"

My endeavor to forget about Seth—to assess what I wanted, apart from him—was not going well. "I have no idea."

"You know exactly."

"Twelve times."

"And?"

She wanted gritty, sticky details, but I had no desire to provide them. Maybe someday, when sex with Seth became routine—or at least, less overwhelming—I could talk to Sara about the mechanics involved. For now, I told her what I realized I had been dying to tell her.

"So, a few mornings ago, we had sex. And afterward I wanted some water. And Seth swore up and down that his dad was at his girlfriend's and wouldn't be home for hours, so I went into the kitchen completely naked and got myself a glass."

"Bold," Sara said.

"I was, like, sprinting back down the hall and trying not to spill all over the carpet, and I could hear Seth cracking up in his room. And then once I was safely inside, I just stood there, hydrating. Nude. And at first I was like, *What are you doing? Put some clothes on.* But then I thought, why wouldn't I stand naked in Seth O'Malley's room and drink a glass of water? You don't need any clothes to drink a glass of water, especially not when your boyfriend is looking at you like you're the sexiest woman alive."

Sara rolled toward me, shielding her face. Through the cracks between her fingers I could see she was smiling.

"I don't know," I said. "I just always thought sex would be more embarrassing. I didn't know I could feel so comfortable with someone and so excited by him at the same time. I thought it was one or the other."

Sara hesitated, then said, "I know Seth makes you feel like a sexy hydration queen, or whatever, but maybe a lot of guys would make you feel that way? Maybe he's just the first?"

"Have you ever felt that way with someone?" I asked her.

"No," she admitted. "Never."

Before my interview the next morning, Sara took me to see an apartment. The studio she'd found would have struck me as perfect if I'd been able to forget, for one second, that it was laughably out of my price range. The place was small—just one room plus a kitchen and a bathroom, both closet-size—but, as the building manager pointed out, it was the details, like the original hardwood floors and glass doorknobs, that made the place *truly special*. The guy looked at Sara as he spoke. Of the two of us, I guess she appeared to be the most likely candidate for pricey city living.

"I can't afford this place," I whispered in her ear.

Whoever had recently vacated the apartment had left a bed pushed against the wall beneath the window. A fitted sheet had slipped from one corner, revealing the blue, scaly mattress underneath.

"Well, not now," Sara agreed. "But a year from now? After you've worked for a while?"

We were speaking under our breath, but even our whispers echoed in the empty space. The building manager shook his collection of keys. "A basement unit is opening up soon," he said, "if you're looking for something a little more economical."

"That would be great," I said, pivoting, ready to follow him back into the hall. Sara grabbed my shoulders and turned me around for one last look.

"Goals," she insisted.

But all I saw was the abandoned bed.

Seth and I had only ever slept together—literally *slept* together—in one bed, at the Paradise Cove Motel. I wanted to share more beds with him. My bottom bunk at home, the lumpy bed back at the hostel. Beds in guest rooms, dorm rooms. Hospital beds. Air mattresses in tents. Our own bed.

It wasn't like I wanted to select the man with whom I'd share every bed, forever. I had absolutely no desire to fast-forward time, or to be a day older than I already was.

I just wanted to choose Seth, right now. And again tomorrow. And possibly every day after that.

My interview with Greg lasted seven minutes, during which he did not ask me a single question.

Maybe my reasoning had been naive, but I hadn't actually expected the director of Capitol Hill Assisted Living to mention the video. Obviously, he had seen it, but I didn't think that selecting his employees based on their accidental Internet fame was a hiring policy Greg would necessarily own.

His hair was short and gelled, and he was wearing a silky wine-colored shirt, a black tie thrown over his shoulder. After I shook Greg's hand and sank into the plastic chair across from his messy desk, he opened a laptop and navigated to YouTube. Even as it dawned on me what was happening, I held out hope. Maybe he only wanted to show me a promotional video for his business, or a conversational parrot.

Greg sat back in his chair as *California Teen Hero Saves Life of a Friend* began to play. I didn't particularly want to watch it, but I didn't know where else to look. The top comment—which I'd checked last night, while Sara was showering in our hostel's moldy bathroom—was still, *I want them to take turns sucking my ****.*

Why had DoomChild97 censored himself? Did he imagine he was, by any definition, being polite?

Normally, when I watched the video I watched myself. It was impossible to forget that hundreds of thousands of strangers had seen this version of me—pit-stained and unattractively hunched, but also calm, also resolute. Watching the video with Greg forced me to see those sixty seconds through a stranger's eyes. Namely, I saw Cameron. Her discolored face, slack and unresponsive. And I remembered how, despite appearances, I hadn't felt calm and resolute; I had felt simply terrified.

Neither of us had requested that the moment be filmed and aired on television, or uploaded to the Internet, but Cameron was the only victim. Of her own body, of all the unwanted attention. Her life had almost ended, and then— maybe thanks to me, or maybe thanks to a team of highly trained medical professionals—it hadn't. Wasn't that the whole story?

Seth had been right. Instead of accepting an invitation to appear on the *Steed County News*, I should have gone to see Cameron in the hospital, accepted her thanks. Nothing more.

I lowered my gaze to a dark smudge on the fake wood of Greg's desk. I listened to the tinny sound of the waves crashing, until the video's line of dialogue promised it was almost over.

Greg closed the computer, satisfied. "Obviously you're a quick thinker. You have a good memory for detailed instructions. You can stay calm under pressure."

He was listing the qualifications from his own Craigslist ad.

"You're skilled, courageous. If there's anything else you want to add . . ."

Greg was on the verge of offering me the job. Did he think that by hiring me, he'd be adding a hero to his staff? Or did he just enjoy the novelty of my face having been viewed three million times?

I'm barely famous, I wanted to tell him. *I'm actually no one.*

Instead, I cleared my throat and said, "Uh, no. I guess not. I guess that covers it."

"Can you start in two weeks, day after Labor Day?"

I froze. If he needed an answer right now, the answer was no.

"Want some time to think it over?" he asked.

I nodded, numb.

"Fair enough." He heaved a sigh, like nothing was fair or ever would be. "It's a big move. Let us know by Monday morning, okay?"

Monday morning was five days away.

I nodded again, standing and leaning across the desk to shake Greg's hand again. Mine was clammy, cold. Greg looked surprised, then curious, wondering how a girl with such gross hands could have used them to save a life.

That night, after having dinner in a Thai restaurant downtown, Sara and I followed 1st Avenue all the way up to Pine Street, making a left where the road plunged into Pike Place Market. Beneath our feet were red bricks, all slippery with rain. Sara grabbed my hand so we didn't get separated as we entered the market and wove through throngs of people waiting to buy bouquets of roses, or fish with their eyeballs still intact. Above us, neon signs pointed to bakeries and butcher shops. The air smelled like mold, coffee beans, and patchouli.

I wanted this, though—all the people not necessarily looking one another in the eye, minding their own business. Anonymity felt right to me. Safe, even. Like I could make an embarrassing mistake and hardly anyone would notice, but also like I could scream for assistance and all sorts of people would come running.

Chances were, one of them would be able to help.

At the back of the building—home to a psychic's stall curtained with beads, and also to a glass display of soaps made from the milk of Washington-raised goats—Sara and I pushed through a set of doors onto a concrete stairwell, where we encountered the most stunning view I'd ever beheld from a vantage point that smelled mostly of urine.

The Puget Sound had absorbed the ink-blue dusk, the orange flares of the sunset. My chest tightened. It hurt, to be this happy and simultaneously apart from Seth. I wanted to text him a picture of the view and write something cliché, like, *Wish you were here.* But I knew the picture would hardly show up on his flip phone, and that he might not even open the file, which would cost him twenty-five cents to retrieve.

It was just a nice view, anyway.

It was just more scenery.

Soon, Seth would be clocking in for his shift. I felt drained by the thought of everything that needed to happen over the next five days. I needed to fly home to Crescent Bay, reunite with Seth, work back-to-back nights, and make my choice.

If I was being honest, a part of me doubted my ability to up and move to this city. Even if Seth hadn't been a factor, did I know how to live alone? Could I function without my mother telling me when to wear a coat, or my dad correcting my grammatical errors, or my little sister mouth-breathing all through the night?

And what if I got sick? Maybe I would pull myself together and trek through the rain to obtain my own NyQuil and Gatorade—or maybe I would just curl up and die.

If leaving home was a far-fetched fantasy, staying in town to be with Seth hardly seemed more realistic. At this distance, all the early morning hours we'd logged together felt hazy and unverified, like something I'd dreamed. And I wasn't sure I could let a dream—even the best one I'd ever had—define my entire life.

Leaning over a green-painted railing, Sara side-eyed me. "You okay?"

"Can we go back to the hostel?" I asked her.

Surprised, she checked the time on her phone. "It's still early. Don't you want to see more of your maybe-future city?"

I shrugged. "I've seen enough."

TWENTY-EIGHT

We brought the rain home from Seattle. As Sara and I stepped from the plane to the tarmac, we had to hold our backpacks above our heads to keep from getting drenched. Her dad picked us up outside the terminal, his car smelling like spearmint gum and air freshener. Politely, Mr. Quintero quizzed us on the details of our trip, and Sara answered him while I rested my forehead against the cold window and watched the familiar countryside flashing by.

Sara was saying, "Audrey aced her interview, obviously. Now I just have to hope she doesn't run off to Seattle and get too cool for Elliot and me."

The dirt road to Seth's house was coming up. Abruptly, and without looking at Sara, I leaned toward the front of the car and said, "Mr. Quintero, do you mind taking the next left?"

He made eye contact in the rearview mirror. "Did your family move?"

"No, but could you drop me off at my boyfriend's house?"

Sara's dad seemed unsure, as if maybe I was allowed to fly to Seattle and interview for a job, but not to visit my boyfriend on a Thursday morning. Finally, I said, "I'll text my parents and let them know," and Mr. Quintero put on his turn signal. I could feel Sara's eyes boring into the side of my face, but this wasn't up to her.

After Mr. Quintero drove away, I cut through the long, wet grass surrounding Seth's house, soaking the bottoms of my jeans. I had never snuck up on Seth before, but I identified his window by the sticker meant to resemble a sheriff's badge, which he'd stuck to the glass however many years ago.

One of Seth's Labradors caught me before I could knock. Instead of howling, Faith made her eyes wide and anxious and thumped her tail against Seth's bed. Seth threw off the covers, ejecting both dogs and his cat from their haven between the sheets.

Seth was close to naked.

"You need a better watchdog," I said as he lifted out the screen and pulled me through the open window. Flannel shirts, jeans, and hoodies littered his bedroom floor.

"Who could be better than these two?" His voice was groggy, but full of love for his pets as he nudged open the door to the hall, encouraging them to vacate. Obediently, the trio filed out of the room.

"I could have been a burglar," I said.

"They know you're not a burglar. They know you."

Seth wrapped his arms around me and stooped to bury his face in my hair. His skin warmed mine, even through my damp clothes.

"How was Seattle?" Seth asked, pushing my jacket off my shoulders.

I didn't have an answer.

"You and Sara have a good time?"

Seth lowered the zipper on my sweatshirt. In another second, the sweatshirt had joined his collection on the floor.

"Do you always sleep in just your underwear?" I asked.

"Yes," he said, undoing the button on my jeans.

"What if there's a fire?"

"Then I'll put on pants."

"What if there's no time?"

"Then some firefighters and probably Mrs. Rivera will see me in my boxer briefs. I'll be humiliated."

"Who's Mrs. Rivera?"

"My neighbor. She's always asking me to change her watercooler."

Now I was almost naked. He was pulling me into his bed, pulling the covers over our bodies. I breathed in the peppery smell of Seth, post–night shift.

"How was your interview?" he whispered.

"I don't want to talk about my interview."

He slid his hand between my thighs. "What do you want to talk about?"

"Mrs. Rivera's watercooler."

Seth's laughter was compromised by exhaustion. He'd only been home for a few hours, after spending all night mopping hallways and scouring chili residue from commercial-size soup pots. I could still smell the antibacterial soap on his fingers.

We had been headed in the general direction of sex, but now, as Seth wrapped his arms around me, I felt us both succumb to a heavy, dreamless sleep. The kind of sleep that only strikes when there are no alarms set, no voices in the hall, no sunlight breaking through the blinds—nothing to remind you of wherever else you're supposed to be.

When I finally opened my eyes, Seth was already awake, lying flat on his back and staring up at the popcorn ceiling. His domed light fixture doubled as an insect graveyard; my mother, if she could have seen the carnage, would have lost her mind.

Again, he asked me, "How was the interview?"

"They offered me the job," I admitted.

He tried to keep his voice neutral. "Are you going to take it?"

I glanced at his ancient clock, resting on a stack of shoeboxes and old textbooks. I still had days to make my decision, but I found myself telling Seth the truth the moment it occurred to me.

"I don't think so."

All along, I had been counting on a change of scenery to change my life. Warm and happy in the cocoon of Seth's bed, I thought I finally knew better.

He rolled toward me. A grin tugged at the corners of his mouth, threatening to undo his serious expression. "Really?"

Casually, I said, "You wouldn't be there, would you?"

He shook his head, the grin complete. "I'll be here."

It was exactly what I'd expected him to say.

TWENTY-NINE

Maureen was berating me for my failure to spread a clean sheet across a plastic-wrapped mattress with one expert flick of my wrists. An air vent above the bed had thwarted my efforts, consistently blowing the sheet to one side just before it fell into place. According to my supervisor, the task had taken me "three or four tries, *at least*." Now, as we dug into our steaming Lean Cuisine Hot Pockets, she was explaining, "I know it seems like a small issue, but all the wasted seconds add up to wasted minutes, which add up to wasted hours, which—"

"For sure," I interrupted as pleasantly as possible, grabbing my phone as it shivered across the break room's table. "I'll be faster next time."

I'd grown immune to Maureen's lectures, which were as frequent as they were petty. She took so much pleasure in bossing me around; most nights, I didn't have the heart to fight back.

My phone had alerted me to a new e-mail.

The e-mail was from Cameron Suzuki.

Hey, Audrey,

**So, a girl from Under Your Breath contacted me
and asked for my side of the story. I don't know
if you've ever read UYB but it's an online journal I
really love. They publish a lot of girly, feminist stuff,
and I thought it'd be nice if when people looked me
up they found this magazine, and not just a ton of
clickbait.**

**Anyway, they want to interview you, too, so I
promised I'd ask. They're going to call me Saturday
night at 6 p.m. Come over if you want and we can
talk to them together.**

**Oh and they're paying $100 each. I negotiated them
up from $50 each which I thought seemed low.**

**See you soon, I hope,
Cameron**

My supervisor was still philosophizing about the passage
of time, but I tuned her out as I stared at the screen, reread-
ing the message.

Obviously, I had expected to cross paths with Cameron
Suzuki at some point. Given what she had been through
this summer, it was hard to imagine her parents letting her

leave town anytime soon, even for college. In the back of my mind I'd been dreading running into her at the Fish Shack, or the Qwick Mart, or on the muddy trail leading up to Cape Defiance. Ever since I'd confessed to Seth that I'd gone on the *Steeds County News*, he'd allowed me to believe that Cameron more or less hated me.

But there was no hate in Cameron's e-mail. There was nothing but the casual, unassuming friendliness I'd always associated with the most popular girl in school. I was relieved, and intrigued—so intrigued that I wrote back right away, telling her I'd be there. It wasn't until I had returned my phone to my pocket and attempted to refocus my attention on Maureen that an uneasiness washed over me, pricking my palms and constricting the nerves at the back of my neck.

Maybe Cameron had never resented me for going on the news—for testing how far my haphazard heroism could get me—but Seth had.

Would things between us be different if I had ignored Kristy Summers? If I had refused to talk to the reporter from the *Sacramento Bee*? Maybe Seth would have encouraged me to escape to Seattle if I'd gotten the job on the merits of my application, nothing more.

Maybe he even would have considered coming with me.

"Audrey?"

Maureen was standing in front of the open refrigerator, the Diet Coke in her outstretched hand an obvious peace offering.

Reflexively, I opened the drink. Then, instead of pouring the artificial sugar down my throat, I set the can on the table and told Maureen I'd be right back.

In the last few minutes of my lunch break there was someone I needed to see.

For once, that someone wasn't Seth.

Because I was staring at my phone as I entered room 64, trying to verify that my quick reply to Cameron had been normal-sounding and free of typos, I didn't immediately notice the boxes stacked against the wall. When I looked up, poised to greet Tamora with a question, she wasn't there. Soon I realized what else was missing—the mugs, the teakettle, the Pendleton blanket, the photo albums.

Someone had packed up Tamora's things.

My first impulse was to rush back to the break room and ask Maureen what had happened—whether a heart attack or a stroke or a bad slip in the shower had necessitated Tamora's transfer to Health and Rehabilitation, or if Tamora, tired of around-the-clock care, had finally requested an apartment in the Independent Living wing. She was not dead. Tamora had not died while I was playing hooky, running around

Seattle with my best friend. That wouldn't make sense, wouldn't be fair—and I was about to turn on my heel and make sure of it, when, behind the closed door of the bathroom, the toilet flushed.

My heart rate slowed as I listened to Tamora wash her hands, waited for her to dry and moisturize her manicured fingers one by one. She emerged then, fully dressed and unsurprised by my presence.

"Nurse Nelson. Did you have a good vacation?" Slowly, Tamora lowered herself to the edge of the bed. She appeared pleased, not at all injured or compromised.

"I was sick," I said, sticking with the story I'd told Maureen. "Are you going to explain why all of your stuff is in boxes?"

Tamora admired the stack of them. "I'm checking out. First thing in the morning."

"You can't just check yourself out. It's not a hotel."

Her lips curled. "It's funny, I always thought the same thing. But it turns out, you *can*. Chelsea—she's the daytime you—filled me in on the details. Do you know Chelsea?"

"Yes," I admitted.

"She explained my rights to me. Evidently I'm a grown woman and I don't need anyone's permission to . . ."

I raised my eyebrows.

"To blow this Popsicle stand," Tamora finished.

My arms were crossing, my head shaking from side to side, and I wanted to tell her that she was mistaken; she required full-time care, my nightly assistance. But really, I knew she didn't and never had. I wanted Tamora to stay because she was the highlight of my job at the Crescent Bay Retirement Home. Without our nocturnal talks, my shifts would drag through the twilight, past midnight, and on until dawn.

"What does Jackson think about this?" I asked, knowing that full-time care had been his idea and his preference all along. Tamora had agreed to the plan simply because he'd asked her to.

"He's fine with it!" Her insistence came on too strong. She began to ramble. "He needed some reassurance, naturally. We're going to hire someone—a girl like you—to come check on me from time to time. And Jackson and his husband are going to make an effort to visit with some regularity. Plus, I've rented a house in one of those schmaltzy beachside communities without a postal code. The house has no stairs, no empty elevator shafts—but even if I *do* manage to stumble, I'm sure I'll only have to holler before one of my meddling neighbors has the sense to phone an ambulance."

"Um," I began, but Tamora wasn't finished.

"It's a horrible place, based on Jackson's description. Everyone has wind chimes affixed to their porches and tacky driftwood sculptures guarding their front doors. *But—*" She caught herself. "Not as horrible a place as this. The rooms won't smell of rubbing alcohol and mortality." She nodded her head. "At least there's that."

I took a breath, hoping Tamora would be inspired to do the same. "Are you sure this is what you want?"

She had gone from confident—cocky, even—to semi-hysterical in a handful of seconds. My lunch break was over, but it didn't matter; I wasn't leaving until I was sure she was okay.

Tamora sighed and admitted, "What I wanted was to live with Jackson in the hills outside Sacramento until I died."

"But that's not what Jackson wanted," I said gently.

"This house I've rented is only a few minutes down the highway. I really think it's the next best thing. And when it truly becomes necessary, when I'm so senile I can't remember my own mother's name, or what Reba McEntire wore to the Country Music Awards in 1987, *then* Jackson can roll me right back to the old folks' home. Or to the funeral parlor. Whichever seems most appropriate."

"I don't think Crescent Bay has a funeral parlor," I said.

Tamora narrowed her eyes. "Then what do you do with your dead?"

"Bury them at sea?" I guessed.

She waved an elegant hand. "That's fine."

Minutes earlier I had burst into Tamora's room wanting something definite from her, but I no longer remembered what, exactly. All I knew was that Tamora had given me yet another reason, or another excuse, to stay.

"I'll come visit you," I said, making the promise faster than I could think through its long-term implications. "Once a week, or as often as I can. And I'll help you interview home health aides. Maybe I can even help you move in tomorrow, after I get some sleep. If you give me the address, I can—"

"Audrey." Tamora silenced me. I wasn't sure I'd ever heard her refer to me by name. Either she called me Nurse Nelson or she called me nothing at all, so rarely was anyone else in the room with us. "You can't take care of me. You have places to be."

"I don't," I argued.

"You expect me to believe you were home sick the last three nights? You don't seem like the kind of girl to be conquered by the common cold."

Again, my head was shaking against my will. I was not going to tell her about Seattle, or that I'd led Seth to believe my mind was already made up.

"You cannot stay in this one-horse town just for a boy," she said.

I laughed, frustrated. "How do you know everything?"

"I'm extremely old."

"I have to stay. The boy in question won't go with me."

"You'll regret it."

But I would regret breaking up with Seth even more. I knew this as fully as I knew that Tamora wouldn't believe me if I asserted how much I loved him. Probably she remembered falling for some chiseled California cowboy at the tender age of eighteen—and probably it was clear to her, now, how her life would have been diminished, had she molded it around his. But Seth O'Malley wasn't Tamora's first love. He was mine, and I was nowhere near ready to let him go. He had only ever given me reasons to pull him closer.

"Maybe," I conceded.

Because I knew Tamora might be right, someday, even if she was wrong right now.

THIRTY

Tamora had not accepted my offer to help her move, or to interview aides, or to step in as the overzealous daughter she had never dreamed of having. She did, however, make one request. She wanted a housewarming party. Allegedly, she and Jackson had christened every home they'd ever owned or rented with a raucous celebration, attended by everyone who was anyone within the California contingent of the country music scene. "But since Jackson's through with all that," Tamora had said, "and since I don't personally know anyone in this quaint town of yours, I'm relying on *you* to assemble a guest list."

I had been slightly embarrassed to admit that the only guest lists I'd ever made included my two best friends, my siblings, my parents, and no one else—but Tamora was undeterred: "Throw in the boyfriend, and we'll be set."

I had agreed, and the party was planned for Sunday night, hours before I would finally have to call the retirement home in Seattle and decline the position. Probably, I reasoned, Greg had already given up on me and offered the job to a local CNA with years of experience, a girl whose name generated only a modest number of Google search results.

Whoever she was, she deserved it more than I did.

On Saturday, I drove over to Cameron's house about a half hour before the person from *Under Your Breath* was supposed to call. Her family lived in one of the newer gray-shingled cottages at the edge of town. From their driveway it was a short distance to the grassy dunes that hugged the beach.

Cameron came to the door in running shorts and an oversized sweater. She did not look like a girl who had almost died in July. Ridiculously, when she leaned in to hug me, I was scared of hurting her. I spent most of my nights maneuvering people whose bones I might actually shatter. What did I think I was going to do to Cameron?

Her chatter was immediate and overwhelming. She led me into the kitchen, saying, "You have to try some of this lemonade I just made—assuming you like lemonade. Most people do. Even if you don't, please try it. I'm reasonably confident I make the best lemonade in town. The trick is to not add too much sugar *or* too much lemon juice to a base of club soda, and then garnish the whole thing with some fresh mint, which my dad grows in the backyard. Does your dad garden? Do you like mint?"

"Uh, sure," I said, accepting the glass she was forcing on me.

Cameron had seemed more subdued in her e-mail. Obviously, I remembered her going on about the Duraflame logs on the Fourth of July, but I had always attributed those nerves to her surprise at seeing Seth.

Now I had to wonder if I was the one who made her nervous.

As we entered her bedroom, I braced myself. I had this idea that Cameron's room might be full of Seth-detritus, like maybe he kept extra flannel shirts or bandannas hanging from a hook on the back of her door.

He didn't. The room was free of any evidence that Cameron had dated my boyfriend, except for one strip of pictures—I recognized the black-and-white, high-contrast style of the local arcade's photo booth—stuck to her mirror. The pictures featured a younger, shorter-haired Seth kissing a giggling Cameron on her perfectly smooth cheek.

She noticed me staring, but made no apologies as she perched on her bed and sipped her lemonade. "So, the girl from the magazine should call any minute. I don't know if you're the anxious type, but she told me it would be really relaxed. They're just going to ask us questions about what it was like to accidentally star in a viral video. They're looking for candor, I think. Honesty. But you can say as much or as little as you want."

"Honesty?" I echoed.

"Yeah. It won't be like when what's-her-face from the *Steeds County News* made you out to be such a—" Cameron stopped herself. "Sorry. It's just, she made a lot of assumptions."

"Agreed," I said. And I would have assured her that she didn't need to be sorry—I knew exactly what she'd meant; on air, Kristy Summers had reduced me to a small town teenage saint—but being in Cameron's bedroom unnerved me, for some reason. I kept expecting her to invoke her own heart attack, to thank me for saving her life or to demand an apology for how I'd handled myself in the aftermath. But the confrontation never came.

Apparently, Cameron was saving her story for the press.

In another second the phone was ringing. Cameron laid her cell on the bed between us and enabled speakerphone. She was right, it turned out; the interview was nothing like the ones I'd done before. The girl from *Under Your Breath* introduced herself as Lila and sounded only a few years older than we were. She actually listened to what we said, and asked follow-up questions in the manner of a person engaged in conversation—not just someone looking to confirm things of which she was already convinced.

"So, tell us what it felt like when you first saw the video," Lila prompted Cameron.

Cameron took a breath. "It was really scary."

"Did you see the video the first time it aired on the local news?"

"No, I was in surgery. I saw it the next morning, on You-Tube."

"How many hits did it have by then?"

"Just a few thousand. It was super shocking to see myself looking so . . ."

". . . Dead?" I ventured.

Lila chuckled softly, but Cameron nodded at me. "Right, because before then I didn't really understand how close I'd come to dying? Like, I don't remember collapsing on the beach, or Audrey doing CPR, or even being conscious in the ambulance—which I guess I was, for a second. I just remember waking up in the hospital thinking I'd been in a car accident, or something."

"Was anyone with you when you woke up?" Lila asked.

"My parents and my . . ." Cameron hesitated. "My ex-boyfriend."

"Wow, really?" Lila sounded all too eager for Cameron to elaborate.

"Yeah, my ex-boyfriend . . . who happens to be Audrey's current boyfriend."

"No way!"

I cleared my throat and confirmed, "True story."

"So, this is way messier than anyone even realizes," Lila posited.

Cameron looked at me. With so much kindness it practically stung, she said, "Nah. We're all friends."

After an obligatory murmur of support for our three-way friendship, Lila moved on. "So, Cameron, this is the first time you've spoken publicly about your heart attack, correct?"

"Yup," Cameron said.

"But, Audrey, you've agreed to lots of interviews?"

"A few." My gaze was fixed on the paisley print of Cameron's bedspread.

"And Cameron, how did it make you feel when Audrey answered questions without your input?"

"How did I *feel*?" Cameron repeated.

Lila rattled off a list of possibilities. "Used? Confused? Angry?"

My cheeks burned. Somehow, a stranger had thought of the one question I most wanted to ask Cameron myself.

"Oh, I don't know." Cameron spoke quickly, dismissively. "I guess it made me feel like something sort of traumatizing had happened to both of us, and like Audrey didn't actually have any control over how many people saw that video. No more control than I had. And like, even though the video's awful and embarrassing—and of course I wish I could erase it from the Internet, and from my mind—a viral video is still a pretty fair price to pay for my . . . life?"

Our eyes met, and we grinned at the absurdity of the question, at the absurdity of the last two months. We had been famous for a single summer. By this time next year, no one outside of our small town would remember our names.

I knew Cameron must have, on some level, resented me for going on the news, guaranteeing extra airtime for a video she wished had never been filmed. Still, I was glad that my own selfishness wasn't the part of the story she felt compelled to tell.

Toward the end of the interview, Lila asked us how our respective lives would change, come September. I kept my answer vague, reporting that I was planning to stay in Crescent Bay for the time being, to continue working at the nursing home and save some money. I fully expected Cameron to say that she, too, would be hanging around. She had already talked about the anxiety that had plagued her just after her heart attack, admitting to the weeks she'd spent immersed in reruns of *The Bachelor* and hardly ever leaving her house.

But now, Cameron revealed that she was sticking with her original plan to go to UCLA and share an apartment with her favorite cousins. The three of them were already making plans to decorate the place. Cameron wanted to string white Christmas lights across every doorframe.

Before letting us go, Lila thanked us for our time and promised to link us both to the article the moment it was published. With a sigh of relief, Cameron ended the call. Through her window—the pane of which was half covered in printed selfies of Cameron and her multitude of friends—I could just barely see the ocean foaming, lapping at the sand.

Cameron Suzuki was leaving. It was possible that she was braver than me.

"You know who else is going to UCLA?" I asked her.

She smiled and squirmed. "Yes."

"Are you still interested?"

"In Elliot? Yes."

"Want me to tell him?"

Cameron considered the offer, but shook her head. "I'll tell him myself." Then, pushing on my knee, she said, "Why aren't you going to Whedon? It's such a good school!"

"For a lot of people, maybe. But not for me."

"You know, you've got Seth thinking you're a flight risk."

I blinked, unable to imagine Seth talking about me

behind my back. He never breathed a derogatory word about anyone, not even the anonymous driver of the BMW who had aggressively tailgated us for twenty miles on the 101 last week. "What a dick," I'd said, and Seth had replied so charitably, "Maybe his wife's in labor."

"He said that?" I asked Cameron.

"He didn't use those exact words, but it's obvious he's worried about losing you."

"Not happening," I said. She appeared unconvinced. Either because Cameron had employed that therapist's trick of saying nothing—giving me no choice but to fill the silence—or because it seemed, somehow, like she might be able to fix this tightness in my chest, the desperation I felt whenever I caught sight of the waves crashing outside her window, I kept talking. "Besides, even if I was a flight risk, even if I left him behind, don't you think he might be better off? I'm all reckless and impulsive, and Seth is never impulsive."

Cameron agreed. "He can't even decide what to order at a restaurant before the place shuts down for the night."

Seth and I had never been to a restaurant together. Nothing was ever open during the hours we were hungry. "He's happy here, and I'm not. Maybe if I stay we'll just end up hating each other."

"Seth could never hate you," Cameron said. "Trust me."

"I'm pretty sure he's hated me before."

She rolled her eyes. "I know he gave you a hard time about the *Steeds County News*. I'm sorry. Seth can be sort of judgmental. He has certain convictions and he gets, like, majorly disappointed when the people he loves don't automatically share them. It's not really fair."

Our conversation was slipping into dangerous territory. *Judgmental* was not a term you would use to describe Seth O'Malley unless you knew him extremely well. His judgments were sneaky, subtle, hidden behind wide smiles and buried within bear hugs.

Still, I loved him for believing in a world where a girl could suffer a dramatic coronary event at the age of eighteen and no bystander would assume it was his story to break. No one would sit at home asking who was hotter—the almost-dead girl versus the girl performing CPR—or trying to determine whether it was even plausible, that a young woman's heart had stopped beating and another equally young woman had known what to do about it. Concluding no, it was too far-fetched. We had staged it for the attention.

Seth believed in a world where we got to choose how much of ourselves to share, and I couldn't hold that against him.

"Nah," I told Cameron, pleased to be an authority on the subject of Seth O'Malley. "He's not judgmental. He's just old-fashioned."

I was still parked outside of the Suzukis' house, watching the sun melt into the ocean as I dialed Seth's number. For once, his phone wasn't dead or missing. He answered on the first ring. Because Seth's caller ID was nonfunctional, I always savored the moment just after he realized it was me. I said hi, and a smile tore through his voice. "Audrey Nelson. Where are you?"

"Just leaving Cameron's."

"How was the interview thing?"

"Fine. I let her take most of the questions."

Seth didn't respond, but his breathing was measured, relaxed. Some static disrupted the silence, a hazard of living so far from any major city. I was always surprised when I used my phone on vacation and the line was crystal clear.

"Will you take a trip with me, someday?" I asked him.

"Like to San Francisco?"

"Like to Paris. Or Berlin. Or Shanghai."

Seth hesitated. "Shanghai. That's a long flight."

"We'll sleep through most of it."

"I think I might be scared of flying."

I laughed at him. "Supposedly it's one of the safest things

you can do. Safer than whatever you're doing right now." I paused. "What *are* you doing right now?"

His sigh was so deep, I imagined his chest rising and falling. "I am sitting behind the wheel of my Jeep, staring at the entrance to Dot's Tavern."

"Um, why?"

"Because my dad has been inside for the last three hours. He already has two DUIs on his record and a suspended license—none of which will stop him from attempting to drive himself home tonight, which is why I'm sitting here, like a dog, waiting for the door to swing open and for Steve O'Malley to stumble out."

I had told Seth about my mother's affair. I had waved my phone in his face, begging him to bear witness to the mortifying details she'd published to the Internet. Once, I had even subjected him to a full-blown Nelson family crisis, performed in the overcrowded venue of our kitchen. But I'd never really asked him about his dad's drinking. Had I assumed he didn't want to talk about it? And was there any truth to that assumption? It wasn't like Seth had shied away from Tamora's demand that he spill his life story. Nor had he seemed at all reluctant to introduce me to his father, that first time in July, before we disappeared inside Seth's bedroom.

Maybe I had never asked because I didn't want to know.

Maybe it was too hard for me to acknowledge the validity of all the things tying Seth to Crescent Bay.

"Do you want company?" I asked him.

"Nah," he said. "You shouldn't spend your night staking out Dot's Tavern."

Neither should you, I wanted to say.

"Go home," he told me.

"What will I do at home?"

"Sleep. Eat. Pick a fight with your little sister."

He was teasing me, and I let him get away with it. We said *good night* and *I love you* and *see you tomorrow*. Neither of us mentioned Shanghai or Berlin, the long-haul flights we would or wouldn't take.

I let him get away with that, too.

THIRTY-ONE

The next night, I was trying to get ready for Tamora's housewarming party while my little sister soaked in the tub. She had dropped an aggressively scented bath bomb into the water and now the room smelled like a cloying combination of roses and cake. Having already applied concealer and blush, I was sharpening an eyeliner pencil. It was more of an effort than I'd made on prom night, or maybe ever, but I was nervous. Expecting to spend an inconsequential evening with my siblings, my best friends, my separated parents, Seth O'Malley, Tamora Sinclair, and Jackson Moon seemed akin to casually counting on a miracle.

"Hey, Audrey?" Behind the shower curtain, Rosie sounded forlorn. I could hear her idly splashing at the water, reminding me of all the baths we'd shared as little kids.

"Yeah?"

"If Mom and Dad break up for real, who do you think gets me?"

I smiled, appreciating the way she seemed to consider herself the prize. "I don't know, Ro. Who would you rather live with?"

"I don't want to live alone with either one of them. Think about it. Either I'll have to survive on instant noodles with Dad or, like, spend my entire high school career fighting with Mom about why I can't just throw on a turtleneck and call it a day."

"High school is not a career. You don't get a salary, and you have to carry a large plastic spoon to the bathroom."

"Um, what?"

"It's the hall pass." Having smudged the liner across my left eyelid, I was tasked with making my right eye match.

"Will you live with me?" Rosie asked.

I froze. It had only ever dimly occurred to me that, if Mom and Dad divorced, I would be faced with the same choice as Rosie: Professor Turtleneck versus Professor Instant Noodles.

There were five years between us. By now, shouldn't I have had more options than my little sister?

"I mean, if you don't get that job in Seattle," Rosie clarified.

I stood back and studied my made-up face in the mirror. My family didn't know that I'd been offered the job on the spot. Technically, I still had until tomorrow morning to call

Greg and claim the position. But I knew I wouldn't, and sometimes I wondered whether I'd made a mistake, going straight from the airport to Seth O'Malley's bed. If I had given myself a day to think it over objectively—Sethlessly—would Seattle have stood a chance?

"Sure, Ro," I said, trying not to sound as despondent as I felt, promising, "I'll stick with you."

Her sigh of relief was audible. It wasn't the worst sound in the world.

And then our father was knocking on the door. "Girls?" He spoke with all the confidence of a man interrupting his teenage daughters in the bathroom. "Do you think we should maybe . . . go?"

I checked the clock our mother had hung on the wall, years ago, after a recurring hot-water shortage inspired her to suggest that Rosie keep her soaks to fifteen or fewer minutes. We were, in fact, running late—but it was unlike Dad to care. He was normally the one who needed to be literally dragged from his work, his fingers still twitching against an imaginary laptop's keys.

I vacated the bathroom, allowing Rosie her privacy. Dad was pacing the hallway, dressed in pressed khakis and a button-down shirt that didn't advertise a single university—an ensemble that typically meant he was on his way to a seminar. By the time the three of us were buckled into the

MINI, Dad's anxiety was palpable. It took him three tries to insert the key into the ignition.

"You're acting unhinged," Rosie pointed out.

With a sigh, Dad pressed his forehead to the steering wheel. "I know it."

I had figured he was nervous to shake hands with Jackson Moon, or that he doubted his ability to adhere to social norms after spending the entire summer alone in our kitchen, laboring over an unpublished manuscript that was, technically, old enough to be enrolled in the third grade.

Now, I realized, he was terrified to see our mother.

My sister had already caught on. "Mom's your wife, remember? You've known each other for a hundred years?"

"Twenty-nine years," Dad said, as if Rosie's exaggeration had been a mathematical error.

"So. What do you think she's going to do? Throw her drink in your face?"

The color drained from Dad's cheeks as he considered the possibility. Desperately, I wanted to help him. I thought about suggesting that he book one of the long-haul flights Seth was too scared to take, whisk Mom away to someplace she'd never been, and show her that she wasn't really as trapped as she felt. But I didn't know if a vacation would be enough to change my mother's mind. And I didn't know exactly what had happened between Iris and the guy in

Italy—whether their lips had touched, whether they'd slept together. Or if their courtship had been only aesthetic, tailor-made for an anonymous blog. Sunsets and shellfish. Sandals half buried in sand.

No part of me wanted to know these things.

"Don't worry," I told Dad. "She wants to see you. She misses you."

The engine was running, but we hadn't left the driveway. "She said that?" he asked. "Verbatim?"

It was typical of my family to insist upon knowing whether someone had said something *verbatim*. What had Mom said, exactly? Outside the nursing home, she had called Nelson *infuriating*. But she had also admitted that he'd never left her mind. The two sentiments, I figured, could easily amount to missing a person.

Unable to resist editing my mother's words—giving my father more hope than was strictly warranted—I lied and said yes.

Tamora had sent me her new address, which I entered into my iPhone and mounted to the dashboard. Getting there was the same as getting anywhere; we turned onto the 101 and followed the curves of the highway. The exit sign for Tamora's neighborhood was about ten miles south of Crescent Bay proper and said only, COMMUNITY OF SLAB CREEK, POPULATION: 167.

Even without the address, I would have recognized her house instantly. The vintage mint-colored Thunderbird parked outside was perfect, the vehicular version of Tamora herself. I flashed upon the night I met her—how she had rejected the nursing home's meat loaf in favor of a more delicious memory.

Now that she had her car, and her freedom, she could drive the hundred miles to the nearest In-N-Out Burger whenever she pleased.

Among the cars already parked along the road was my family's aging minivan. With its museum of Whedon College bumper stickers and its dented side door—the result of Jake procuring his learner's permit at the first legal moment—the minivan looked incongruous behind the shapely BMW that could only have belonged to Jackson Moon.

The absence of Seth's Jeep made me nervous. We were a little bit late, and Seth was almost always on time.

As we approached the house, Dad unbuttoned the collar of his shirt, suddenly clued in to the evening's lack of dress code. No wind chimes hung from Tamora's porch, and no driftwood dragon guarded her door, which she'd left wide open. We could see through the kitchen and the dining room—both spaces a maze of boxes—and straight into the backyard, where Mom and Jake were sitting with Tamora and Jackson, plus a stranger in white linen pants.

Tamora waved and welcomed us. The patio had been cracked by tufts of sea grass. An old concrete birdbath was crumbling into one corner of the yard—but Tamora looked at home and at ease, seated around a glass-topped table with half my family and all of hers.

Something compelled my mother to stand and give my father a formal kiss on the cheek. Most likely she was trying to set a precedent for good behavior. Still, my heart ached for Dad. Did he really deserve to be greeted the way she greeted guests at faculty parties?

As Jake got up to hug us, he eyed his chair nervously, as if someone might steal the prime spot beside Jackson Moon. Taking the hint, I seated myself on the opposite edge of the table.

The retired country legend was the first person to say anything of substance.

"Audrey, I have to admit, the last time we met I didn't realize you were such a celebrity."

I stared at Jackson, feeling distinctly like the butt of a joke.

"I showed him your video," Tamora explained.

"Oh." My cheeks burned. In the presence of his tenured fame, I had forgotten about my video. "I'm not a real celebrity. I mean, it's just YouTube."

"It's a viral sensation!" said the stranger in linen pants.

"I'd seen it long before Jackson put two and two together. I'm Clyde, by the way." Jackson's husband extended his hand and I reached to shake it. His pants were paired with a matching linen shirt that begged to be ravaged by red wine. But unlike the rest of the adults, Clyde wasn't drinking wine. Instead he clutched a murky, greenish concoction pierced by a bendy straw.

"She's not famous," my brother said hastily, "I mean, not like—"

"Of course she's famous!"

Sara's voice rang out across the backyard. She was carrying a massive tray of shrimp cocktail, Elliot hovering shyly at her shoulder. Beyond grateful for the interruption, I jumped up to relieve Sara of the shrimp. I delivered the tray to the table and introduced everyone as fast as possible.

"Where's Seth?" Sara asked, claiming a spare chair beside Clyde.

"Not sure." I tried to sound flippant, unconcerned.

"I thought he was coming," Elliot said.

"I thought so, too."

"Why don't you text him?" Sara suggested. "Find out where he is."

"He'll be here," I promised, because I was unwilling to send a message and receive bad news. I needed him here.

A lengthy silence was interrupted only when Clyde whispered, "Who's Seth?"

"Boyfriend," Tamora mouthed.

Prolonging my time in the spotlight, Sara cried, "Audrey, I haven't talked to you since Seattle! Are you taking the job?"

From across the table, I gave her a look: *Please don't.*

"Wait a second," my mother said. Deep lines creased her forehead. "I was under the impression that you hadn't heard back."

"Same here," Dad said.

Tamora snapped her fingers. "I *knew* you weren't really sick last week."

Sara was guiltless, already admonishing me. "Audrey! It's your dream job!"

"It's exactly the same as the job I already have," I argued.

"Except that it's day shift, pays twice as much, and it's in Seattle!"

"You turned it down?" Elliot caught on. "Why?"

"Yeah, why?" Sara demanded.

I closed my eyes. To my friends, Seth O'Malley was still the guy with the ponytail who wore cowboy boots to places other than the rodeo. In their minds he was forever occupying the hall at school, forever hugging one Crescent Bay girl after another; there was no reason for me to get in line.

"Come on," Sara said. "I saw your face when we were standing in that apartment."

"What apartment?" Rosie asked, reminding me of the casual promise I'd already made her. Soon I'd be nineteen, then twenty, and still staring at the sagging underside of my little sister's top bunk.

To Sara, I said, "I was looking at the mattress someone had left behind. I was thinking about Seth."

My father cleared his throat, lest I expand on the connection between my boyfriend and mattresses.

"Audrey," Elliot said suddenly, causing more than one person to straighten their posture. "Remember junior year, when your Environmental Science class took that overnight field trip to Mount Shasta?"

"I didn't go," I reminded him.

"Right, but remember how weirdly excited you were to go?"

I shrugged. "It's an active volcano. It might have exploded."

"Right, and you missed an active volcano maybe exploding because the night before the trip, you let Sara drag you to Cape Defiance for the seniors' end-of-the-year bonfire and Sara got so drunk that you had to drive her home and make sure she didn't inhale her own vomit in her sleep. Then, in the morning, you told Mrs. Quintero that Sara had been poisoned by a bad batch of clams at the Fish Shack and you skipped the field trip to spend all day administering her Tylenol and holding back her hair."

Remembering his audience, Elliot glanced at my parents and added, "Sorry."

"Our innocence, forever shattered," Dad said.

"Mount Shasta's not likely to erupt for another four hundred years," Jake said. "Just, for the record."

"Phew," said Clyde.

My mother continued to frown, while Sara gazed at me with affection, her chin resting in her hands. "I'm going to miss you. My own personal nurse."

"That's not the point!" Elliot said.

"We get the point." I sighed.

"Do you?"

"You're comparing my boyfriend to a bad hangover Sara had one time."

"I'm just saying that you have a *tendency* to put other people before yourself."

"That's true," Sara admitted. "You do."

Both Tamora and my mother murmured their agreement. I looked between the two of them, stunned. Mom, of all people, knew exactly how selfish I'd been this summer, whereas Tamora hardly knew me at all.

Jackson Moon took the opportunity to lift the guitar I

hadn't realized was roosting beneath his seat. My future forgotten, Sara grabbed a bottle of Coke from the assortment of beverages on the table and poured herself a drink. Her eyes were trained on Jackson, like he might, without warning, burst into one of his hit singles.

All he did was strum a few chords, aimless and angsty. For the first time I noticed the pearl buttons on his fitted flannel shirt. He had dressed to please Tamora, I realized— like a kid decked out in the clothes his grandmother had given him for Christmas.

Under my breath, I told Elliot, "I really don't think I'm making a mistake."

He shrugged. "There will be other jobs, other cities. You can always change your mind."

My phone remained dormant in my pocket, and I still hadn't heard the rumble of Seth's Jeep. His lateness was getting to me. My throat tightened when I thought, irrationally, through all of the worst case scenarios.

Tamora leaned back in her chair and said to my parents, "How did you two kids meet, anyway?"

Dad's cheeks caught fire and Mom winced. My siblings and I traded looks of alarm. Our parents had met in a bar during grad school. They had always led us to believe it was a harmless story, as benign and conventional as the Connecticut town they'd lived in.

"We were at school in New Haven," Mom began.

"Just say Yale," Jake advised. "It's less pretentious."

She shook her head, but made the correction. "We were both at Yale, halfway through our PhDs. Nelson's in English, mine in political theory. Two blocks from my apartment there was a bar. Not a nice establishment, more of a . . ."

"A dive bar," Nelson said, lifting his wine to his lips.

"Right. And the bartender there—"

"Lou," Nelson supplied.

"Lou played this game with her customers. The game was that if you could correctly identify five consecutive songs from her very eccentric playlist—"

"It wasn't a *playlist*," Dad said. "It was the nineties."

"Then what was it?" Mom asked him. "A jukebox?"

"Probably a collection of mixtapes," Dad said.

"Well, either way, I was there with a girlfriend one night and we were on a roll. Between the two of us we had named four songs, and we were one tune away from winning ourselves a free pitcher of PBR."

"Classy," Rosie said.

"I love this story." Clyde spoke dreamily, leaning closer to my parents.

Mom glanced at Jackson and blushed. My brother's eyes widened with panic as he realized where, exactly, this story was headed. Clenching his jaw, Jake sent Mom a silent message: *Don't you dare insult the most famous person at this party.*

"What were the four songs you had already guessed?" Tamora wanted to know.

"Oh, you can't possibly remember," Dad said, issuing a challenge.

Without missing a beat, Mom recited, "'Wild Horses' by the Rolling Stones, 'Stars Fell on Alabama' by Louis Armstrong, 'In Bloom' by Nirvana, and 'Africa' by Toto."

My brother's jaw dropped. Dad sported a proud smile and my friends sat back in their chairs, as entertained by my family as ever.

Carefully, Mom continued her story. "So the fifth song comes on, and it's a country song. Neither of us know it. We're openly despairing, because we're—"

"Drunk," Dad said.

"Because we're poor, thirsty graduate students!" Mom argued.

"You were never poor in grad school," Dad said. "You won every single grant."

Iris shook her head, but her pleasure was obvious. "Well, to make a long story short, a boy from the booth behind us slid in next to me and whispered the name of the song in my ear."

"What was it?" Clyde asked, giddy.

Those with the last name of Nelson already knew the answer, but Dad confirmed it. "The song was 'Shotgun Wedding' by Jackson Moon."

A wave of appreciative laughter swept over the group. Almost imperceptibly, Dad raised his drink in Mom's direction and took a sip of his wine. Even Jackson seemed charmed; a wry half smile worked its way up his left cheek. And finally Tamora's party felt like a party—like an event that could warm a house, make it safe and habitable for years to come.

Someone's hands pressed down on my shoulders.

"I'm sorry I'm late."

At the sound of his voice, I shouted with relief. "Seth!"

"Audrey!" he shouted back, equally jubilant. And the way he proceeded to embrace my friends, my parents, even Jackson and Clyde—you would think they had all played for the same football team or fought in the same war. He apologized a second time as he greeted Tamora, but she just waved away his regrets.

"Pour yourself a drink, Seth. Have some shrimp."

"I'd love that, and I will, but first—"

Seth dropped to his knee in front of my chair.

My mother gasped. Rosie clapped a hand over her mouth, stifling her own scream.

"Um." This could not be happening. I wanted to grab

Seth by the armpits and hoist him back into a standing position before he ruined everything that had ever been good, forever.

Finally, he became aware of his own posture. His cheeks turned crimson and he shut his eyes. "Everyone thinks I'm about to propose, don't they?"

Mutely, I nodded.

"I'm not proposing."

My heart unclenched as my dad muttered, "Thank God," his long exhale like a tire losing air.

"But I do have an idea," Seth said.

I nodded, receptive. Now that marriage was off the table, I was sure I could handle whatever he had in mind.

"Okay. You know that old motel in town? The one right on the beach, with the freezing cold pool everyone's always breaking into?"

"Sure," I said. "The Surfside Inn." It was one block west of the Fish Shack, two blocks south of the arcade. Guests of the motel were always leaning over their balconies, exhaling cigarette smoke toward the sea.

"They're turning it into apartments. I was on my way to the Qwick Mart and I saw the NOW LEASING sign. I went inside and talked to the manager. That's why I'm late."

"You talked to the manager?" I clung to my confusion, unwilling to follow Seth's train of thought.

Maybe it wasn't a proposal, but it felt uncomfortably close.

"Yeah, and he showed me one of the units. Full disclosure, the place smells pretty moldy. Probably from people hanging out in their wet swimsuits all the time. But if they don't replace the carpets before we move in, I can do it myself."

"Before we *move in?*"

"The rent will be cheap. Between my job and yours, we can totally swing it." Seeing my shock, my hesitation, Seth turned to address my parents. "I know you guys wanted Audrey to live at home and go to Whedon. And I realize you think I'm this brainless janitor who shouldn't be dating someone as smart and ambitious as Audrey—"

"We don't think that," Iris assured him.

Nelson looked at her as if to say, *We don't?*

"I just think we'll both be happy," Seth said, facing me. "I mean, it's within walking distance to the nursing home. We could go to work together every night, wake up together every afternoon."

As always, the idea of sharing a bed with Seth made me smile. Beds were central to my Seth-based fantasies.

My smile encouraged him. "We'd have a balcony with an ocean view. Easy access to the Fish Shack for takeout. I'll build you a campfire on the sand whenever you want one."

There was so much hope in Seth's eyes.

Softly, I said, "We've never even talked about it."

And then disappointment settled over his features. He looked like someone who had run out of energy halfway through a performance—like Sara when she'd used up all her fake tears before the cop had finished writing her a speeding ticket.

Big announcements and grand gestures were not really Seth's style. Did he think this was what I wanted? For him to be spontaneous, and impulsive?

A little bit reckless, like me?

All I knew was that I wanted to calm him down. I wanted him to know that I loved him, that everything would be okay. And because we had an audience, each member on the edge of his or her lawn chair, there was only one thing I could say.

"All right. We'll check into the Surfside Inn. Permanently."

I ignored my brother burying his face in his hands, my friends exchanging one of their patented looks—*we tried*—and my father asserting, "We'll discuss this later," as if Seth and I weren't eighteen years old and in possession of our own futures.

Enduring their live reactions was worth the return of the O'Malley grin. There were no seats left, but Seth grabbed the Igloo cooler Tamora had stocked with bottles of white wine and he sat on that instead. Lacing his fingers through mine, he whispered, "I know it's not Seattle. Or Shanghai. But we'll have the whole place to ourselves."

Part of me wanted to laugh. Part of me wanted to sob.

Accidentally, I locked eyes with my mother. She was looking at me like she wanted to check my vital signs.

Clyde reached for a mason jar of what appeared to be pond water. "Would anyone like some kombucha?" he asked. "It's home-brewed."

Dad took the jar and inspected the liquid. "Is it safe?"

"Not likely," Tamora said, just as Jackson strummed a random minor chord. Irritated, she smacked him on the shoulder. "Either put that thing down or play us a song."

I took for granted that Jackson, who had been silent since the start of the party, would settle for option A and return the guitar to its battered case. When instead he began to play, I was too surprised to immediately recognize the song—too surprised, and too busy ensuring that my pop culture junkie of a brother kept his phone buried deep in the pocket of his shorts.

Then, Jackson began to sing.

When your dad grabbed his shotgun
I didn't have a choice

but I still can't stand
the sound of your voice.

Jackson was a good singer, but he took himself too seriously. The playful lyrics turned maudlin in his mouth.

The wedding was simple
if simple means drunk.
Your family's prized moonshine?
I'm through with that junk.

My parents were squirming, staring into their drinks. Even Tamora looked pained, as if Jackson had forgotten everything she'd ever taught him about pleasing a crowd.

And then you were moody,
calves swollen and blue.
You screamed until the nurse passed out
and now there's two of you

Jackson sang the entire ballad, narrating the couple's first tumultuous year with their daughter, the wife's affair with some scoundrel in town, and the slow death of the family's beagle. By the time the song was finished, only Clyde appeared enamored with his husband's talents. The rest of us were eyeing the house, wondering who would be the first to make a beeline for the bathroom, if only for a moment free of secondhand embarrassment.

"Wow," Sara said finally. "That was special."

"Sure was," Seth agreed.

Jackson's smile was tight. Accustomed to his legions of boot-stomping, whiskey-shooting fans, he was obviously disappointed by our lack of enthusiasm.

Iris said, "I guess there's a reason that's our song."

She was talking to Nelson, and only a trace of regret prevented the comment from sounding flat-out flirtatious. Tamora, unfamiliar with the nuances of my mother's voice—and also a little bit tipsy—said, "You two are still young. You have the rest of your lives to work things out."

Dad pointed to her as if she'd said something profound. "Thank you. That's exactly why Iris should just come home."

For a second, my mother appeared to consider it. Her eyes rolled skyward and her finger skated along the rim of her wineglass. Then she shook her head, returned her gaze to earth. "The problem, Nelson, is that you're not the only one who's made mistakes."

Later, it would occur to me that Mom had been referring to her Italian suitor, about whom Dad still knew nothing. Soon, before my parents could officially settle the score—

either calling it even or calling a divorce lawyer—Mom would have to confess to Nelson that she'd cheated on him.

But in this moment, I thought she meant a different mistake entirely.

Seth had just finished pouring himself some Coke and was offering the two-liter bottle to my little sister, who appeared as panicked as she always did when addressed by my boyfriend. Giving up, Seth set the bottle down and sipped his soda. I was asking too much of him, subjecting him to my family's ongoing drama. Our arguments, insults, and sudden revelations. Our unpredictability.

I was asking too much of him, and I wasn't going to stop.

At the exact moment he reached for some shrimp, I said, "Seth, I can't live in a water-damaged motel with you."

He blinked. He retracted his arm. "You can't?"

Sara's lawn chair squeaked as she inched it closer. I ought to have pulled Seth into the privacy of Tamora's house; privacy was what he would have preferred. But what I needed to say to him felt both urgent and fleeting, like if I didn't spit it out, this instant, I might permanently lose my nerve.

"I'm moving to Seattle."

There was no way they'd already given the position to someone else. I was Audrey Nelson. I was *California Teen Hero Saves Life of a Friend,* and I was damn good at my job.

"I need to get out of this town, because if I stay here

another year I will come to loathe absolutely everything we both love about it. I'm tired of driving up and down the same stretch of highway. I'm tired of knowing about every speed trap and pothole and blind corner. I'm tired of never meeting anyone I haven't met before. I'm tired of sand in my sheets. And I swear to God, Seth, I cannot eat another clam strip."

I was running out of breath. He was looking at me the way you look at someone who is suffering from a clam strip–induced crisis.

Also: the way you look at someone who is breaking your heart.

"I just need to figure out who I am, apart from this place, apart from my friends, apart from"—I gestured haphazardly to our audience—"all these people."

Several minor protests came from Sara, Dad, and Jake. Nothing from my mother or Tamora.

Seth had his hands behind his head, fingers buried in his hair. It was his way of saying *I don't know,* and *slow down,* and *let me think.*

I wasn't sure what was more unlikely—that I had fallen for the most popular boy in Crescent Bay, or that I had managed to thoroughly overwhelm him.

Maybe it wasn't the worst thing I could do to the love of my life.

"So you're taking the job," he said.

."And I need you to come with me."

I tried to make my need sound as indisputable as the weather.

Seth's cheek twitched. "What?"

"I will be miserable if I go without you. I will be miserable if I stay, and I'm pretty sure you'll be miserable, too."

Dropping his voice, Seth said, "Is this how we're going to make all of our decisions? Assemble your friends and family and blindside each other with plans?"

"I hope so," Jake said.

"No," I said to Seth, unsure if he was more mad at me or amused by me. "If you hate Seattle, we'll come back. And anytime you're worried about your dad, we'll visit. The second you need something as bad as I need this, I swear, I'll make sure you get it."

Seth angled his chin toward the clouds. I could see the patches of scruff on his neck, the stubble that felt more abrasive against my skin than he probably realized. Seth wasn't perfect. He loved unconventional flavors of beef jerky and asked me, too frequently, if I felt like *tossing a ball around*. He was overly friendly. He smiled too much.

He had been a Boy Scout from the ages of ten to seventeen.

"Okay," he said, dipping his chin. "I'll go."

Someone emitted a single inappropriate cheer. I wasn't willing to tear my eyes away from Seth, but my money was on Clyde.

"You will?"

"It's a pretty good offer. You should have made it months ago."

"I barely knew you months ago."

Seth grinned and took my hand. He pulled me to my feet. "You barely know me now."

We kissed in front of my best friends, my entire family, a rebellious senior citizen, a retired country music legend and his kombucha-drinking husband. We kissed amid the sea of chairs and empty glasses, the uneaten shrimp, the weeds and the crumbling birdbath. It was mortifying. It was exhilarating. And maybe it should have bothered me, Seth's idea that I barely knew him after everything we'd been through this summer. Everything I'd almost given up for him.

The idea didn't bother me at all.

I suspected I would love him, whoever he turned out to be.

THIRTY-TWO

Seth left the party early, anxious to talk to his dad and his brothers about his now imminent move to Washington with a girl from school. Jackson urged the rest of us out the door when Tamora's eyelids began to droop, and it became clear that she might, for once, be persuaded to retire before midnight.

I didn't know how to say good-bye to her. The two of us had never hugged, and even though she followed me out to the driveway—where she rested a hand on the hood of her Thunderbird and looked at me like, *Your move, Nurse Nelson*—I didn't feel capable of wrapping my arms around her small frame, or of insulting her with a perfunctory kiss on the cheek.

In front of my friends and family, I said to Tamora, "Thank you for not dying this summer."

My mother cringed and Rosie dissolved into weary giggles. Sara and Elliot took the opportunity to pat me on the shoulder, climb inside of Sara's pickup truck, and quit this whole scene.

Tamora was the only one who took my gratitude in stride. "Thank you for not attempting to save my life," she countered.

"I would never. I heard your Do Not Resuscitate order loud and clear."

Tamora's smirk soon yielded to a yawn. "Whose clown car?" she asked, nodding to the MINI Cooper parked across the gravel road.

"My dad's."

"Then what is he doing, unlocking the door to that utility vehicle?"

I followed Tamora's line of sight. My father was taking his old place behind the wheel of the minivan. Mom had claimed the passenger side while Jake and Rosie, presumably, had already loaded themselves into the back.

Had my parents forgotten they were supposed to be separated?

Were they drunk?

Iris, I knew, rarely had more than a drink in a sitting. Dad, too, had a penchant for respecting his limits.

"All right." I was confused, and a little annoyed. "I guess I'm driving home alone."

Tamora shook her head. "Ride with your family. You can

come back for your car in the morning. Bring Seth with you. I have some advice for that boy."

Wary, I asked her, "What kind of advice?"

She rolled her sea glass eyes. "Fashion advice. What else?"

The Nelsons were waiting for me to get in the van. Whether my parents were making a statement or an absent-minded error, I played along.

As I squeezed in beside Jake and Rosie, they both stared straight ahead, seat belts fastened and hands in their laps. None of us so much as glanced at the MINI as we left it behind. None of us said a word until the turnoff for Tamora's neighborhood was firmly in our rearview mirror.

When we were safely on the 101, Jake heaved a sigh. "I bet you'll make so many new friends in Seattle."

"Oh, really?" I asked, not falling for it.

"Yeah. You'll play bingo, catch the early bird special at Denny's. Did you know that cups of coffee are only a buck if you're fifty-five or older?"

"That's a really good deal," Rosie deadpanned.

To my brother, I said, "You were the one who begged me to meet Tamora Sinclair. Did I not come through for you? Plus, I got you into a party with the two most famous people in Crescent Bay."

"Was that man in the white pants a musician?" Dad

asked. "I missed that. I thought Mr. Moon was the only celebrity guest."

"Um, I think Audrey was counting herself as famous," Rosie explained.

"Oh!" Dad said. "Interesting."

All of us became simultaneously aware of Mom's silence. She wasn't attempting to rein in our ribbing, to act as referee, or assure me that I'd always be a celebrity guest in her heart.

"Hey." Dad reached over the center console to nudge her knee. "What did you mean, before, when you said I wasn't the only one who'd made mistakes?"

"Yeah, Mom." Rosie's attempt to lean forward was so abrupt that the seat belt locked, pinning her to the seat. "What did you mean?"

Mom turned to Dad. I studied her profile, unable to tell if her eyes were damp or just reflecting light from the dashboard. "I'll tell you, but not in front of the kids."

"Back at the house?" Dad asked. We had already missed the exit for Professor Hale's beach cottage. We were denying its existence, the same way we were denying having arrived at a party in separate cars.

"Back at the house," Mom confirmed.

I wasn't necessarily expecting them to forgive each other. I wasn't even expecting my mother to stay the night. But in that moment, I felt as I always had, pressed against my siblings on the backseat of the minivan. Like we were five people with nothing in common. Five people too weird to belong to anyone else. Five people who defined home by the same house, the same stretch of ocean, the same highway—for another few miles, at least.

Acknowledgments

Endless thanks to my agent, Susan Ginsburg, who could not be kinder, smarter, or more generous with her time. I'm also grateful to the amazing team at Dial, especially to my editor, Namrata Tripathi—whose thoughtful notes and compelling questions improved this book on every level—and to Stacey Friedberg, whose comments on an early draft were invaluable. More thanks to Stacy Testa at Writers House for years of swift communication and publishing prowess.

I also want to thank Vikki VanSickle for her encouragement at a crucial stage, and for all those conversations over all those blueberry pancakes.

Thanks to Wes, who can't read yet, but whose arrival has served as a crash course in patience, multitasking, and astonishing love.

And to Dan Schillinger, who is the reason I remember everything.